THE MAN WHO COULD SEE ALL EVIL

J. S. RAYNOR

Beaten Track
www.beatentrackpublishing.com

The Man Who Could See All Evil

Published 2023 by Beaten Track Publishing
Copyright © 2023 J. S. Raynor

This is a rewritten, re-edited edition of a previous story by the same author.

Paperback ISBN: 978 1 78645 640 3
eBook ISBN: 978 1 78645 641 0

Cover design: Debbie McGowan

Beaten Track Publishing,
Burscough, Lancashire.
www.beatentrackpublishing.com

Dedication

I dedicate this book to my family. My wife Aleth, son James and daughter Kimberley. All suffer the effects of having to live with someone whose mind is always in the midst of new story ideas or engrossed in typing manuscripts in the office.

In addition, I would like to mention how the Royal National Institute of Blind People's Talking Book library has inspired me. After many years of being unable to read physical books, I felt liberated when, in 2011, I bought my first talking-book device and started reading their books. In the twelve years since, I have read over five hundred books. The superb stories created by such magnificent authors as Lee Child, Stephen King, Tom Clancy, Nelson Demille, Jack Finney, Dan Brown, Tess Gerritson, Jackie Collins, Dean Koontz, Harlan Coben, Robert Ludlum, James Herbert, Peter James, Clive Cussler and E.L. James have all intrigued and inspired me to use what I hope is the ability to create all the stories I have written so far and will write in the future. My wish is that I can continue writing stories for many years to come.

Prologue

C APTAIN ALEX McCLOUD looked up when he heard the all-too-familiar sound of sniper fire. It was uncomfortably close to the base camp at Kandahar.

"Jack! Quick! Come with me!"

The two men ran towards the camp entrance and soon saw the crumpled bodies of the two young Afghan soldiers who had been guarding the camp's main entrance gates. A third soldier was calling out for help and trying to revive the two unfortunate men who were far beyond any earthly assistance.

Alex and Jack were soon by the man's side. The young captain was familiar with all three Afghans, who had been willing to assist American and British forces in an attempt to rid the country of Taliban insurgents. To make it worse, all three men were related.

"Did you see the attackers?"

"Yes, Sir." He looked devastated at the loss of his cousins. "There were four Taliban." He turned and pointed toward the car racing away from the camp.

Alex wasted no time and ran with Jack towards a light-armoured vehicle. "Watkins! Adamson! Come with us, quickly!"

Within seconds, they were in pursuit of the dangerous killers.

Alex had been assigned to take charge of flushing out the many groups of Taliban fighters entrenched near the villages where they could intimidate and keep pressure on many thousands of frightened residents. Now he had a job to do. *Just get this right!* he told himself.

While Jack drove, his foot pressed hard on the accelerator, Alex was on his radio, instructing a helicopter pilot to take off and assist in this dangerous mission.

After a few minutes' driving at speed on poorly maintained roads through villages, they emerged into the countryside with just the occasional small group of dwellings. The car with the Taliban fighters came to a halt near a mainly open area. They quickly jumped out of their vehicle and ran away in the direction of a simple building. It was one of several similar buildings in this area.

Jack pulled up without getting too close to the other vehicle in case it had been booby-trapped. All four ran after the escaping insurgents.

The first three Taliban fighters made easy targets and were quick to dispatch. When another fighter retreated into the small, ordinary-looking building, Alex's unit followed, unaware that it was a deadly trap.

As the man ran inside the room, he quickly hid behind a stack of boxes, waiting for the British soldiers to enter. When he was satisfied that several soldiers were inside the building, he shouted, "Praise be to Allah!" and detonated a huge bomb, ensuring not only his own death but that of several of the infidel fighters.

In the explosion that followed, Alex's sergeant and best friend, Jack Prentice, was literally torn to pieces, while Corporal Doug Adamson was decapitated, and a third soldier, Private Bill Watkins lost both legs.

Alex felt the full force of the blast, his clothes immediately catching fire, while he received a great number of shrapnel wounds to his face and one side of his body.

Luckily for him, the force of the explosion hurled him away from the structure and out of further danger from the now fiercely burning building. A second massive explosion ripped through the air, making it impossible to retrieve what was left of the bodies of his three unfortunate comrades.

Alex was uncertain what happened next, but somehow, he stumbled away from the blazing inferno that had trapped them and was quickly dragged away by his fellow soldiers, who had disembarked from the helicopter and come to his aid. While enemy snipers were firing at Alex, he was quickly rolled on the ground to extinguish the flames from his burning clothes. Alex was not only dazed but also completely blinded from the frags that had painfully torn into his face, making it impossible for him to help himself. Blood streamed down his shattered face, giving the young soldier quite a ghoulish appearance, somewhat reminiscent of a horror movie.

As the men in his troop realised Alex's difficulties, they literally picked him up and carried him to the helicopter, which, thankfully, had returned for them. It was pretty undignified yet life-saving, as they bundled their inert captain inside. They all scrambled in quickly after him, allowing the heavy machine to lift off while still being targeted by small-arms fire.

Alex remained unconscious for about three hours, coming round in the military hospital at Camp Bastion.

He would always remember that day vividly. The antiseptic smell, the air of quiet efficiency, but most of all, the strange feeling of isolation. Not just the fact that he was lying in a hospital bed, but for all he knew, the ongoing battles could be a million miles away or even have ended, though he knew this was not likely.

He turned slightly in his bed in a vain attempt to get a little more comfortable and winced from the sharp pain.

Out of the darkness, a familiar voice gave him a start. "Hello, Alex. You're back with us, then?"

Alex recognised the deep, calming tones of Derek Connolly, his commanding officer.

He wasted no time and asked the all-important question. "What happened to my men?"

There was an uncomfortable, meaningful pause before the reply came. "A secondary explosion prevented us from getting the others out. Prentice, Adamson and Watkins didn't make it, I'm sorry to say."

Alex had feared the worst but had still hoped. "Oh, shit! What a mess! I should have guessed it was a trap."

Major Derek Connolly could not agree with the young officer. "Don't blame yourself, Alex. If we did not react in case everything was a trap, we would get nowhere. The important thing now is to get you better and out of that bed."

Dreading the answers that may be given, he asked the next important question. "What happened to me? Why can't I see anything?"

Again, another short, yet meaningful pause. "You received about twenty per cent burns, mainly to your left side. The frags caused extensive scarring, particularly to your face and upper body."

"What about my eyes?"

"I'm sorry, Alex. The probability is that loss of sight to both eyes is permanent."

Alex felt as though he had been hit by an express train. Burnt skin and frag wounds could heal, but the news that he would never see again hit Alex badly. He took a deep, involuntary breath before asking, "Are you certain about my eyes?" He feared that he knew what the answer would be even before Derek replied.

His commanding officer sounded apologetic. "The front portion of both eyes was damaged so severely that corneal implants could not even be considered. I'm terribly sorry, Alex, but that is the situation as explained to me by the medics."

Right then, Alex wished he had died in the battle along with his men. He could not understand why his life had been spared while his future had been so finally and brutally destroyed. *There's no future in the army for a soldier without sight,* he thought, somewhat bitterly. He could not imagine life without sight, unable to see the magic in a woman's smile or the wonderment in a child's innocent face. Even to see the creases and fine lines in his own face as he aged would be denied to him. His silence said everything.

Alex's feelings of hostility and despair were not aimed at Major Connolly. It was his superior's job to be honest, sometimes to the point of brutality, with the men in his command. One of the disadvantages of climbing up the ranks was the inevitable task of breaking bad news when a death or serious injury occurred.

"Listen, Alex. Tomorrow you will be flown back to the UK, where you will receive the very best medical treatment. If there is any way that your sight can be restored, then it will be done. I'm just telling you the situation as it is at this moment. Okay?"

"Sorry, I didn't mean…"

"It's all right, Alex. I do understand your frustration. We now have to put our trust in the specialists back home."

The flight back to England was a very sobering experience. Alex was one of three who were on stretchers along with one female and five male soldiers whose injuries were less severe, allowing them to sit in normal seats.

It was heart-wrenching to realise that as well as the injured, there were two soldiers in coffins. Soldiers whose lives had been cut far too short. *What a fucking mess!* he thought. For the men in his unit who had died in the huge explosion, their bodies would remain in that God-forsaken country, the dignity of being buried on British soil being denied to them. All that was left were the memories of these three brave individuals.

Within a couple of hours of landing, Alex and the other seriously injured soldiers were flown, by helicopter, to Queen Elizabeth Hospital at Edgbaston in Birmingham. This famous hospital had only opened the previous year and already had a world-renowned reputation for the care and rehabilitation of military personnel injured in conflict zones.

The care Alex received was superb. He was fortunate to have burns that were not quite deep enough to need skin grafts. There were many blisters from his shoulders down to his abdomen, causing him extreme discomfort, but with a great deal of patience and expertise by the medical staff, they would, eventually, be replaced with new skin.

Debbie and Susan handled him with the same care as they would a premature baby. They gently bathed him and applied liberal quantities of lotions and dressings where appropriate. The bed in which he lay had an electric ripple-effect mattress, designed to prevent contact sores normally associated with lying in one position for protracted periods of time.

The injuries to his face were, however, a major cause for concern. The metal fragments had torn deep into the flesh, and it took surgeons four hours to remove any remaining pieces of metal and repair the facial tissue as much as possible.

Chapter One

20th April 2011

"SHIT!" THE BANDAGES were unbearably tight around Alex's head and he wished somebody, anybody, would loosen them enough to ease the throbbing pain in his damaged skull. There was little of his head not tightly bandaged apart from his nose and mouth. He tried, with fingers that did not feel like his own, to fumble with the gauze, but try as he might, he was unable to find a loose end.

"Shit! Shit!" He was not, under normal circumstances, the kind of guy who casually uttered even this mildest of profanities, but now, in his present situation, it felt excusable.

The effort exhausted him and he gave up, sinking back onto the bed, defeated and deflated. Naively, he hoped that nobody had observed him pulling at his bandages, but a nurse had and rushed over to his bedside.

"Alex! Please leave your bandages alone. They're tight for a reason."

Alex grunted. He knew she was correct, but that did not lessen his frustration.

Seeming to sense it, Debbie—his nurse—softened a little. "Is there anything I can get you, Alex?"

There was not a hint of humour in his voice as he replied, "How about a new body?"

She gave a wan smile. "You do have a good body, believe me." She wasn't saying it merely to please him. She'd seen him naked many times and couldn't help wishing she had a guy with such

7

a muscular frame in her life. With Alex, everything, and she really meant *everything*, was in the right proportion.

Debbie was single, and at twenty-eight, after a few forgettable relationships, she wondered if there would ever be someone special in her life. Her past sexual partners had, to put it simply, not come up to expectations. Why a man should think that a two- or three-minute fumble would be enough to satisfy a woman, she could never comprehend. Why was it that men found it impossible to understand what a woman really needed?

She thought Alex might be the kind of guy who did know what a woman needed and had even said as much to her colleague, Susan. Ever since Alex had been flown from Afghanistan and brought into the Intensive Care Unit, three weeks earlier, the two women had bathed, cleaned and assisted him to use the bedpan. They had fed him intravenously and then by hand when he was incapable of looking after himself as a result of the heavy cocktail of drugs necessary for pain relief. They knew every inch of his body in far greater detail than anyone else, even including himself. Her blushes, at these most intimate thoughts, went unseen.

"You're healing well," she said, "and with a little patience, you will make a full recovery."

He struggled to speak clearly, his voice not following his thoughts, coughed a little and then tried again. "I could do with a drink, please, Debbie. My mouth is so dry."

"Of course." She pressed the controls to raise the head of the bed, making it easier for her difficult patient to drink. She placed the cup into Alex's hand and, using a straw, he gulped down a few welcoming mouthfuls of fruit juice.

"Better?"

"Yes, thanks. Much better. I'm sorry for being such a pain in the butt." He lay back, irritated that even the slightest effort, such as sitting up, exhausted him. Never in his life had he felt as incapable and useless as he did now.

"Don't worry, you're getting better each day, and I'm not joking when I tell you that we have had much worse patients than you." Debbie hesitated, uncertain if she should tell Alex of one of her more memorable experiences, which had left her in tears, but then, after only a moment's hesitation, continued, with some bitterness in her voice. "About ten months ago, a colonel was admitted into this unit. He had lost his leg after being caught in a Taliban suicide bombing. He received the same amount of attention as everybody else in Intensive Care, but that was never enough for him. One day, I was late with his medication as a consequence of one of the more critically ill patients dying, and I was upset, as the unfortunate young soldier had been a war hero. To my mind, the string of obscenities and insults from the colonel was completely unjustified and unnecessary." Brushing away a tear at these painful memories, she added, "I could never imagine you emulating that officious colonel."

Hearing her story, Alex realised how truly dedicated all the nursing staff were, and in that moment, he was determined not to make their jobs any more difficult. "I'm so sorry, Debbie."

"Don't worry about it. It's all part of the job, and I really do love my work here." The diligent nurse adjusted Alex's bed again using the remote control, made certain he was as comfortable as possible and quietly returned to the nurses' station.

Alex had smelled her perfume as she'd leaned over him, and the sweet, distinctive scent lingered after she had moved away. *Nothing wrong with my sense of smell*, he thought. It was not the only sense that had survived, of course, but like most young men, it had always been lurking just beneath the surface. *Wonder if she is good-looking.* He imagined that she had slim, attractive features, bright, seductive eyes, a small, angular nose and full, soft, delightfully tempting lips.

What he did know for sure was that she had long, silky hair, as it had touched his arm when she'd leaned over him a few days earlier. Had Debbie strictly followed hospital regulations, she should have had it tied back, but there had been occasions, perhaps on her late shift, when she had temporarily let her hair down.

Wonder what colour it is. He could ask her, but for some inexplicable reason, he was a little reticent. In his mind, her hair would be jet black, contrasting against her soft, milk-white skin. He imagined her naked, displaying her small, firm breasts, slim waist and slender hips. He knew that he might be disappointed if the reality did not meet up to his erotically vivid imagination, but well, it helped to pass the time.

Bet she's great in bed, he thought, remembering stories in his youth of the many sexual antics indulged in by members of the nursing profession when off or even on duty, but, of course, that did not mean that these rumours were true. Still, imagination worked wonders when the body was incapable of much, if any, action.

Apart from this interest in the females looking after him, Alex's feelings were a mixture of anger, boredom and regret that he was unable to see or do anything useful for himself, just as if he was an infant once again.

Before all this, he was a picture of physical fitness. As a twenty-four-year-old captain in the British Paratrooper regiment, his six-foot-two-inch, twelve-stone muscular frame enjoyed the admiration of both men and women alike. He not only had strength of body but was also extremely confident, self-disciplined and perfect material for the strict requirements of the British Army.

At twenty, he had undergone rigorous training at Sandhurst Military Academy, leaving as a commissioned officer, and when he was posted to Afghanistan in 2009 as a second lieutenant, he knew it this was exactly what he wanted. He certainly did not relish the idea of a regular occupation, a mindlessly boring, nine-to-five desk job, five days a week for the next forty-odd years. For many, it would have been perfectly acceptable and infinitely preferable to having no job at all. For Alex, it would be like living in a permanent state of limbo with no challenges and no excitement.

He had wanted action, adventure and, of course, a certain degree of danger. His parents, however, were not so convinced and, fearing for his safety, had tried to persuade him to take a less leading role in military activities, but he had always been that way. At the age of six, he'd declared that when he was grown up, he was definitely going to be a soldier. All through school, as well as achieving good results in academic subjects, he had excelled at swimming, rugby, football, gymnastics and long-distance running. He not only had great strength of body but was also determined enough to excel in anything that would assist his military future.

It was not as if there had even been anyone in the close family with a military background. His father, James, was a barrister and his grandfather, Richard, an accountant, both, in Alex's opinion, quite sedentary, extremely boring occupations.

The one exception to this was his mother's brother, Uncle Robert. After ten years in the Royal Air Force, he was now a senior pilot with Singapore Airlines. He was the only one who could understand the hunger for military action so apparent in the youngster. When he had the opportunity to talk to Alex in private, he would tell of his own military experiences, particularly his missions in defence of the Falkland Islands, and generally encouraged the attentive Alex, even creating a degree of tension with his sister and brother-in-law when they realised how his words were influencing their son. Yet nothing would dissuade the determined youngster from his goal.

Both Louise, his mother, and James knew their son had ambitions to have a combat role and were disappointed, though not surprised, when he left the UK for a six-month tour of duty. During that time, he had shown great courage and strength of character and was a worthy example of a commissioned officer.

Alex had been involved in many risky manoeuvres, coming close to death on numerous occasions. On one of these, he managed to rescue a teenage girl and her family after they were threatened and attacked by the Taliban, all because the girl was determined to be well educated, something which the Taliban feared and did their best to prevent. The girl had been injured but, thanks to the intervention of Alex and his combat group, not seriously. He could not understand the Taliban mentality. Did they really fear domination by women? Was that why females seemed to be so dominated by men and repressed within the Islamic faith? He had heard of young, unmarried women who had been brutally stoned to death after being discovered in an intimate relationship, while the man, apparently, would escape without fear of any punishment. Why should women accept anything less than full equality?

It was a great relief for his proud parents when he safely completed his six-month tour of duty and returned to the UK as the newly promoted Captain Alex McCloud.

He had everything going for him. A career he loved and Helen, his fiancée, who had been an important part of his life for the past three years.

The problems started when he returned to Kandahar Province in Afghanistan in December 2010. The troubles were escalating, and the Taliban were proving to be ever more resourceful in their efforts both to evade and attack foreign troops.

Chapter Two

22ⁿᵈ April 2011

WHEN HELEN, ALEX's fiancée, visited him just three days after his return to the UK, he was apprehensive about her reaction. There was a slight hesitation when she entered the ward, and then, without saying a word, she walked up to his bed and planted a tender kiss on Alex's lips. It had been five long months since they had last kissed, but the taste of her lipstick and the smell of her perfume reminded him of much happier times. On that day five months ago, shortly before he went out to Afghanistan, they had done much more than kiss, but how long would it be before he could make love again? How long before he could be a real man?

She gripped his hand tightly. Although Helen considered herself lucky that Alex had survived the conflict, it was heartbreaking to see him in his present condition. "How are you feeling, darling?"

"Better now you're here, sweetheart. It seems like ages since we were together." He relaxed a little, yet within a few seconds, a virtual black cloud appeared at the back of his mind. Somehow, something seemed different and troubling. All his life, Alex had been self-confident and assured, but nothing seemed certain anymore. Did he have anything to look forward to? Would Helen still want to marry him, now he was blind? He wished he could see into the future if only to know what to expect.

"Are you in a lot of pain?"

"The medication helps. The painkillers make me so drowsy that I do sleep quite a lot. Then, there are the headaches, far worse than I've ever experienced. At least I'm alive, unlike poor Jack."

Helen knew of Alex's long friendship with Jack and would have liked to give him a big hug, but she dared not in case it caused him even more pain. "Oh, darling, I'm so sorry."

She sat on the chair at the side of the bed and tenderly held his hand. It was as if it was made of delicate China and may break if she held it any tighter. "When are the bandages going to come off?"

"I don't know. The staff change the bandages regularly to clean and check how the flesh wounds are healing, but I really don't know how long it will take."

Helen sympathised. "Oh, it must be awful. I suppose it will take a while for your eyes to heal before you can see again?"

Alex was stunned by her question. "Didn't my parents tell you about my eyes?"

Her blushes went unseen. "Well, yes. They said both your eyes were damaged, but I thought that surgery would be possible to recover some sight." She was already regretting that she had asked what now seemed like a stupid question.

The hopelessness in Alex's voice was evident as he replied, "You have no idea how much I wish that was true, but the ophthalmic surgeon told me there was too much damage to both eyes to ever have the possibility of seeing again."

An awkward silence fell on the young couple, broken only by Alex's parents and younger sisters, Lucy and Amelia, entering the single ward. His mother sensed the tension between her son and potential daughter-in-law but knew better than to make the situation worse by enquiring about the noticeably chilly atmosphere.

Messages from relatives and friends, some quite humorous, were passed on to Alex by his parents, and the conversation soon took on a lighter tone.

Lucy found the sight of her brother in such a bad way deeply upsetting and shed many tears while squeezing his hand tightly. Thirteen-year-old Amelia was equally upset but somehow managed to stem the flow of tears, having shed so many when she first heard the news about her big brother suffering extensive injuries.

Later, when all the visitors had left, Alex thought again about Helen's question. He had a sickening feeling that everything that had happened over the past three years between them was soon to fall apart. She had not said anything more about his lack of sight, but the disappointment in her voice said it all. Why should anything spoil his chances of a happy marriage?

Over the next few weeks, Helen's visits became less frequent. Alex had feared that would happen but had hoped her feelings were too strong to be affected by his hopeless medical condition.

His depression deepened, noticed by the vigilant medical staff. On top of this, he suffered from many chilling nightmares, where he relived the experience that had so effectively changed his entire life. Reliving the agonising death of his friends and comrades terrified him beyond belief, each nightmare scribing deeper and deeper into his already tormented soul.

On several occasions, the nursing staff had to wake him as he screamed and threshed around in his bed, with the potential to damage his slowly healing wounds.

When Helen did visit, he sensed a barrier between them. She tried to say all the right things to lift his spirits, but there was now an emotional chasm where once their hearts had been deeply entwined. It was almost a relief when visiting time came to an end, as he found it difficult to hide the hurt he was feeling inside.

He surprised himself when he admitted his concern about Helen to Jane, the psychiatric counsellor, a middle-aged woman with a soft, caring voice, who listened attentively to the young man's worries.

"It's not uncommon for relationships to suffer after such a trauma. You may find that she resumes the relationship when you are more mobile. Would you want that?"

Alex had to think about his feelings for Helen. "I think so, but I know I'm a huge disappointment to her."

"Don't be so hard on yourself, Alex. Many blind people can still lead a full, active life."

Even the word *blind* made Alex aware of a deep-rooted fear. Why was this five-letter word so short yet so powerful with his emotions? Why should it happen to him?

"I know, but I never wanted to depend on somebody else. I'm the one who should be looking after my partner."

Jane could understand his feelings of inadequacy. In her job, she had come across similar situations many times, and saying the right words to injured servicemen was never easy. "Give yourself time, and I feel certain that your situation will improve."

He knew she was probably right and tried, with great difficulty, not to worry about his own situation and difficulties.

To add to Alex's anxiety, the painful headaches persisted. For this reason, the specialists responsible for his care decided to carry out a brain scan.

The anticipation of this worried the young soldier even more, as the thought of having not only lost his sight but also having impaired mental abilities was just too much for him to accept.

Peter Jacques, the neurosurgeon who analysed Alex's brain scan, tried to be reassuring. "In most respects, your brain scan appears to be absolutely normal, Captain McCloud."

The 'in most respects' part of the surgeon's statement caused immediate concern to Alex. "What does that mean?"

"As far as we can establish, there are no lesions. This means that there is no neurological impairment to your mental abilities."

"Good." Alex felt a little easier but still knew that there must be something more to explain. "So how is my brain different?"

The surgeon sounded reassuring. "There are signs of increased activity in the right hemisphere, which usually means heightened cognitive reasoning. This could have been caused by the impact on your skull when you were injured in Afghanistan."

Still puzzled, Alex asked, "Is that a good thing?"

"Oh, yes. Individuals with higher activity than normal in this area tend to be more aware, more perceptive and, in some cases, have an unusual gift or talent, such as increased memory retention or the ability to mentally solve complex mathematical calculations."

This took the young man by surprise. "You mean I may now be a genius?"

The specialist, who was quite a big guy, laughed with surprising volume. It was almost a Brian Blessed laugh. "Genius is a bit of an emotive term, but certainly mental capabilities higher than the average, and don't forget, the downside is the problem of continuing headaches."

"Those bloody headaches!" Alex would happily exchange any improvement in his mental abilities for the absence of mind-numbing pain.

The surgeon smiled apologetically, though it went unseen. "I can prescribe medication, but as you probably know, their effectiveness diminishes and can lead to higher, undesirable doses. I would be grateful if you could keep me informed of any unusual side effects that you notice. I'll put my card on your bedside cabinet.

Alex thanked him for the information but doubted he would ever be phoning the surgeon with amazing revelations. For now, his future did not seem to lie much beyond this bed and in this hospital.

Gradually, over the next few weeks, he was allowed out of bed more often as his body began to heal from the burns. It came as a relief to be able to stand after such a long time when he was unable to leave his bed. His legs were weak, and he was shocked to find that he had lost over two stone in weight.

With regular physiotherapy, exercise and a good supply of food, he would regain his body mass, but this would do nothing to bring back his sight.

It was an even greater relief when the dressings were finally removed from around his head. The scarring from the shrapnel wounds was annoying, and the nurses had to keep reminding Alex to leave them alone.

Before the bandages had been removed, Alex had wondered if there would be any vision left. A faint light, perhaps? Moving shadows as people crossed his line of vision? Anything at all would give him some sign of hope, but the inky blackness that surrounded him told him that his dreams were just that. Pointless, stupid, hopeless dreams!

It was the worst feeling he had ever experienced to be immersed in a pitch-black, inky sea of nothing. How deep was this seemingly bottomless, empty pit? Would it ever come to an end?

As he thought about his hopeless, current situation, Alex suddenly remembered an earlier part of his life, which in some ways was reminiscent. When he was about fifteen, he had a phase when he was crazy about potholing. He knew it could be dangerous but enjoyed the excitement of finding as-yet-undiscovered underground caverns.

It was on one of those expeditions that he had nearly lost his life. His group was making its way back to the surface when, without warning, a sudden rock fall blocked his path. What made it worse was that he was isolated from his friends, the rock fall separating them. His torch had been damaged by the fall, leaving him on his own and in complete darkness. He had many anxious thoughts during his imprisonment and wondered if this was how his life was going to end.

It took several hours of delicate rock removal before the emergency services could release him from his cramped, unlit cell in the rocks, and it was an experience he'd hoped never to repeat, yet his current situation had so many similarities.

After this brief exposure to unseen natural light in his present world, small, individual protective dressings were placed over each eye, these being concealed by dark glasses.

In the middle of Alex's feelings of desperation and hopelessness, he thought of his best friend, who had lost his life in the explosion. For Jack Prentice, the blackness would be everything and permanent. He would not feel the soft touch of the nurse's skin or any other woman's, come to that. No earthly exercise would strengthen his muscles. Poor Jack. His death had left a huge gap in Alex's life.

They'd first met at secondary school. A tall and, at that time, quite skinny boy with a cheeky, infectious grin, Jack had always had the nickname of 'Jack Sprat' because of his build, but it never bothered him. The two eleven-year-olds made friends immediately. Intellectually similar, they remained in the same teaching group throughout their school years. They joined the cadets together, and it was obvious to everyone who knew them that both were destined to lead a military career. Both had achieved ten, high-grade GCSE passes and were able to continue studying for their A' Levels, although divergence also came during this time.

Jack had fallen for Suzanne, a good-looking, nicely proportioned girl from their form. Their somewhat stormy relationship had cost him any decent grades in his exams, spoiling his chances of going to Sandhurst, much to his parents' disappointment. Jack had later admitted to Alex that when he should have been studying maths and English for exams, he was instead enjoying studying the birthmarks on Suzanne's nicely rounded backside.

Meanwhile, Alex had resisted the attention of several girls to concentrate on his studies. He did, however, remember how envious he was of Jack, who lost his virginity at least two years before Alex had.

"What is it like to come inside a woman?" he'd asked enviously.

"Fantastic! Mind-blowing! There's just no comparison, especially when you both come at the same time. To feel her body give that final shiver of excitement and then just collapsing into each other's arms. Amazing!"

Alex had seen the longing, lusting look in Jack's eyes, desperate for the next time when he and Suzanne would make love, and it had added to Alex's frustration at never having come anywhere close to experiencing it for himself. To his credit, Jack had realised how Alex felt and tried not to say anything more to frustrate his friend. There were several girls in their year whom Alex had been attracted to, and he'd suspected, no, was *certain* that they would have gone to bed with him if he'd had the courage to approach them. Instead, he'd put his studies above everything else and had been rewarded for his efforts, but was it worth it?

The two friends still kept in touch even though their paths were leading in slightly different directions. Jack had many girlfriends after Suzanne, none lasting more than a few months. He then joined the army at nineteen, while Alex was at Sandhurst.

Alex found the fitness and leadership tests harder than he could ever have imagined, but, thankfully, he was accepted by the world-famous military academy. After twelve months of even more rigorous training at Sandhurst, it was gratifying to be able to enlist in the same battalion as Jack, and the two companions continued their friendship as though nothing had happened.

Of course, there now was a difference. Jack had more military experience, but his rank as sergeant was less than Alex's position as second lieutenant and, in the British Army, keeping within one's rank level was important.

However, Alex had ignored this so-called protocol, treating Jack as his equal, so it was, on that fateful day, Jack who'd led the charge into that cursed building, only to be blown apart by the Taliban's bomb.

Alex was deeply affected by the loss of his good friend, and the memories of thirteen years growing up together were precious to him. He was also saddened by his departure from Intensive Care, as he had grown fond of the two nurses who had looked after him, particularly Debbie. He liked her sense of humour and had a good feeling whenever she was near. Indeed, it was the contrast between Debbie and Helen that played on Alex's mind. Debbie accepted him as a man and treated him normally, while Helen … Well, Helen must have had her own reasons, but when she'd visited him only a few days earlier, she had broken off their engagement.

"I'm so sorry, Alex, but I don't think I can handle what has happened to you. I do feel terrible."

Well, fuck you, Helen Dennison! So you bloody well should! thought Alex, but he said nothing.

Tears filled her eyes as she continued, "I think it better we leave things alone for now and see how we feel after a while. But I'm not certain I could manage to be a good military wife."

Alex's anger was bubbling under the surface, yet he restrained himself. She must have realised the possibilities of him suffering injury or death, as his ambitions for a military career had always been known to her.

"If that is what you want, Helen." He remained cool, distant and impassive.

Again, she repeated, "I'm so sorry."

After she'd left, he thought back to how they had met. His parents had organised a big celebration for his twenty-first birthday, which, fortunately, coincided with his military leave. Helen Dennison had been the Occasions manager at the Hilton hotel selected for his celebration. There had been a mix-up in the catering arrangements for the seventy-five guests expected at Alex's party. Helen had managed to resolve the problem with quiet efficiency but still felt it necessary to apologise to him in person.

The chemistry between them was instant. Within days, they had their first romantic date, and within six months, they were engaged. Alex's career made it difficult to arrange the wedding, especially since both parents wanted to organise huge celebrations and, ironically, they were to be married two months after his current tour of duty. All of that had disappeared with Alex's hospitalisation and Helen's change of heart.

That was the last he'd seen of her after three beautiful, enjoyable years together. Three years of laughter, love and passion. Many times, he had imagined having at least three, possibly four children with Helen, a life full of happiness and companionship. He felt deflated and cheated and was more scared of the future than at any time in his life.

How he hated the Taliban for what they had done. The death of three of his comrades, the loss of his eyesight resulting in the ending of his military career, and to cap it all, the woman he loved had now finished their relationship.

A memorial service had been held for Jack and his comrades, together with other soldiers whose lives had been cut far too short through the actions in Afghanistan, but sadly, Alex's condition prevented him from attending. He did, however, 'watch' the news on television, where the memorial service was covered in detail, with a very moving, descriptive commentary. He felt a mixture of anger and sadness at such unnecessary loss of life and realised that, even though his eyes were useless, his tear ducts were still functioning.

Since Alex was now more mobile, he was able to use the bathroom, giving him back some of his dignity. He had been given so many bed baths and had suffered psychologically by having to use bedpans, that it was liberating to finally use the toilet in private. Debbie had shown him where everything was located in the bathroom, and he soon mastered the controls on all the appliances. Alex had always preferred to shave using the traditional wet razor, feeling that they gave a much closer shave than their electric equivalent. He had thought it would be impossible to shave without being able to see his image in a mirror, but in fact, it was an unnecessary luxury. In reality, one just had to feel around the face, instinctively knowing which areas to avoid.

One morning, feeling particularly depressed by his hopeless situation, Alex realised while shaving that he could end all his problems. The solution lay in his hand. All he had to do was slice into either his neck or wrist.

He stood motionless for what seemed an eternity, thinking of his situation. Would anybody really care if he was dead? He still longed for a military career, but without sight, how could this ever be possible?

The wrist is probably easier. All I have to do is find the main artery, slice into it and the heart would do the rest pumping the life blood out of my body.

He felt for the pulse, knowing that one quick slice of the razor would be enough.

What happens, though, if Debbie finds me before I am dead? She would do everything to try and stem the blood flow and, after that, I would not be allowed to use a razor again.

Then I'd be put on a suicide watch, and everybody would think I was a coward.

Another thought hit him.

How would it affect my parents and younger sisters? Could I really put them through so much heartache?

Alex mulled it over for what seemed hours rather than minutes but pulled himself together when he heard Debbie's voice through the door.

"Are you all right, Alex? Do you need any assistance?" The vigilant nurse had noticed how unusually quiet he was and decided to check.

"Fine, thanks, Debbie. Almost finished shaving."

"Good. I have your medication here when you are ready."

Unknown to Alex, the nursing staff was already keeping a close eye on him. The depth of his depression had been noticed, and everyone had been advised to be alert to the possibility of suicide.

Alex finished shaving, washed his face, patted it dry and applied aftershave. In those few seconds, he had decided not to end his life and was determined to face the future, whatever it may bring.

Chapter Three

15th July 2011

T HE MOVE FROM the ICU was not to another ward in the same hospital. Instead, Alex was driven over ninety miles to Moorfields Eye Hospital in London. He felt useless, having to be guided to enter and exit the car, almost hitting his head on the car roof, yet he could not complain about any of his treatment or the attention given to him.

The nurses were sad when it came to the time for Alex to leave the ward that had been his home for the past four months. Debbie, in particular, astonished Alex by giving him what could only be described as a passionate hug and a tender, meaningful kiss on the lips. He had always liked her but was surprised by the emotion expressed by her. He had to admit that he enjoyed and responded to it warmly, reliving the experience many times during his long journey.

At Moorfields, he was escorted to the consulting room of a Professor Goldman.

"Please take a seat, Captain McCloud."

His voice was confident, warm, yet professional. It seemed odd that, after many years of assessing individuals by their looks and actions, Alex no longer had that luxury. Everything had to be ascertained by voice alone. As to Professor Goldman's age, his voice was not the easiest way to assess, but Alex guessed he was in his late forties, plus or minus ten years.

The young soldier's hand was placed on the arm of the offered chair. Clumsily, he took a seat.

"As you are no doubt aware, your eyes suffered a great deal from the explosion. Both corneas were damaged beyond repair or possible transplant." Professor Goldman paused, but without any response from the young soldier, continued. "Normally, in such circumstances, both eyes would be completely removed and inactive prosthetic replacements inserted."

"Why do you say, 'normally'? Why am I different?" Alex was puzzled. His eyes were useless, so why not take the bloody things away?

The professor spoke in a relaxed manner, unfazed by Alex's almost hostile reaction. "This standard procedure can still be carried out, but I wanted to put an alternative suggestion to you."

"Is there any alternative?" Alex could not imagine why they were dragging out this painful, psychological torment.

"When the medical team dealing with your injuries contacted me, they described the trauma in detail. There had been considerable scarring of tissue, particularly around the eyes, with a possible loss of aqueous humour, which is ninety-nine per cent water, indicating probable permanent loss of sight. As a result, I asked them to keep the remaining receptive areas of your eyes protected with a special dressing that would assist in preserving what remains of the retina. You were probably not even aware of this, but by taking these precautions, we now have an alternative to permanent blindness."

Was this the reason why he had seen nothing when the bandages were removed? Had there really been another layer he was not aware of? Alex's curiosity was now getting the better of him. "Tell me more."

"Well, if the eyes are removed completely, then there can never be any chance of seeing anything again, as the optic nerve would be severed."

Stating the bloody obvious, thought Alex.

"In your case, the retinas and the optic-nerve connections are still intact, while the front portion of the eyes is severely damaged."

Alex's attention and hopes were raised by the professor's words. "Does it mean that I may be able to see again?"

"I don't want to raise false hopes, but at Moorfields, in conjunction with the University College of London's Institute of Ophthalmology, we have been carrying out a great deal of research into synthetic lenses and pupils. We are at the point of looking for somebody to test the very promising results of our research."

Alex was stunned by the professor's words. "You want me to be a guinea pig?"

The professor chose his words carefully, fully aware that Alex already felt hostile and defeated by his current loss of sight. "We are at a very advanced stage of research and believe we are ready to test it in a live situation. Ideally, we need a physically fit person who is self-disciplined. Would you be interested?"

Alex now understood why he had been the obvious candidate for the research and that many who lose their sight would not be suitable. "I'm interested, but I need to know more before I agree."

"That's fair. What do you want to know?"

It was obvious what Alex's first question would be. "Will it enable me to see normally again?"

"There is a fair chance, but it may never approach the full vision potential of normal sight. The human eye is a truly fantastic piece of engineering, and any man-made replacement is bound to be inferior."

Alex's hopes lost some of their initial expectations. He had heard of light-sensitive chips being used where normal sight was impossible. While successful, the resolution was extremely limited and could not provide much visual use. The ability to distinguish between light and dark with vague, shadowy images did not appeal to him. In Alex's mind, a low-resolution camera built into spectacles and with a connected battery pack would not give him much useful vision and would make him look decidedly odd.

Curiously, the professor seemed to realise what Alex was thinking. "You have probably heard about chip implants, but let me assure you, Alex, what we have achieved here is infinitely superior to those early implants."

"In what way?"

"What we have achieved is almost a complete replacement for the human eye. The only parts we retain are the retina and the connecting optic nerve." It was clear from the professor's voice that he was proud of the achievements of his team. "Powerful microelectronics are embedded into the prosthetic eye, giving it capabilities never thought possible."

Alex thought of a potential flaw. "Electronics need power. How do you achieve this?" He did not wish to have unsightly wires coming out of his head, leading to an external battery pack. *I don't want to look like Frankenstein's monster.*

"You're quite correct. Micro-photovoltaic cells are used to generate the tiny amount of power needed." Before Alex could ask, the professor added, "Capacitors are used to store the power for up to twenty-four hours, so as long as the wearer has some stimulus from natural daylight or even artificial light every twenty-four hours, that is sufficient to power the devices without the need for any external electrical source."

Alex's curiosity was now aroused. "I'm impressed. Tell me more about the resolution, and is it monochrome or colour vision?"

"Over the past few months, we have managed to increase the resolution from eight hundred by six hundred to nineteen hundred and twenty by twelve hundred. The colour palette is sixteen and a half million. Do you think that is enough?" The professor had deliberately emphasised the word 'colour' to leave Alex in no doubt about the capabilities of his prized invention.

"Those specifications sound like those of a computer monitor or television."

"That's true. The basic technology is identical. In truth, the human eye can only distinguish about ten million colours, so the spec is more than enough."

Alex now had hope in his voice. "It does sound remarkable, and yes, I am extremely interested."

The professor slid open a drawer and carefully lifted out a small package. "This is an earlier prototype, but it will give you some idea of the size. He handed the device over to Alex, who turned the tiny object around in his hand, feeling its shape and size. It was about twenty-five millimetres in diameter, yet not a perfect sphere. The front portion was of smaller diameter than that where the retina resides at the back of the eye.

"How does the weight compare to that of a natural eye?"

"A typical weight of a human eye is about twenty-eight grams, while the one in your hand weighs thirty-two grams when filled with the necessary fluid. The extra weight is marginal and quite manageable. The muscles surrounding the eye can handle up to about thirty-six grams."

Satisfied that these remarkable implants could give him sight once again, Alex agreed to stay at Moorfields for the next few weeks to undergo testing, fitting and training.

Professor Goldman took him to one of the many laboratories within the hospital and asked Alex to lie on a bed. He needed to inspect the remains of Alex's eyes and carefully removed the dressing from one. "Excellent! The tissue in the orbit appears to be in good condition, and there is no sign of retinal detachment."

"If my eyes are still working, shouldn't I be able to see something now? Even just light?" To Alex's logical mind, this was an inconsistency.

"Sorry, Alex. I should have explained. The dressing is in two parts, and in here, I dare not remove the lower. This can only be done in absolute sterile conditions and when you are anaesthetised."

That did sound logical to Alex, yet there was still a big question in his mind.

"What I can't understand is why the microelectronics are necessary. Surely, if the retina is still working, all it needs is a small lens to focus the image on the retina?"

Professor Goldman had anticipated this question. He knew Alex was intelligent enough to work out this simpler solution. "There is a good reason, but I am not the person to explain it to you." He looked at his watch. "The person who can tell you more will be arriving in about forty-five minutes. Until then, I would ask you to be patient, and hopefully, everything will be explained."

Alex was curious about the identity of this mysterious individual. The professor carefully replaced the dressings around Alex's eyes and then escorted him to the room where he would be staying for the next few weeks.

He introduced Amy, a nurse at Moorfields. "She will show you where everything is in your room. We want your stay to be as comfortable as possible. I'll see you later."

"Hello, Alex. Do you mind if I take your hand to show you where everything is?"

"No, not at all." Amy took hold of his right hand and, with great care and understanding of his situation, showed him the location of his bed, chairs, locker and wardrobe. Her hand was cool and gentle as she placed his on each item in the room.

"Where's my case?" he asked.

"Don't worry. It's in the bottom of the wardrobe. I can help you unpack if you wish."

"It's okay, Amy. I'll manage. What about the toilet? I hope it's not far."

"You have your own private bathroom and toilet. Come, I'll show you."

Again, she took his hand and led him into a well-fitted bathroom. There was a bath, shower, toilet and washbasin, all positioned to make location easy.

"It's like a four-star hotel. From what you've told me, I even have my own television in the bedroom."

"You do," Amy confirmed and showed him the controls on the uncluttered remote, making certain that he knew how to use it.

"Is everything okay now, Alex?" She had a very pleasant, soft voice with a slight, almost imperceptible Irish accent. "Is there anything else I can do for you?"

There was, but he knew it would not be included in her job description. He smiled at her. "No, thanks. You've been very helpful."

"If you do need assistance, just pick up the phone and ask for me. If I am off duty, ask for Helen."

The mention of this second name brought back painful memories of his ex-fiancée.

Amy noticed the sudden change in his expression at the mention of her colleague's name. "Are you all right, Alex?"

Snapping out of his thoughts, he regained his composure. "Yes, difficult memories returning. Sorry, I…"

"Don't worry, it's understandable. Right, I'll leave you in peace. Just remember, if you have a shower, don't wet the dressings around your eyes."

As soon as he was on his own, Alex checked the time on his talking watch. He had requested some way of knowing the time and date several weeks earlier and had been provided with a fairly bulky wristwatch which had a strong, rather sombre-sounding male voice. Sometimes, he found the voice extremely irritating, but at least he knew what time of day and date it was.

"Four thirty. Probably another thirty minutes before my visitor. Enough time to freshen up."

As he carefully washed his hands and face and changed into more formal clothes, hopefully suitable for the visitor, many troubled thoughts ran through his mind.

When he had been in hospital in Afghanistan, he had been told that the chances of having any useful vision were minimal. This had been reinforced by the medical staff at the hospital in Birmingham, yet he was now being given the opportunity of having his sight restored. Why? Something must have changed, but what?

A knock on his door disturbed his thoughts. He opened it.

"Are you ready to meet your visitors, Alex?" It was Professor Goldman.

"Visitors? As in plural?"

"Yes, there are two people I would like you to meet. I'll escort you to the boardroom where we can talk in comfort."

Alex took the offered arm of the professor and followed him along the winding corridors. He still felt uncomfortable and embarrassed holding on to a man while he was perfectly happy to be escorted by a woman. Somehow, it offended his masculinity.

Chapter Four

A s they entered the boardroom, Alex heard chairs being scraped on the floor as the strangers stood up. Who could they be? Alex was curious to find out.

Professor Goldman spoke. "Could you introduce yourselves, please?"

"Certainly." The first man walked up to Alex, took his hand and shook it firmly. "Brigadier General Paul Marshall. Pleased to meet you, Captain McCloud." His typically military voice indicated someone not just of high rank, but something even more exclusive and important. There was no way in which Alex could accurately determine the appearance of this senior official, but he imagined a stout, erect figure with gingery-coloured hair and a tidy moustache. He was probably one of a long line of military leaders in his family, of whom there were no doubt many portraits on the walls of his ancient manor.

In spite of all this, there was something about him that Alex did not like. Was it something in his voice or mannerisms? Alex could not work out what it was, but for whatever reason, he felt wary of this distinguished army officer. His experience of most, but not all senior army officers had never instilled him with much confidence. In fact, he considered many to be pompous, arrogant pricks. *Guys do not get to his rank by being nice*, thought Alex.

The man relaxed his grip, allowing the other person to move closer to Alex. This voice surprised him even more than the brigadier general's.

"Major Jennifer Sherlock. Very pleased to meet you, Captain."

Her handshake, while not as strong as the brigadier general's, was warm, firm and conveyed a great sense of discipline, confirmed by her senior rank. The most surprising fact was that she was not English. Her voice sounded American and yet not quite.

With a sudden inspiration, he asked, "Do I detect a slight Canadian accent in your voice, Major?"

She laughed. "Well noticed. My family came from Canada, but we moved to New York when I was twelve, so my accent is a mix of both countries. Probably the worst."

Professor Goldman, eager to get the meeting underway, interrupted these pleasantries. "Shall we all take a seat?"

Alex's hand was placed on the arm of a comfortable chair. All four took their seats. It was the brigadier general who started the conversation.

"I'm sorry for the lack of information given to you, Captain McCloud. Hopefully, we can clear up any confusion or misunderstandings."

"Good! I would like to know why the use of microelectronics is necessary, but even more, I would like to know why I was told that I probably would never see again."

"I must admit that, when you arrived in the field hospital, the specialist there felt there was too much damage to your eyes to retrieve any useful vision."

"So what changed?" Alex was not going to be overawed by this senior-ranking official.

"One of the specialists at the military hospital in the UK found that while there had indeed been major damage to both eyes, parts of the retina may still be functioning and receptive enough to provide some useful vision, providing the remainder of the eyes could be prosthetically replicated."

The professor spoke. "This specialist contacted me at Moorfields to explain your prognosis and enquired about our recent research. The problem is that not all of the retina's receptive area survived. Focusing light through a conventional prosthetic lens would provide some useful sight, but the field of vision would be severely restricted, perhaps even distorted." He paused to let this information be absorbed by the attentive Alex. "The technology we have been developing here can overcome this problem by electronically manipulating and enhancing the image before it is received by the retina."

Alex understood what was being said, but still had a problem. "Why all the secrecy?"

"The fact is that our research is just that. If this micro-implant is used, you would be the first person on the planet to receive it."

"And that is where we come in," the brigadier general interrupted. "As head of Military Intelligence at MI6, your situation is of considerable interest to us."

"But why?" The frustration in Alex's voice remained.

"Perhaps I can help." It was the softer voice of Major Sherlock. "Have you heard of augmented reality?"

"Yes." Alex was hesitant. "I've heard of it being used in video games."

"It has much wider use than gaming. The military already uses it in some situations, and it can prove very useful. I work in a small, elite unit in the US Defence Department, where the benefits of augmented reality are studied and utilised to our advantage. But we are still at an early stage."

Alex was beginning to understand. "So you want to create augmented reality within my eyes?"

"In a nutshell, yes."

Alex could sense the excitement in her voice. These people wanted to use him as a human guinea pig, but there was still something that had not been said, something he was missing. He raised his head and, hopefully directing his question at Professor Goldman, asked, "There's a catch, isn't there? What are you not telling me?"

The professor remained quiet, but the brigadier general gave a little cough and answered Alex's question. "You are quite correct, Captain McCloud. To the outside world, you must still appear to be blind. Nobody, apart from a select group of people, must know that you can see. This military advantage must not be known to the individuals your missions will involve."

Everything had now dropped into place, but Alex's anger was rising. The events of the past few months raced silently through his tormented mind. "I don't know whether any of you know or even care, but my fiancée dumped me because she could not handle the probability of looking after me, as a blind person, for the rest of my life." There was silence in the room. Had he been unfair to expect something, anything from these three disparate individuals? "I'm sorry, it just upsets me to think about how my life has been turned upside down, and you want to meddle with my eyes to suit your military needs."

Professor Goldman broke the silence. "You don't have to decide now. Take as long as you want."

Alex ignored this. "If I do agree, what do you want of me? You would want something for such an investment?"

Major Sherlock picked her words carefully. "Criminals and terrorist groups, both here and in the States, are becoming ever more resourceful, and this technology could bring many benefits. We would like you to undertake specific special missions jointly between British and American forces. For this, you would receive jointly from the two governments a payment of two hundred and thirty thousand US dollars each year. That's about—"

"One hundred and fifty thousand pounds," interrupted Alex as he swiftly calculated, using the approximate exchange rate of one point five dollars to the pound. That was a considerable amount and far more than he had been paid by the British Government during his military career and even more than David Cameron, the present Conservative Prime Minister. It was a very attractive inducement.

If he turned down the offer, he would receive injury compensation and a meagre pension. It could be a very uncertain future without the means to earn a decent living. He could go back to living with his parents, but that would be a burden on them, and what would happen as they became old and infirm? He did not want to imagine such a bleak, empty future.

His thoughts were interrupted by the brigadier general. "On top of your salary, we would provide a place for you to live, rent-free, here in London."

With the current property prices in the capital escalating at an unprecedented rate, that was an even greater inducement, but it was not what changed Alex's mind. The thought of being on secret missions with their inherent danger intrigued him.

"Okay. I will agree to be your guinea pig. Just don't get it wrong. My future depends upon it."

The three men and one woman stood up, and handshakes were, again, exchanged. Alex was surprised to hear Major Sherlock say to the professor, "I'll cancel my return flight to Washington and book into a local hotel."

"My secretary will assist you in finding somewhere to stay. There are many hotels within a short distance from Moorfields. The Crown Plaza at Shoreditch is only about ten minutes' walk from here."

Alex could not resist the temptation to ask, "What is your involvement in the next stage of my treatment, Major?"

"The electronics developed here at Moorfields needs some software enhancement to include the facility to add A-R and that is my specialty. I will be here as long as is necessary. I'm afraid that you are going to see a lot more of me."

This thought excited Alex. If she looked as good as she sounded, the day when he would be able to see again could not come too soon.

The brigadier general added, even though Alex had not asked the question of him, "My involvement here is finished for now, and I'll leave you in far more capable hands. I will be more involved when the missions commence. I wish you every success, Captain McCloud." With that, the brigadier left the room. Alex had the impression that he enjoyed being the centre of attention and was relieved the senior officer had departed.

"Would you like to take my arm, Captain?" Surprisingly, it was not the professor who offered this but the much preferable Major Sherlock.

"Yes, thanks." Alex wondered if she understood his discomfort in being guided by a man. He did realise, while they were walking along the corridor, that she was quite tall. Perhaps five feet nine or ten? He found it difficult to guess her age, but with her rank, the probability was that she was older than him. Perhaps in her late twenties or early thirties?

After leaving Alex at his bedroom door, she went with the professor to the office, where she could organise her accommodation.

Alex remembered how, less than two weeks earlier, he had contemplated suicide and was thankful that he had not had the courage to take his own life.

His spirits now lifted, Alex was more optimistic about his future and decided he needed to rebuild his military physique. He was not in bad condition but had not carried out any strenuous exercise for quite a long time. He changed into tracksuit pants, sweatshirt and trainers.

Fifty press-ups, a break and another fifty was a good start. He wished he had the pull-up bar to strengthen his arm muscles and checked the doorframe to see if it was able to take his weight. He had to admit to himself that the doorframe construction was not designed for a twelve- or thirteen-stone man to suspend himself from and had to make do with stretching exercises. Still, it was a start.

He was sweating when Amy knocked on his door. "I've brought your dinner, Alex."

She wheeled the trolley in and served Alex's meal, placing his plate and cutlery on the adjustable table, positioning it so that Alex could sit in a comfortable chair.

His exercises had given him an appetite, and he managed to persuade the young nurse to give him an extra portion of beef and fries.

After eating his fill, he pushed the table to one side and was about to relax when he heard another knock at the door. "Come in, Amy," he called, assuming she'd come to clear away his dishes, and was surprised when Major Sherlock entered the room.

"I hope you don't mind me disturbing you. I'm at a bit of a loose end in my hotel and thought it might be a good opportunity to find out a bit more about you."

Alex was pleased. "No problem. Pull up a chair, Major."

She laughed. "Let's get rid of these military titles. Please call me Jen."

"Okay, that's fine by me. What do you want to know?"

Jen was very probing and particularly interested in his childhood, asking many questions about his family, education and military training.

He answered all her questions as accurately and honestly as he could and then decided to balance the conversation a little by asking, "Which part of Canada do you come from?"

Her gentle laugh was quite pleasant and endearing. "You won't have heard of it. Innisfil is a tiny town on the west shore of Lake

Simcoe in Ontario. When I lived there, the population was less than thirty thousand and nothing much ever happened."

"Was this the reason your family moved to New York?"

"In part, yes. There were too few opportunities to do much in such a tiny, rural place. My parents wanted me to have better chances than they had."

"Any regrets?"

It did not take much thought for her reply. "None at all. Don't get me wrong, Innisfil is a beautiful place, but if I had stayed there, I would probably now be a logger's wife with half a dozen kids running around the house and an addiction to antidepressants."

They both laughed. Alex sensed from her remark that Jen put career above family life but still asked, "Is there a Mr. Sherlock?"

Again, she laughed. Her character was relaxed and quite amiable, bolstering Alex's thoughts about her. "Only my dad! I travel around too much to settle down, and I love my job."

"I can tell that you're very enthusiastic about your work." Alex was feeling a bit restless, and as he moved to become more comfortable, he accidentally pressed the button on his talking watch. As the stentorian male voice announced that it was nine forty-three, Alex apologised. "Sorry, I didn't mean to press it. It's a bit too sensitive. You know, I can't stand the voice."

She seemed surprised. "Why? It sounds quite manly."

"That's the problem. It gives me a shock, especially when I press it accidentally, which happens often. I would have preferred a more soothing, softer voice."

Jen showed interest. "Let me have a look at your watch, Alex." He slipped it off his wrist and handed it to her.

It was quite bulky, with an analogue display and four buttons, two on each side of the face. Thoughtfully, Jen said, "We need to provide some interface between the chips in your eyes and the internet. We could include it within a wristwatch and engineer a more acceptable voice at the same time."

"Really?" Alex was impressed. He was constantly amazed by the miniaturisation of complex electronic circuitry.

"We could easily manufacture a much smarter watch, combining all the functions needed." Jen stood up. "Anyway, it's time I was leaving you in peace and going back to my hotel."

Alex had enjoyed the evening, even the probing questions and deep discussions about his background. Still, he felt certain that they would be seeing a lot more of each other and was quite happy with this situation.

Chapter Five

OVER THE NEXT two weeks, Alex's patience was severely tested as numerous measurements were taken and software tweaked to optimise the quality and reliability of the tiny chips. He was desperate to reach the point where he could see something, anything. To him, the past few months of blackness had seemed an eternity, even to the point where he had difficulty remembering what it was like to have normal vision. Just to see the rich greens of grass or bright, blue skies seemed far too difficult to recollect. His frustration, together with his continuing headaches, had been making him feel quite irritable and ill-tempered, but somehow, he managed to repress his inner anger.

True to her word, Jen retained a keen interest and, when she was not working, spent many hours with Alex.

Even with all the attention, he still had a strange, empty feeling. A feeling that would not leave him, no matter how hard he tried to shut it out. One evening, he was in his room, eating his dinner. The radio was on in the background. He had come to hate the silence and used the radio for company, almost like a child's soother.

The five-o'clock news was, however, depressing with riots being sparked off in London, following the fatal shooting of twenty-nine-year-old gangster, Mark Duggan, by a police marksman in Tottenham. Anger was spreading at what seemed, to many, to have been an assassination, since Duggan was, apparently, unarmed, although a gun was found only twenty feet away, suggesting that Duggan had discarded it on seeing the police.

Thankfully, the music was more uplifting in Simon Mayo's 'Drive Time' on Radio Two. Since it was Friday, listeners could request the artist and soundtrack they would like him to play.

One listener talked excitedly about his girlfriend. The two of them would be travelling to Barcelona for a romantic holiday the following day, and he wanted to hear music that reminded him of her, particularly the colour of her eyes.

It was his choice of music which caught Alex's attention. 'Brown-eyed Girl' by Van Morrison was requested. This track, released long before Alex was even born and superbly sung by the talented Morrison, was still frequently played on the radio, and now he listened to every word and phrase in great detail.

The guy who requested it probably had never listened closely to all the lyrics, which were painfully reminiscent of Alex's own situation and not one of lovers about to go on holiday together. Helen's eyes were, indeed, a beautiful, deep shade of brown, but the song was remembering the times together before they had separated. As with Alex, they were now only distant memories. Even the line about the waterfall had significance, as they'd had this same experience, two years earlier while walking along a narrow, slippery path near a powerful waterfall in the Cumbrian hills on a hot, August day. Alex was missing Helen more than he had expected and, like Van Morrison, finding it so hard to continue with life as usual.

After the song finished, Alex sat motionless for several minutes, turning the skilfully crafted words around in his mind. Illogically, he now both loved and hated it and wondered if Morrison had suffered a similar, painful break-up of a wonderful relationship, inspiring the emotional words. He was on the edge of tears, held back only by a stubborn belief that this was not something a real man should do.

Eventually snapping out of his morose mood, he finished his meal but was still troubled by these pervasive thoughts.

THERE CAME A time when no further work could be done at Moorfields, as the final chip had to be manufactured in a special facility, which was more normally used for assembling the complex electronics used in satellites. Even so, the production would be given top priority and constructed in a very short time frame.

Noticing that Alex was becoming ever more restless, Jen asked, "Would you like me to go with you for a walk outside the hospital?"

"Would I? That would be great! I'm tired of being restricted to my room and the laboratory."

Jen smiled, understanding his frustration. "Right, I'll call at your room in fifteen minutes, and we'll see how far you can walk. I've checked with Professor Goldman, and he says that it's fine for us to go out."

"Good. I don't know what to wear. Is it cold, outside?" After being restricted to indoors for so long and with no visual feedback from the outside world, he felt uncertain.

"It's actually quite bright, sunny and fairly warm. A perfect day for a walk."

Emerging from the hospital entrance, Alex breathed in the fresh air and held on to Jen's arm as they walked down the steps onto City Road. This was the old entrance, which Jen preferred to use rather than the newer Cayton Street entrance around the corner.

She guided him expertly, letting him know as they approached any steps up or down. He found her pace quite comfortable, not too fast nor slow, and felt quite confident in her care. He was wearing dark glasses, but even so, some people still managed to bump into him. He accepted their apologies, without complaint, when they noticed his situation, but in truth, he really did not mind. He felt so exhilarated by the feeling of the sun on his face, the noise of the city and the strange array of smells in the air. He was like a baby, learning new sensory experiences, and was relieved that the bomb in Afghanistan had not damaged any of his other senses.

They did not walk very far from the hospital since both hardly knew their way around the bustling city and did not wish to get caught up in the current riots, which had now spread to other parts of the UK. Jen did, however, know the route to her hotel in Shoreditch and used this knowledge to their advantage as they walked around the streets of London.

Jen was fairly talkative as they strolled along, and as Alex had already noticed, conversation with this young, vibrant woman was quite easy. As a comparative newcomer to London, she was fascinated by the royal family, particularly Princes William and Harry.

"What I can't understand is why the royals need so many palaces. Apart from Buckingham Palace, there's also Kensington, St. James and Hampton Court." After a moment's thought, she added, "And then there's Windsor Castle as well! Just how many palaces does the royal family need?"

"You have a good point, but after so many years of royalty, they inevitably accumulate many historical buildings."

"Yes, but who pays for the upkeep and maintenance of all these buildings?"

"Partly through tax payments, but the queen does pay for a large part of the cost of upkeep. Tourism also brings in a terrific income to offset all the expense, so it's not quite as bad as you may think." After a moment's thought, he added, "At least we don't have to maintain Nonsuch Palace!"

Jen almost did a double take. "Nonsuch Palace? It sounds like a Disney creation."

Alex laughed, half-expecting such a reaction from someone who lived across the Atlantic. "Henry the Eighth decided to build the best palace in the world to celebrate the birth of his first son and named it 'Nonsuch' because there would be nothing as good to compare it with."

There was a hint of curiosity and perhaps a slightly mocking tone in Jen's voice as she asked, "So what happened to…" She paused, finding it difficult to repeat such a strange, untypically British name. "Nonsuch Palace?"

Their discussion was temporarily interrupted at this point, as they crossed over the busy road, Jen guiding him, particularly at the up and down kerbs.

"Poor Henry never saw its completion. He died a few years before it was finished. Apparently, it did live up to its name and was built in Henry's hunting grounds in Surrey. It passed down the royal lineage, and by the 1680s, it was in the hands of Charles the Second, who, foolishly, gave it to one of his mistresses."

"Lucky woman! So, it's no longer a royal palace?"

"Worse than that. His mistress had enormous gambling debts and had the building torn down, selling all the materials to pay off her debts. From that point on, Nonsuch Palace ceased to exist and became 'No such Palace'!"

Jen laughed. "I really don't know whether I should believe this story. It has a strange yet ridiculously plausible sound to it."

"Would I lie to you?" Alex smiled, knowing how ludicrous the story must have sounded. He had thought the same when Helen had told him of the long-demolished royal building, but the internet had confirmed the facts.

"Check it on Google and you'll see."

After walking for nearly two hours, they returned to the hospital and back to Alex's now very familiar room. As he sat on the bed, he said, "It's crazy, Jen. I feel exhausted, and yet what we have done today is nothing compared to normal daily army routines."

"Don't worry. You have been inactive for quite a while. It will take time to get back into shape."

Alex's smile was one of gratitude. "I know. Thanks so much, Jen. I'd be lost without you. Literally!"

She laughed at his quip. "No problem. I enjoy your company."

He stood up and, hoping his effort would not seem too clumsy, took hold of Jen and leaned in for a kiss. It was a miscalculation on his part.

She pulled away and stood back from him, surprised at his bold approach. "Sorry, Alex. I'm not sure that's a good idea."

The young man dropped his hands, feeling foolish and admonished. Naively, he asked, "Why? You just said that you like me."

There was a note of exasperation in her voice. "I do, but I want to keep our relationship professional. The last thing I need is to return home and try to maintain a long-distance relationship. Sorry, but it's just not going to work, Alex."

He could see the sense of her argument but still had hoped for a better response. During the past few weeks, they had spent many hours together, and he had felt great comfort in Jen's company, but more than that, he had longed to make love to her. When struggling to fall asleep at night, he had, on many occasions, imagined Jen pulling the covers back and climbing in naked beside him, her wandering hands discovering every intimate part of his body. Her fragrance and the touch of her skin, although only in his imagination, had aroused him, and he'd wished these fantastic, sensual dreams would, somehow, come true. *Perhaps there is someone in her life, back in the States*, he thought.

For Jen, the budged attempt had not been a complete surprise. She'd noticed a change in Alex. Now he was getting over Helen, he probably felt that she was fair game for a new romantic involvement. Jen did really like him, but it was too soon for such a relationship. For her, it was nearly three years since she had been intimately close to anybody, and she was still hurting from the experience. The thoughts of her ex-lover filled her mind and brought great sadness to her, after his horrific killing.

Their thoughts and discussion were interrupted by the arrival of Professor Goldman. He was excited, and if he did sense the awkward situation, he showed no sign. "Alex! We've just received the prosthetic eyes from the lab. We're lucky the package managed to reach here, considering all the riots in London and around the country."

"Great!" His enthusiasm at the news was slightly tempered by the continuing violence and Jen's not unreasonable rejection of his advances. "When can they be fitted?"

The professor looked at his watch. "We have some final tests to ensure that everything is okay, but I see no reason why we can't fit them tomorrow morning."

It would be a relief to end his world of blackness, and Alex knew that if it was not for the dedication of this brilliant professor, this chance would not even be possible. The ophthalmic surgeon left the young couple to return to his work.

Recovering himself, Alex said, "I'm so sorry, Jen. Of course, you are right."

"It's all right, Alex. I can understand your situation and, I guess, you're still missing Helen."

The mention of his ex-fiancée's name made Alex realise that Jen's words rang true. The pain of separation was immense, and it would be very difficult for any other woman to ever replace her. Yet he knew Jen was someone very special. He felt incredibly stupid for making such an amateurish pass and blamed it on his sexually starved hormones.

Jen suggested that Alex get a good night's sleep, ready for the work of the following day. She held his hand and kissed him gently on the cheek, which Alex gratefully accepted as consolation.

He still found difficulty sleeping, thinking about his fudged attempt at intimacy with Jen. Was she really a 'Helen substitute' or was she someone he wanted to have a long-term relationship with?

Chapter Six

IN A QUIET road in London, not too far from Moorfields Eye Hospital, Tony Bradbury was at the wheel of his smart, six-month-old Mercedes C-Class. He was quite early for his meeting and drove at a leisurely pace. Twenty-eight-year-old Tony was a confident, successful criminal who had made most of his money from dealing drugs. He never dealt with end users, preferring to act instead as a middleman or, as he preferred to think of himself, as a wholesaler.

Over the past few years, he had enjoyed spending the fruits of his crimes on numerous luxuries, giving him the confidence of one who had made it. A smart, West End apartment, expensive personal jewellery and a bank balance in excess of two million all helped Tony believe he was untouchable.

Sitting behind him was heavily built Jake Mitchell, Tony's business partner of five years and his muscle. Both men were looking for possible traps, never trusting those they were involved with to do exactly as expected. Tony and Jake were armed and ready to kill anybody who may decide to cause them a problem.

Tony parked the car at the quiet entrance to an ancient-looking warehouse, as agreed with their contact.

"I don't like this area," said Jake. "There's something about this that gives me an uneasy feeling."

"Relax, Jake. Just keep your eyes alert and we'll be all right."

Within a few minutes and precisely on time, a man of medium build, probably in his early thirties and carrying a briefcase, approached the car.

Tony unlocked the doors and opened the front-passenger door just enough to indicate where the man should go.

Pulling the door fully open, he took the front-passenger seat and placed the briefcase on his lap. After closing the door, the man said, "Impressive car, Tony."

"It should be for the price I had to pay." Tony did not like small talk and asked, "Do you have all the money?"

"Of course. Do you have the goods?"

Tony was almost offended but ignored the question and lifted a briefcase onto his knees. "You show me the cash and I'll show you the goods."

The man seemed quite casual as he turned his briefcase to allow inspection of the contents. He flipped the catch and lifted the lid. A high-pressure *whoosh* of eight litres of sevoflurane gas was instantly released, giving just enough time for the man to fit a small, protective breathing mask to his face before the effects could be felt by him.

For Tony and Jake, there was no such escape, both men losing consciousness within three seconds. Jake had started to draw his gun but was unable to complete his defence.

The rear door opened, and another man, similarly fitted with protective mask, slipped into the vacant seat. He shut the door and held out his hand expectantly. The man in the front seat took two long ice picks out of the briefcase and handed one to the other. Within seconds, both Tony and Jake had the ice picks rammed into the backs of their necks and up into their brains, ensuring that their deaths would be swift and with minimum loss of blood. Some had spilled out of the small wound and run onto the expensive, tailored shirt and suit Tony wore.

One man opened the window just long enough to dissipate the gas and make it possible for their masks to be removed. The dark-tinted windows on the Mercedes had assisted these two killers in their carefully executed plan. They were meticulous as they wiped their prints off anything they had touched.

Danny Jackson and Paddy Conroy stepped out of the car, each carrying a briefcase. One had not much more than a small amount of cash and the mechanism for releasing the gas, while the other contained three kilos of high-quality cocaine.

Once they had walked far enough away from the Mercedes to avoid suspicion, Paddy took a phone from his pocket and dialled a number. His message was brief and concise. "Business transaction completed successfully."

Danny smiled. "Gianni should be very pleased with today's work."

Paddy agreed. "Shame about the car. I wouldn't mind one like that myself."

The two men continued their walk until they reached their own car a few blocks away. Satisfied with the success of their mission, they drove away from the area.

Chapter Seven

9th August 2011

A LEX LAY, ANAESTHETISED on the operating table, a clamp holding his head steady, allowing the gowned surgeon to begin the very delicate operation. The tiny dressings that had been protecting the retinas were removed, and the prosthetic shells, complete with their miniature electronics, were gently inserted into the vacant orbits. The clamps holding the facial tissue were slowly released, allowing the muscles to grip the shells and fill the anterior chambers with aqueous humour.

When he was satisfied that Alex's replacement eyes were correctly aligned, Professor Goldman motioned to Jen to inspect the final appearance. He lifted the eyelids to show Major Sherlock.

"They appear fantastic and so real-looking. I just hope Alex is going to be able to see again."

"We'll know as soon as he comes round from the anaesthetic."

A very groggy Alex began to come back to consciousness about forty minutes later. While under anaesthetic, he had experienced a strange, almost realistic dream of two men being silently killed, which, considering his military background, was not surprising, yet for some inexplicable reason, he felt that this was closer to home than Afghanistan. The pain in his head seemed too much to bear but eased as he returned to full consciousness.

As his mind cleared, he realised that a mask had been placed over his eyes, and he moved his hand to take it away.

Professor Goldman noticed. "Are you ready, Alex?"

"Yes, of course. I've longed for this moment for months."

The surgeon carefully lifted the mask off and helped the younger man to sit upright. "Tell me what you can see."

Alex prayed this was going to work and looked in the direction of the professor's voice.

There was definitely something different. The inky blackness had disappeared and was now replaced with a pale, insipid-looking mist surrounding him, but then he noticed that the mist was gradually becoming more and more patchy, with haphazardly positioned blotches of other colours slowly invading his visual field.

"Yes! I can see some light!" Concentrating his efforts, he stared intently at the older man. "How do I focus the image?"

"Exactly the same as you have always done. Just look at the object you wish to see, and the muscles will adjust the focal length to achieve the sharpest image. The electronics in your new eyes are self-calibrating for optimum acuity. It may take a little while for you to get used to."

As Alex stared at the professor, the image slowly changed from a blurred, fuzzy outline to a more distinct shape in his brain. He could see a figure dressed in a light-green, surgical gown. Gradually, the details became sharper, and the man was smiling at him. "I can see you!"

Professor Goldman took off his surgical cap. "What colour is my hair, Alex?"

With noticeable enthusiasm in his voice, he answered, "Mainly black, but I can see some greyish areas!"

"Isn't that just typical of my luck! Give a guy sight and the first things he notices are my grey hairs! Don't look too closely or you will also see the wrinkles on my forehead."

They laughed, and then Alex realised there was another person in the room. He turned his head to see a woman standing close to the wall on his left. She was quite tall with short, blonde hair, clear, blue eyes and pale, golden skin. "Jen? Is it you?"

She laughed. "Right first time, soldier. I deliberately stayed out of your main field of vision to see if you noticed me. The implants appear to be working."

The smile she gave him made Alex realise that the reality was even better than his vivid imagination. She truly was beautiful. Her amazingly bright, blue eyes seemed to sparkle in the stark, fluorescent light of the operating room. Alex's thoughts began to meander along new tracks. *Wow! What a beauty! Sorry, Van, but no more brown-eyed girl.* Elton John's 'Blue Eyes' seemed more appropriate for Jen.

"How many fingers am I holding up?" asked Jen.

Without any hesitation, he answered, "Four!"

"Correct. Now, how many?"

Alex saw Jen swiftly move her hands, concealing them behind her body. "I don't have X-ray vision, so I've no idea. You're holding your hands behind your back!"

"Great!" They all laughed, happy that this scientific gamble appeared to have paid off.

The professor, eager to be assured that everything was working, said, "Now, Alex, look at the chart on this panel and read the letters for me, please." The professor switched the rear illumination on the reading-test page.

With increasing confidence, Alex read down the screen, only finding difficulty with the very bottom line.

"Don't worry, Alex. Look at the bottom line again and concentrate. Really focus on working out what the letters are."

To Alex's amazement, the letters became larger, making it possible to read every single character without any difficulty. "Fantastic! I can zoom in, just like a camcorder! How do I zoom out?"

Again, the professor chuckled. "Look away from the smallest letters and the zoom will decrease. You'd better zoom out before you look at my hair again, or you'll see even more grey hairs!"

Alex was like a small child with a new toy. Fascinated, he looked at everything in the room, zooming in and out at will. He even sneakily zoomed in on Jen's face, hoping that she wouldn't realise she was being studied at close quarters.

Why is it that women from North America and Canada seem to have such perfect teeth? Alex thought. Her lips were full and delightful. She was wearing pale-pink lipstick, which seemed to sparkle. He did wonder if it had been applied especially for his benefit, but whatever the reason, she looked superb and absolutely stunning.

Bringing him back from his thoughts, the professor added, "Just like a camcorder, if you zoom in too much, the image will become pixelated, but I'm sure you can live with that."

"Yes, I certainly can. This is truly amazing! Thank you both, so much." The smile on Alex's face said it all.

The professor asked, "Are you okay for me to make some further tests of your eyesight?"

With his newfound vision, Alex's mood had lightened considerably. "Yes, of course. I'm ready for anything."

Professor Goldman smiled, and now Alex could see his expression clearly. More clearly than he had ever imagined possible. "Come into the other room, and we'll carry out a field-of-vision test.

Alex remained motionless, now used to being escorted from room to room. Realising what he had done, he cursed himself for being so stupid and meekly followed the other two into an adjacent room.

"Take a seat, here, Alex."

He took the offered seat. The older man placed heavy spectacles on him and placed a disc in the frame to cover his right eye.

"Now, rest your chin on this support and look directly at the spot in the centre."

Alex was facing a large black hemisphere and concentrated on the white spot at its centre. He was handed a small unit with a prominent push button.

"When I start this equipment, you will see another white spot close to the midpoint. It will move away from the main spot, and I want you to press the button when it disappears out of your field of vision. Okay?"

"I understand, Professor, and ready when you are."

The older man started the unit and the second white spot began to move away from the centre. Alex waited until it had disappeared from his field of vision and quickly pressed the button. The spot swiftly returned to the centre and this time moved in a different, random direction. About ten minutes later, a complete field of vision had been mapped and stored for Alex's left eye.

After the disc was removed from the spectacle frame and inserted to cover his left eye, the whole process was repeated.

The ophthalmic surgeon turned the lights up in the room and spread the computer printouts on the desktop in front of him.

"So, how's my field of vision?" Alex nervously enquired.

After a painfully long pause, Professor Goldman looked up at Alex. His face held a broad smile. "Fantastic! Your field of vision is even better than we had expected or hoped for. The accepted normal field of vision is about ninety-five degrees out, sixty degrees up, seventy-five degrees down and sixty degrees in. This is typical for a man in his early twenties, but in your case, we have managed to extend this by another five degrees in all directions." The professor looked with incredulity at the printed results.

"Quite remarkable!" he exclaimed. "Even your blind spot is minimal. It is the brain which fills in the gaps created by the blind spot where the optic nerve is attached, but somehow, the electronics have also compensated and assisted in the process."

Alex's face lit up at the news. "Congratulations, Professor. You've created prosthetic eyes with superior capabilities to normal human eyes. Thank you so much."

Jen had been listening and joined in with the praise. "It is a truly great achievement. When the AR is activated, the vision will be even more superhuman."

"There's another test I would like to carry out before we make a start on the enhancements." The professor operated a dimmer control, which adjusted the level of lighting in the room. After turning it quite low, he said, "Tell me how much detail you can see now that the light level is low."

Alex looked around the room. "I can tell that the light level is lower, yet … It's strange! I can see everything in perfect detail."

"Excellent! Now, see if you can read this." The professor lifted a sheet of paper off the desk upon which he had previously handwritten a message.

Alex laughed. "My birthday is in three days' time. Friday, twelfth of August."

The professor was lost for words. He turned the paper to face Jen. "Can you read this?"

Jen stared at the paper and shook her head. "No, I can't make out a thing." The professor turned up the light until she could read the message.

"That's incredible! You already have the best vision in the world, even at low-light levels.

Alex was elated. "This is a terrific early birthday present."

Jen decided that now was the time for the next phase. She handed a small box to Alex.

Inside, he found two smart brushed-stainless-steel wristwatches. They had the appearance of high-priced Swiss-made precision watches. "Now they're cool-looking watches! Thanks, Jen."

"You're welcome. The two watches are identical. I felt it prudent to have a backup in case one gets damaged or lost. Oh, and they're waterproof down to fifteen feet."

He placed one on his wrist, admiring his new, stylish timepiece. It had a neat digital display and no buttons.

"It's touch-sensitive," Jen explained. "Just touch the display on the right-hand side."

When Alex did so, it came as a pleasant surprise to hear Jen's voice emerge from the tiny speaker. "The time is eleven thirty-five a.m."

Alex laughed. "That is such an improvement on my present talking watch. Your voice is so clear yet calming."

"Thanks for the compliment, Alex. Now press the lower edge of the display."

When he did as instructed, the voice on the watch said, *"Today is Tuesday, August ninth, 2011."*

Jen gave him further instruction on how to set the alarm by touching the top of the display. "Now, here comes the tricky bit, Alex. Look at me and then touch the left and right side of the display at the same time. I think this is going to be a bit embarrassing, for me, at least."

Alex wondered what she meant but tried it. To his amazement, text appeared at the top of his field of vision. It read:

Jennifer Kimberley Sherlock
Rank: Major
Nationality: American/Canadian
Date of birth: May 11, 1984
Marital status: Single
Occupation: Advanced technology researcher,
US State Defence Department.

Alex was stunned. "Incredible! How on earth does it work?"

Jen smiled proudly. "The image from your eyes is fed, via the watch, to a powerful image-recognition computer, and providing it can find a match in the database, the text is relayed back to your eyes. As soon as you look away, the text will clear.

Intrigued, Alex turned his head to look at the professor. The earlier text was replaced with new information, reading:

> Name: Daniel Michael Goldman
> Title: Professor
> Nationality: British
> Date of birth: January 4, 1961
> Marital status: Widowed
> Position: Head of Advanced Ophthalmic Research at
> Moorfields Eye Hospital, London, England

"Wow! This is mind-blowing!"

Jen, proud of her contribution, added, "Sorry the date format is not European. The data is US-based, so month comes before day, but I'm sure you can live with it."

"Please don't apologise. What you have developed is truly fantastic."

"It could lead to information overload if this was permanently on, so, to stop it, just touch the left side of the display again."

He did this, and instantly, the text disappeared.

There's more," said Jen. "Touch the left and top of the display together."

Again Alex did as instructed and was shocked at what happened next. Instead of seeing what was in the room, a new image appeared in his eyes, but he was uncertain about what was being displayed. "What is it showing?"

"This is the tricky one. Many spy satellites are constantly monitoring the Earth and, what you can see is a real-time image looking down on this part of London. You should be able to make out the outlines of Moorfields Eye Hospital and the surrounding roads. Try concentrating on one part of the image, say, the road next to Moorfields."

As he did so, the image zoomed in until it was possible to see fine detail such as people and cars moving along the busy road. "This is unbelievable! But it's presumably only this good on a fine day?"

Jen shook her head. "That was a major consideration when designing the software. If the weather is cloudy or during the night, infrared cameras take over, allowing you to, still, see human activity at any time, day or night, even through heavy cloud cover."

Alex was now beginning to understand the military significance of the project. This was why it all had to be kept a secret. "Dare I ask how much all this technology is costing the American and British taxpayers?"

Jen hedged the question. "You really don't want to know. Let's just say that it was over two million dollars."

This did not surprise Alex. "So, I'm the man with the million-dollar eyes?"

Jen laughed. "I suppose that, allowing for inflation since *The Six Million Dollar Man*, that's probably about right just for the eyes!"

The young man felt like a character out of X-Men, someone with superhuman powers, but he hoped that this 'gift' would benefit the world. He had a thought.

"It's going to be difficult for me to act as if I'm blind, now I've got superhuman eyes."

Jen handed a small case to Alex. "Try these on."

Alex looked at the pair of spectacles she held out for him. "Won't it reduce the capabilities of my eyes if I have to wear dark glasses?"

"Not with these. To anybody else, they look like any ordinary pair of sunglasses, but the lens is specially made to allow you full freedom of vision." She sounded very confident. "Try them on, Alex."

He seemed doubtful but took hold of them and put the glasses on. "That's amazing! I can still see as clearly as though I was not wearing them. And they look quite fashionable."

"Good! I'm glad you like them. We fashioned them on the Ray-Ban sunglasses brand."

Professor Goldman looked at the newly confident young man and felt very satisfied with the results of his extensive research.

He had been working on this project for over three years and had wondered, on many occasions, if anybody would ever benefit from his efforts. Alex's injuries had made him the ideal recipient, and at last, the professor felt truly vindicated.

On many occasions, Daniel Goldman had been severely criticised by his colleagues, who felt that he was wasting his time and, more importantly, precious research budgets. Still, he had persisted, even more since the sad death of Pamela, his wife of twenty-seven years, to breast cancer in 2008. Always a dedicated worker, the professor now spent even more long hours, working late into the night on his 'special' project.

When he realised the full military significance of his work, the professor had contacted the Ministry of Defence. At first, they showed very little interest, but when the deeply committed professor mentioned the possibility of adding augmented reality to the prosthetic eyes, their interest soon became apparent.

He only appreciated the extent of their interest when he was invited to a meeting at MI6 at Vauxhall Cross, where he had to sign a secrecy agreement. That was where he met the larger-than-life Brigadier General Paul Marshall for the first time. He was invited to explain, in detail, how the high-tech prosthetic eye worked and how soon a fully working version would be available.

He gave himself a tight deadline of six months and, with new impetus, just managed to keep to his schedule.

During this period, Major Sherlock flew in from the States to join in the progress meetings, and very soon, she was a significant contributor to the design of the miniature circuitry and software contained within the bionic eye.

"Do you need me for any further tests, Professor?"

Alex's question brought Daniel back to the present. "No, not for now. What do you have in mind?"

The young man hesitated a little. "I just would like to see how I look in the mirror in my room. Does that sound very vain of me?"

"No, not at all. It's understandable and quite natural. Can you find your way to your room?"

"I think so. You will hear me if I get lost."

Alex was about to leave the laboratory when he had a sudden thought. "What happens if I have a shower or get caught in a heavy downpour? Are the eyes waterproof?"

Professor Goldman laughed. "I suppose it's a logical question, but the answer is that the electronics in the prosthetic eye are in a sealed unit encased within a resin shell, making them completely impervious to any moisture. Even if you dip your head underwater, there will be no problem."

Satisfied with this answer, Alex smiled. "Whew! That's a relief!"

It seemed so strange to walk along the maze of corridors back to his room without assistance, but he managed it without too much difficulty. As soon as he was in his room, he stripped naked and stared at himself in the full-length mirror on the inside of his wardrobe.

Alex smiled and the man in the mirror smiled back at him. Was this really what he looked like now? Four months of seeing nothing had eroded, even changed, what he thought was his appearance. Of course, his features were slimmer through loss of body weight while inactive in a hospital bed. The areas down the side of his body that had received most of the burns were still pinkish and quite noticeable, but he felt that in a few more months, they would have blended in. Thankfully, his manhood had escaped mutilation during the bomb blast and should still have the capacity to sexually satisfy a woman's needs. *Hope that's not going to be too long a time,* he thought.

The hair on his head was growing back where it had been shaved before his many operations to remove the frags. There were still numerous scars on his head and body, and his face looked a bit uneven in skin tone following the scarring, but of course, what Alex was really interested in were his eyes. Would they appear realistic or obvious imitation replacements? He hoped that they would look more realistic than those of a ventriloquist's dummy.

Nervously, Alex edged closer to the mirror and looked at his 'bionic' eyes. He had to admit that the professor had done a brilliant job in recreating them. How many times had his mother commented on how sharp and bright blue they were just like his father's, and now science had created perfect copies. He found it incredible that the eyes he was looking at and through had been created by Man.

He was fortunate that his eyelids had escaped damage during the bomb blast, as that would have presented many problems in retaining the prosthetic eyes securely in place.

Feeling very satisfied with the results, Alex dressed again. His room had one window. It was quite small, but now bright sunshine streamed into his room, highlighting a rectangular strip on his bed and the wall beyond. He moved closer to the window and peered through with some curiosity. It overlooked City Road, and with the strong, afternoon sun, London seemed so bright and colourful.

When he had walked around the area with Jen, his imagination had filled everything in with drab, varying shades of grey, but now red, blue, green and a multitude of other colours met his incredulous gaze. He found it difficult to tear his eyes away from this new spectacle and enjoyed watching the rich, vibrant colours of the cars, people and buildings. "Whoever said that London was a drab, dull place?"

Glancing up, he noticed a plane, high in the sky. At first, it seemed tiny, but then his eyes zoomed in on the craft, giving Alex an idea. He touched the left and right areas on his watch and, within seconds, text appeared at the top of his vision:

Aircraft: Boing 737
Flight: BA211 from London Heathrow
Destination: Stockholm, Sweden
ETA: 17:50

This clever feature intrigued him. He could have spent many hours just identifying objects in his field of vision.

"What a fantastically clever device! How come I managed to be the lucky guy with vision second to none?"

He cancelled the text with another touch on his watch and, with some difficulty, returned to the present.

His first thought was to phone his parents and tell them of his good news, but he was brought back to reality by the words of the brigadier general echoing through his mind.

"Only a select few must know of the newfound vision."

If Alex's parents knew about his superior eyesight, it would not take long before aunts, uncles and cousins became aware of his secret, and after that, who knew? A casual remark to a journalist and the press would soon have him on the front page. Publicists would be pestering him constantly to tell his story, and then the whole world would know. This scenario had to be avoided, at all costs and he knew that his secret could not even be shared with his own close relatives. Still, he wanted to visit his family and sought out Professor Goldman to ask his advice.

He confirmed Alex's fears. "Your family and friends must not know the extent of your vision, as it may endanger future military missions. But I do think it a good idea to visit your family, especially as it's your birthday on Friday. Another day and we should be finished with all the tests, so why don't you phone your parents and make some arrangements?"

Alex desperately wanted to see them but could envisage several problems. "How do I travel to Bury St. Edmunds as a blind person when I can see better than anybody else? I can't just walk up to my parents' house and knock at the door!"

Jen was listening with interest to the discussion. "Perhaps I can help, Alex."

"How?" Alex could not see any obvious solution.

"There is one other combination of keys on your watch which I have not told you about. Try touching the top and bottom contacts together."

Alex did as suggested, and suddenly, he was again immersed in a sea of inky blackness. The superhuman vision he had known for just a few hours had disappeared in an instant.

"God! How do I get it back?"

"The same touch contacts again will resume full vision."

Alex touched his watch and smiled as his eyesight was, again, fully restored. "Wow! That was so scary. To go back to nothing after what I've seen today was truly depressing."

"But at least it would be convincing." Jen could see that Alex was still doubtful. "I could drive you there if you wish." After a moment's thought, she added, "You could introduce me as someone who works at Moorfields."

Alex looked surprised. "Would you do that for me?"

"Of course I would if it will help you out of a problem. And my work here is just about finished, anyway."

Professor Goldman seemed happy with this compromise and added, "I can provide you with a white stick and other aids to reinforce the impression of being blind."

Alex considered the idea. "Okay, I'll phone my parents this evening."

His mother was thrilled to hear from him but rebuked him for not keeping in touch. "You always seem to be away on your birthday, but we'll make this one very special for you. It's a bit short notice, but we'll manage."

He knew she would pull out all the stops and interrupted her before she could get too far into her planning. "Mum, I don't want a big party. Just you, Dad, Lucy, Amelia and Grandmother. I don't want all my relatives gawping at me while I'm struggling with the food on my plate."

She understood his apprehension and agreed to keep the celebrations just within close family members.

"Would you like us to pick you up on Friday?"

"No, thanks. It's not necessary. One of the staff here will give me a lift."

She sounded surprised. "Really? Okay, see you on Friday."

He was thankful she had not asked any further questions about his escort. She had been upset when Helen had finished with her son. Not surprisingly, she thought it a cruel, selfish decision and at the slightest excuse would make derogatory remarks about her very nearly daughter-in-law. Alex knew that as soon as his mother met Jen, she would begin mentally preparing for a wedding.

Chapter Eight

12th August 2011

ON FRIDAY, ALEX had wanted to pay for the hire car, but Jen had insisted that her expenses included the cost of any transport during her time in London. "Think of it as a birthday present from me and the American taxpayers," she said with a firmness which denied any further argument.

Considering that back in the US, she would have been driving on the other side of the road, she was, obviously, a confident, skilled driver. They wound their way out of the capital. The Audi sped along the M11 towards Cambridge, where they turned onto the A14, following Alex's directions. His parents lived midway between Bury St. Edmunds and the village of Woolpit in Suffolk. As they drew nearer to his family home, Alex felt a mixture of fearful anticipation, excitement and anxiety. When they were within half a mile, he touched the contacts on his watch and was once again thrust back into a chilling blackness.

He had described the house location to Jen, and when he felt the car swing off the road and into the curved drive, he knew the time had come. Alex remained in his seat until Jen came around the car and offered him her arm for assistance. He heard the front door of the house open on his left and knew that his mother would have seen them arrive. Of one thing he could be certain: his mother and sisters would be studying Jen, thinking that she may be a potential marriage partner for him. Jen handed him his overnight case from the back of the car and directed him towards the front entrance door.

It was his mother, Louise, who spoke first. Jen helped Alex to step into the wide hallway, where his mother took hold of him and hugged him as though she had not seen him for years.

"Alex! You're looking so well. Introduce me to your friend."

Freeing himself from the hug, Alex said, "This is Jen. Jen, meet my mother, Louise." As they exchanged greetings, Alex asked, "Are Lucy and Amelia here?"

Lucy's voice trembled a little as she said, "I'm already here, Alex. Come on, give me a big hug as well."

As they held each other, Alex felt terrible. He knew his eighteen-year-old sister was emotional because of his faked 'blindness'. How he wished that he could switch on his eyes and see his family properly.

As Lucy loosened her hold on him, thirteen-year-old Amelia moved in. Although she was at least nine inches shorter than Alex, he could tell that she had grown a little since they last saw each other. Her voice was also a little shaky as she asked, "How are you feeling, Alex?"

"I'm fine, sis, and happy to be home again." The obvious emotion in Amelia's voice touched him. Although he had always teased Lucy, the age difference between him and Amelia made him very protective of his little sister. In truth, he would have done anything to care for and protect either of his sisters, and he was extremely proud of both of them.

Alex's father, James, was not at the house. It was only four-fifteen and another two hours before he was likely to arrive home from the office.

"Shall we go into the lounge? Would you both like a drink?" Louise was fussing as she always did when faced with a new situation. Two now faced her. Her son returning home unable to see his family and Jen, a young, attractive woman who obviously cared enough for Alex to bring him to their house. There were so many questions she wanted to ask, whilst accepting that it would be impolite to do so.

Jen guided Alex into the large lounge, although he probably could have found his way around the house without difficulty, memories of the layout still strong in his mind. His problem was that he would not know where his mother and sisters would be. Jen was now used to this situation and led Alex over to the chair offered by his mother.

The voice of Alex's eighty-two-year-old grandmother, Elizabeth, sounded a little tremulous as she asked, "How are you feeling, Alex, dear?"

"I'm fine, thank you. How about yourself? Do you still have a problem with your balance?" Since her mid-seventies, his grandmother had had problems with her inner ear, causing her, on occasion, to lose her balance.

"It's worse in the morning, particularly when I've just woken up." She gave a little sigh of resignation. "But I'll survive."

He felt certain that she would be around for many years to come. His grandmother was a very strong-minded woman and the only survivor of her generation in the family. Her husband, Robert, had died of lung cancer in 2007, while Alex's father's parents had both been killed in a car accident in 1994. Stupidly, this had been caused by a drunken driver smashing head-on into their car at seventy miles an hour. Alex had been eight years old at the time, but he still remembered them with great sadness. Amelia had not even been born at the time of the accident, and Lucy, who had been only one year old, was too young to remember them. Alex had always felt cheated that only one of this older generation was still alive to pass on information from the past.

Earlier that day, Louise had collected her mother from the warden-controlled flat, where she was determined to look after herself. She always insisted that she did not want anybody to make a fuss of her just because of her age. Thankfully, she still had a very sharp mind and was most insistent that she could manage on her own.

"Tea, coffee or fruit juice?" his mother asked.

Jen chose black coffee, while Alex asked, "Do you have any Tropicana?" This particular brand 'with bits'—as the manufacturer had so proudly promoted in their adverts on television, as if it was clever to miss juicing all the flesh of the orange—was a favourite of Alex's, and his mother knew it.

"You know we will always have your favourite drink in the fridge," she said with a knowing yet unseen smile.

A few minutes later, his mother placed a cool glass in his hand, and as he sipped the refreshing drink, he was, as always, reminded of Wham's hit song 'Club Tropicana'. It was released in the eighties before he was born, but he remembered seeing the video of George Michael, Andrew Ridgely and the two bikini-clad backing singers as a young teenager and ogling the scantily clad gorgeous girls.

The interrogation was about to start. "How long are you staying for, Alex?"

"Only until Sunday. Jen's giving me a lift back." He knew what her next question would be, and he was not disappointed.

"Would you like to stay here, Jen? We do have a spare room."

That was true. It was a large, five-bedroom detached house, worthy of Alex's father's occupation as a barrister, but Louise's hopes were about to be dashed.

"No, thanks, Louise, but it's good of you to offer. I'm visiting some friends in the area."

That last statement was not quite true. During their drive from London, Alex and Jen had agreed that it would be less embarrassing for both of them if she were to stay in a hotel. The two had stopped in Bury St. Edmunds and found that the Angel Hotel had a single room available for a couple of nights.

Louise seemed disappointed, perhaps feeling that possible future wedding plans would have to be shelved, yet again. All she wanted was a secure and happy life for her son, and Jen seemed perfect material for a potential match. Louise would never forgive Helen for 'dumping' her son just because of his loss of sight.

The small talk continued for a while until Jen decided she would leave Alex with his family. "I'll pick you up about eleven on Sunday morning, Alex."

He went out with her to the car. He spoke quietly to prevent being overheard. "God, it's difficult! I really wish I could switch my eyes on again. I miss seeing them."

"Just relax and enjoy being with your family. You'll be fine."

"I'll try. Hope you enjoy your stay at the Angel. It's very historic. Apparently, Charles Dickens has stayed there, but I think he checked out some time ago."

Jen laughed and gave him a hug before climbing into the Audi. He waited until her car had driven onto the road before he turned back towards the house.

Lucy came out and took his arm. "I'll help you, Alex. Do you want to go to your room, yet?"

"Yes, please, sis. I could do with freshening up." He knew the layout of the house perfectly but realised that he may accidentally catch one of the many expensive ornaments his mother had accumulated over the years.

Once in his room, he took off his shoes and relaxed on the bed. As he lay, there, he touched the contact areas on his watch. It came as a great relief to see again. He looked around his room and realised that nothing had really changed since he was last at home. The large dressing table still had the long-abandoned games station, on which he used to spend hours playing, mostly, military games.

"You spend far too much time playing dangerously sadistic games. An absolute waste of time!" his father would say, but even then, it

was a precursor to him joining the army, which both his parents had feared.

The stack of DVDs lined several shelves. Alex wandered over and picked out a few. He had most of the James Bond collection, even dating back to the days of Sean Connery and, more recently, Daniel Craig as the famous secret agent. Even as a small boy, he had enjoyed playing with Action Man soldiers and anything else with a military background or connection.

Pride of place on the cluttered top was a model of a British Chieftain tank, which he had painstakingly constructed from an Airfix kit when he was about twelve years old. Alex had spent many hours assembling the model and even more accurately painting it in fine detail. He still felt proud of this miniature symbol of his dreams and ambitions.

Alex stood there for several minutes, his eyes scanning the mementos of his childhood.

At last, he snapped out of his memories and wandered into the en-suite bathroom where he quickly freshened up, tidied his hair and then switched off his eyes, ready for his family gathering.

As he opened the bedroom door, Lucy reappeared, ready to escort him downstairs. He felt guilty, remembering how horrible he had been to her in his mid-teens. He had teased and made fun of her, but now she cared enough about him to be ready to help when necessary.

Lucy had always been terrified of spiders, and he remembered how he collected as many as he could find only to leave them tactically positioned around her room to scare the wits out of his younger sister. He particularly enjoyed placing the larger ones close to the pillows on her bed for maximum effect. Lucy's screams when she found these eight-legged beasts could be heard right through the house. It would always take a while for her to calm down, and quite justifiably, she would accuse Alex of planting these monsters just to frighten her. He now felt really bad for his role in these typical teenage-brother pranks.

They sat together in the lounge, Louise occasionally excusing herself to go into the kitchen, where she checked the slowly cooking dinner, which smelled fantastic to Alex. Even though the food had been good at Moorfields, it could never compete with his mother's home cooking.

His grandmother had fallen asleep and was gently snoring.

Alex was trying his best to avoid saying much about himself, preferring instead to quiz Lucy on her A' Level examinations, which she had recently finished but as yet did not know the results.

"I feel fairly confident but just hope I've done well enough to be accepted at Cambridge." In some ways, Lucy was, like him, determined to aim for a particular career. However, in her case, her parents were in favour of her studying for a job as a surgeon in the National Health Service. She was a hard worker, and Alex felt certain that she would succeed in the field of medicine.

As for Amelia, she was enjoying the six-week break from school. She was, like her older sister, studious and hard-working but enjoyed any break from the regimented school timetable.

Around six thirty, the sound of the key in the front door could be heard, signalling that Alex's father had arrived home. He walked straight into the lounge and up to where Alex was seated. "Good to see you, son." The hand on his shoulder was as much as he could expect. He could never remember being hugged by his father, but at least he had not avoided the word 'see' in his greeting. So many people when faced with a blind person would jump through verbal hoops to avoid this simple yet obvious word.

"Hi, Dad. How's work?"

The older man gave a little chuckle. "A relief. The case I've been working on recently has been delayed as the defendant tried to commit suicide, otherwise I would have been in Manchester Crown Court today. I'm just pleased to see you on your special day."

Alex knew that he was, indeed, fortunate to see his father. As a barrister, he could be away for days at a time, working on cases around the country. His mother had become used to James's long absences and kept herself busy for most of the time.

This evening, all six of them enjoyed celebrating Alex's twenty-fifth birthday, and Alex really appreciated the meal so superbly prepared by Louise. Alex's grandmother had a few too many glasses of wine and, once again, became quite drowsy after the meal.

Of course, there were presents. A warm, branded jumper, expensive aftershave lotion and a box of chocolate liqueurs were the type of presents he could always appreciate. Lucy and Amelia had joined together to buy him an iTunes voucher.

There was a tricky moment when James asked, "What of the future, Alex? Are you going to be looking for work?"

Alex had been dreading this question, but before he had chance to reply, his father continued. "I've many good contacts and probably could get you an office job of sorts."

Alex could have screamed. Even after all that had happened, his father was still trying to control his life, pushing him towards a boring, business-orientated occupation. "I've already been contacted by the Army Occupational Resources division, and they're keen to employ me as a military advisor. They will even help me to find some accommodation in London."

How he wished he could have seen the look of surprise on his father's face, as he responded, "Really? Well, that's great!" The lack of enthusiasm in his father's voice was very noticeable, but Alex did not care at all and hoped that Brigadier General Paul Marshall could really change his life for the better.

Later in the evening, Louise took her now somewhat relaxed mother back to her flat, after the old lady had given Alex a longer-than-expected comforting hug.

Chapter Nine

THE FOLLOWING DAY was spent quietly with Louise, Lucy and Amelia bringing Alex up to date with family news, while his father, predictably, was working on case notes in his study.

It was a happy, gentle, relaxing day, several hours being spent in the large garden, enjoying the warm August sunshine while in deep conversation with his mother and sisters.

It was Amelia who noticed his watch. "That's a cool-looking talking watch, Alex. Can I hear what it sounds like, please?"

He really had no choice and gently touched the display. Jen's voice sounded very clear in the quietness of the garden where the only other sound to be heard was that of birds singing. *"The time is two forty-five p.m."* He touched the other contact area. *"Today is Saturday, August thirteenth, 2011."*

It was his mother who commented. "The voice on your watch sounds just like your friend, Jen."

Damn! thought Alex. He'd never thought about the possible consequences of having Jen as the voice on his watch. He had no option but to lie. "Jen is an expert in microelectronics, who worked with the RNIB in designing this new watch and offered to use her voice in preference to the usual male voice."

"Really?" Louise was particularly surprised by this information and wondered, again, if there was something Alex was not telling them about his friendship with this young, Canadian/American woman. "It must be nice to hear her voice when she's not there."

Lucy and Amelia were not as interested as Louise in their brother's relationships but both agreed that his watch was really cool and trendy.

Somehow, he managed to get through the rest of that day without any further embarrassing problems, even occasionally switching his sight on to catch a sneaky look at his family.

It seemed so strange to be sleeping in his old bed once again, and by Sunday morning, he had been brought up to date on all the family news.

Although Alex enjoyed being with his family, it was a stressful time and he felt relieved when Jen arrived at the house on Sunday morning. He gave Lucy, Amelia and his mother a big hug and popped his head around the door of the study where his father was, as always, working on case notes.

"When will we see you again, Alex?"

"I honestly don't know, but during the next few weeks, I will be training with a guide dog. I'll keep in touch by phone."

He sighed with relief as he settled in the passenger seat of Jen's car. As soon as they were out of the drive, he switched his eyes on again. "I'd like to go back to London a different route, Jen, if you don't mind a little diversion."

"Not at all. We've plenty of time and it's a lovely day. Where would you like to go?"

"If we turn left at the next junction and keep on that road for four or five miles, we should arrive in a place called Woolpit."

"Sounds a little creepy."

Alex laughed. "Creepy is a good description. I've been fascinated by the place since I was a boy. Apparently, its name has nothing to do with wool. I understand it used to be called Wolfpit, which derives from the pits that villagers used to dig to trap the roaming wolves."

"Really?" Jen sounded as though she did not quite believe him. "How long ago was this?"

"Oh, well over a thousand years ago. But that's only part of the story. During the reign of King Stephen in the early eleven hundreds, a boy and his sister suddenly appeared in the village."

"What's so strange about that?" Jen was clearly puzzled yet at the same time intrigued by this curious tale.

"Their skin was bright green, their clothes unusual and they spoke in a strange language."

"You must be kidding?" Jen wondered if Alex was telling her a tall story.

Alex's expression was serious. "It is well documented, so I feel certain that it was true. The children had appeared out of a cave near one of the many ditches, and the story goes that they lived in an underground colony in a place called Saint Martin but had lost their way and, on coming out of the cave, were stunned by the brilliant sunshine. A group of reapers found them unconscious and carried them to the village."

Jen found the strange tale incredible and asked, "What became of them?"

"Both children were baptised, but unfortunately, the boy died after a short while because he would not change his lifestyle and only ate green beans, yet his sister adapted, learned English and ate many other foods. Apparently, her skin colour became more normal as she grew into a young, somewhat loose woman. She called herself Agnes Barre, married a nobleman and had children."

"That is one hell of a weird story. So why do you want to go there, now?"

"I suppose it's just my curiosity. Woolpit is only a small village, and I wonder what it looks like from the sky!"

Jen now understood. Alex had time to think about the possibilities of seeing the world in a different light using his newfound super-vision.

Within a few minutes, they were in the centre of the village and parked the car next to an ancient pub. It was a beautiful, sunny

August day, and the couple took a seat in the paved garden area at the rear of the fourteenth-century Swan Inn.

A waitress took their order, and within a few minutes, Jen was sipping a soft drink while Alex enjoyed a glass of real ale.

Alex looked thoughtful. "It's strange to think that after nearly nine hundred years, there could be many descendants of the green girl in the area."

Jen thought for a few seconds and, smiling, said, "I think the waitress may have looked a little green, but perhaps that was with envy at seeing me with you."

Both laughed and agreed that it was a fascinating, hopefully true story.

Casually, Alex touched the contacts on his watch, and immediately, his field of view had been replaced with a satellite image of the whole area.

He could see the roof and garden of the Swan Inn and the impressive St. Mary's church, nearby, with the narrow, winding roads surrounding them.

He concentrated on the garden of the Swan Inn, and as the image zoomed in, he could even make out the tiny figures of himself and Jen. Alex was tempted to wave his arm but did not want to look like an absolute idiot. Although he had never been to New York, he understood that in Times Square, anybody could appear on a huge advertising screen if they positioned themselves in the right place within the square. He now understood the reason why so many people did the craziest things just to appear on the screen for all to see.

He moved his gaze around the village but still could not explain, even to himself, what he was hoping to see. Buildings, houses, woodlands and roads but as far as he was aware nothing out of the ordinary.

Then he spotted it. At first, it just looked like a mark on one of the roofs in the village, but as he concentrated on this area, the different colour of this one roof became more apparent, contrasting against neighbouring roofs. He remembered what Jen had said about his vision through the spy satellites. Infrared detectors could identify areas of different temperatures, usually to locate human activity. What he was seeing now was one building where the roof temperature was, apparently, significantly higher than that of the surrounding buildings.

Jen had noticed Alex's change of concentration and asked, "What is it, Alex?"

"I… I don't know." He lowered his voice to avoid being overheard. "I think there's a building on fire."

"Are you sure?"

"I suppose there could be an innocent explanation, but I can't think of one. All I know is that this one roof has a difference of some sort. It can only be that it is much hotter than other surrounding roofs."

Jen took instant command of the situation. "Drink up and we'll check it out."

The two drained their glasses and left the Swan Inn. They walked arm in arm through the village towards the building in Alex's vision. As they approached it, Alex switched from overhead vision to look at the buildings from a normal perspective.

As he did so, a young, dark-haired man was just entering one of the houses in this quite elderly block of terraced houses. It was at the end of this group of buildings where Alex had noticed the heat source, yet from this viewpoint, everything appeared to be quite normal. Alex had expected to find flames licking at the windows, but heavy blinds prevented any chance of seeing inside the building. However, it was not just one house that was affected. The same pattern of a strong heat source and blinds at all windows applied to the last four houses in the block.

"Perhaps the heat source hasn't reached full combustion point yet," said Jen thoughtfully.

A sudden inspiration hit Alex. "Don't make it too obvious that we are looking at the houses, Jen. I think it could be a cannabis farm. The temperature has to be much higher than normal to cultivate the plants."

"You could be right—it makes sense. What we don't want is to get caught up in an investigation, so I'll phone my contact here in the UK and get him to alert the local authorities." She pulled out her mobile, keyed in the number and spoke quietly, passing on the address of the properties. Satisfied that they could do nothing more, she said, "Police will be here shortly. I think it's time we left Woolpit."

Alex agreed, and they walked back to their car.

Inside the house, a young, nervous-looking man watched the couple on a CCTV monitor. He knew they had been looking at the houses with some interest and pressed a few keys on his mobile. He wasted no time on introductions. "Moving out immediately. Parties interested in properties."

The person on the other end of the line understood perfectly the meaning of the brief, coded message and gave a simple acknowledgement.

The young Italian man swiftly put the phone in his pocket. He was sweating profusely, partly through the intrusion by these strangers but also because of the demands of hundreds of plants requiring a great deal of heat and moisture. Plaster was bulging on the walls and ceilings, and many rough holes had been made through the entire structure. The cost of setting up this skunk cannabis farm had been over £30,000, but since the output could generate forty times that every year, it was a very effective investment. The owner of the houses had no idea what his properties were being used for and was satisfied that he was being paid a regular rent. This would now come to a swift end.

There was no way any of the equipment could be removed in the time available, but the man moved quickly around the plants within the four adjacent houses, cutting off the heads of some of the female flowers and dropping them into a leather pouch. He threw this, together with some of the monitoring equipment, into a large holdall and hurried through to the back of the houses.

Taking one last look at this once-profitable place, he realised what a mess the building now looked with sodden plaster on walls and ceilings and access between the houses made through rough openings in the party walls.

Walking swiftly, he escaped along the narrow passages, trying to avoid being observed, and made his way to a small area of wasteland.

Still nervously looking around, he climbed into an ancient van and drove away, knowing that this cannabis farm would no longer be profitable for his organisation.

ALEX AND JEN said nothing as they drove back through Cambridge towards London, aware that in just a few more hours, they would have to go their separate ways. Both had enjoyed their time together over the last few weeks, and although Jen did not want a relationship, they had become good friends. Or was it more than that? Alex mused that, perhaps, he was getting more like his mother, just wanting to settle down and have a family. Louise would have loved to become a grandmother, but Alex pulled himself together. He had a job to do, and the time was approaching when he had to repay the British and American Governments for the precious gift of sight.

The couple, both subdued by their imminent separation, said little as they walked to his room at Moorfields. Once there, Alex switched his sight on again. He looked at Jen and was sure there was a hint of tears in her eyes.

"I'm going to miss you, Jen."

"I know. I feel the same about you." She paused, searching desperately for the right words, hoping this separation would not be too painful for either of them. "I've no choice. I have to go back to the States now that my work here is done."

Alex smiled with a look of resigned understanding. "I know. I do understand. If you ever feel like a holiday, I could show you around the sights of Britain."

"I might just do that. I would really love to visit all the tourist places one day, except anywhere like that creepy place. Take care and keep in touch, Alex."

He laughed at her reference to the strange, historical village. The two hugged, and then Jen was gone. Once again, Alex was on his own with an uncomfortable, empty feeling in his heart.

For the rest of the day, he lazed in his room and his only visitor was the usual nurse who brought his evening meal. Professor Goldman was absent, as he was taking his first weekend off in a long time. Even he would miss the endless days of concentrated effort and felt strange and empty now he had achieved his goal of creating artificial sight for a blinded soldier. *What next?* he wondered.

Alex noticed a small folder on his bedside cabinet, and now that he had the vision to read again, he scanned through the information. It contained a brief history of Moorfields Eye Hospital. Apparently, it was the first specialist eye hospital in the world and was opened as 'The London Dispensary for Diseases of the Eye and Ear' in 1805 by John Cunningham Saunders. Initially, it had been set up as a charitable institution, opened to assist soldiers returning from the Napoleonic Wars in Egypt. Many had contracted trachoma, a blinding, tropical form of conjunctivitis.

The hospital had moved to its present site on City Road in 1899. It retained its charity status until nationalisation in 1948 but had to be rebuilt after receiving a direct bomb hit during the Second World War.

It was quite amazing how the hospital had changed from its historic background into a high-tech centre of excellence known throughout the world.

After this brief period of education, Alex felt restless and, for that evening, he lay on his bed, listening to Radio 2. 'Listening' was not really the right word, as the music and the presenter's voice drifted through his brain without registering anything.

What had puzzled him was why he had chosen to go to Woolpit. It was as if something had drawn him there. Perhaps the gift of 'special sight' had something extra? Did he have a sixth sense and, if so, why?

He watched the BBC news that night and heard the newsreader talk about the discovery of a cannabis farm in a quaint Suffolk village. Nobody had been arrested, as the houses were deserted. It was not a major news item, but Alex smiled to himself, knowing that he and his newfound special sight were responsible for its discovery and loss of income for the illegal growers.

Chapter Ten

B Y NINE O'CLOCK the next morning, Alex had packed his bags, ready to leave the hospital after a total of four weeks in this world-famous institution. When his visitor arrived at ten thirty, Alex said his farewells to the diligent staff and gave particular thanks to Professor Goldman, who had made such a fantastic difference to his life.

The unnamed man introduced himself as Alex's driver and escorted him out of the hospital to the car park. Alex had been told to remain 'blind' for this journey to the Ministry of Defence offices. Within forty minutes, he was walking along the quiet corridors of a large, anonymous building. Eventually, they reached the room where Alex suspected he was, again, to meet the brigadier general.

He was not mistaken. The greeting was executed with the same regimented stiffness and precision as at their earlier meeting. Once the escort had left the room, Alex switched on his eyes and looked around the richly furnished office. A seat was offered to the young man, and he was introduced to the other three individuals around the table.

Adrian King, Paul Adams and Kristin Asher were polite and fairly quiet in comparison with their more senior colleague.

"Every person in this room is familiar with your situation. That is that you lost your sight in battle and have had prosthetic replacements, which have capabilities far superior to those of the human eye."

Alex remembered how he was told that only a few, select individuals would know his secret. Presumably, these were the few apart from Jen, the professor and some senior officials within the American Defense Department.

"I would be grateful if you could demonstrate the capabilities to my colleagues."

"How? What can I do to convince everybody in this room?" As he was talking, Alex looked closely at everyone around the table.

"Don't worry. We're all familiar with the current relatively low resolution of implants within the eye. If you can describe us, this will give an indication of the quality and full extent of your vision."

Alex said nothing as he considered. "Okay." He looked first at the brigadier general and was surprised how close his impression was to reality. "You are quite tall. Probably six feet three, have slightly greying ginger hair, a neat moustache and ..." Alex zoomed in. "Green eyes. Your tie is maroon with grey patterns."

What Alex did not mention to these individuals was the watch worn by the brigadier general. His superior vision had identified a Cartier—one of the most expensive fashion watches available. *He must be on a damn good salary to afford one of those*, Alex thought, somewhat surprised. Even without the detail of the watch, his description was evidently more detailed and accurate than the group had expected.

He continued, "Adrian, you have short, black hair, silver-framed spectacles, a dark-blue suit, white shirt and a grey tie. Paul, you also have black hair, a bit longer than Adrian's. Your suit is mid-grey, white shirt and a light-blue tie."

He paused to look at the only female in the room, knowing that he had to be particularly careful in his description of her. "Kristin. You have shoulder-length blonde hair, bright-blue eyes, and you are wearing a pale-green blouse and light-grey skirt. You also have a fine, gold chain around your neck. A teardrop pendant hangs from this chain."

All four, particularly Kristin, were smiling and noticeably impressed. Alex could also have guessed their ages, but the possibility of getting them wrong stopped him from giving this extra information. Marshall was probably in his mid-forties, while the other three appeared to be in their early to mid-thirties.

"Excellent! Your descriptions are precise and very accurate. Now, as you know, we have a place where you can live in London. After this meeting, you will be driven there, and tomorrow you will begin training with a support dog."

"I thought it was going to be a guide dog?"

"To the public, it will appear as a guide dog, but in reality, it is a police dog with extra training. In this way, the dog will act not just as your eyes but also for your personal protection."

Alex was impressed. "I hope I can get on with the dog or else it may attack me instead."

The military man smiled. "I'm confident it will be a successful partnership." Alex noticed that the brigadier general had a habit of playing with the end of his moustache. Alex was still puzzled by his feelings about this man, as there was nothing to suggest a threat, but still, the uneasy feeling would not escape him.

The older man turned to his colleagues. "Now, I would like you to describe your job functions to Alex. You first, Adrian."

The young man cleared his throat. "I am the coordinator for the Terrorist and Serious Crime Investigations Intelligence Unit. My role is to direct you to specific objectives and locations where you will assist in observing known suspects. Whatever you do, you do not speak to any local police officers about your observations. You will contact only me for directives and feedback. I report back to the brigadier general."

"Okay, understood," Alex replied and thought, *He seems fairly young for such a responsible position.* There was also something about the man's voice that was vaguely familiar. After a moment's thought, he realised that Adrian sounded similar to the London-born presenter and actor, Stephen Fry. Alex wondered if Adrian had a similar sense of humour to the ebullient Fry, or did the similarity end with the voice?

It was now Paul's turn. "My role is in microelectronic aids for operatives. I suppose you could think of me as 'Q' in the James Bond film series but not as glamorous a role. In addition, I am responsible for maintaining the electronics in your communications watch."

Alex had to admit that he did not look like a 'Q'. *Not really a geeky guy*, he thought. "Sounds interesting."

Next, Kristin cleared her throat. "My role is as coordinator between British and American Intelligence. You probably won't hear much from me, as Adrian will provide me with the feedback for the States. Without American assistance, this project would never have got off the ground. Understandably, they have insisted on full and complete information on your progress and assignments."

"That's fair, considering they're paying towards the cost. Okay." Alex had a sudden thought. "Adrian, what happens if I do get stopped by the police? Is there anything I can say or show so they don't interfere with my assignment?"

"A good question. After this meeting, Paul will take you to an office in this building, where your official ID will be created. It should only be shown to the emergency services as a last resort."

"Okay, that's understood. Also, how do I contact any of you if I need to?"

Paul answered. "You will be given a mobile phone, shortly. Although it looks like any other smartphone, it has dedicated and encrypted channels for communication with all of us."

Their discussion ended, Paul took Alex to an operations room. There was an air of quiet efficiency in the large, organised room. Several people sat at desks, all typing and concentrating on their individual screens.

Paul approached a middle-aged, balding man at one of the workstations. "Anthony. Do you have Captain McCloud's ID ready?"

The man smiled and slid a drawer open. He retrieved a small, neat wallet and handed it to the senior officer. "It was completed just a few minutes ago."

Paul opened the wallet and studied the ID. "Thanks. That's fine. How about the mobile?"

Before Paul had finished his question, Anthony had produced what looked like a really smart-looking iPhone from the same drawer.

"Excellent. I'll show you how to contact us, Alex." Paul indicated the keystrokes to call the different disciplines at the headquarters and then handed the phone and ID to Alex. The two of them left the office, Paul directing him back to where Adrian was waiting.

"All done?"

"Yes. Captain McCloud has his new ID and mobile phone."

"Okay, Paul, I'll take over, now."

Alex guessed that Adrian was the senior of these two men, as he escorted Alex back to a waiting car, shook his hand and said, "This man will take you to your new accommodation, and tomorrow, you will be picked up and taken for training with your support dog."

"How long before my first assignment?"

Adrian considered his question carefully. "That depends on how you get on with your dog. Hopefully, within a few weeks."

Alex thanked him and slid into the passenger seat of the black Ford Focus. The driver said nothing as he engaged the gears and accelerated away into the traffic. He obviously knew London well, as he made many turns down the less busy roads, avoiding the traffic snarl-ups so familiar in the capital city. Eventually, he pulled up in front of a group of Georgian terraced houses.

"Your apartment is on the ground floor at number twenty-one. I'll show you around."

The young man climbed out and opened the door for Alex, who had already switched his sight off. He took the arm of the driver, who was also carrying Alex's suitcase.

There were five steps up from the pavement level to the front door, which was shared by all the apartments. The man showed Alex a small keypad at the side of the door. "The combination number for entry is nine four six two."

Alex had a look at the keypad. He could feel a slightly raised marker on one of the keys. "Is it the same as a telephone keypad with number one at the top left?"

"Absolutely right. See if you can find the correct sequence."

Alex pressed the keypad, and after he'd hit the enter button, the lock on the door was released. He pushed it open and stepped into the large hallway, followed by his driver, who closed the main door.

"Your entrance is the first door on the left, hopefully making it easier for you to find."

Alex soon found the doorway to his apartment. He felt for a keyhole, but there was none. "How do I get in?"

"There is a small, flat plate just under the handle. When you place your ID against it, it should open."

Already impressed by the security, Alex took his ID out of his pocket and used it as instructed. The electronic lock clicked smartly, and he was able to push the door wide open. He stood back, allowing the driver to enter first.

"We're now in a hallway with three doors off it. The one in front of you is to the living room, one further along to a bathroom, and the one at the end is the bedroom." He pushed the door open, and the two men walked into a large living room. "It's a living and dining room, and there's just one more door to the kitchen. Would you like me to show you the rooms in more detail?"

Alex was desperate to switch on his eyes but did not know if the driver was aware of his bionic eyes, so said, "It's okay. I'll manage. Thanks for your help… I don't even know your name."

"Terry." He said this quietly and with an obvious reluctance, as though he preferred to remain anonymous.

"Okay, Terry. What time will you pick me up tomorrow?"

"Nine o'clock. Please be ready." The driver seemed to be very precise and had a noticeable lack of humour in his voice. He placed Alex's suitcase against the wall.

As soon as Terry had left, Alex touched the contacts on his watch and was then able to see his new apartment in full detail. The living room was a good size, about nine metres by five, and comfortable with clean, uncluttered lines. It was already furnished with a sofa, two chairs, a dining table, storage cupboards and a forty-two-inch slim television mounted on one wall.

He wandered through to the kitchen to find it equally modern and comfortable. The kitchen units seemed to be very recent and there was everything he could possibly need, including washing machine, tumble dryer, kettle and even a Tassimo coffee maker.

Alex wondered who had lived here before him and how long ago. Eager to see the bedroom, he went back into the hall and down the bright corridor to the end door.

The room was equipped with a double bed, complete with good-quality bedding, and a large, built-in wardrobe. Alex pulled the door open, half-expecting to find a complete rail of clothes, but not surprisingly, there was nothing except some spare hangers. Still, it was immaculately clean, leaving him no cause for complaint.

The last room to inspect was the bathroom. It was not big but had everything he could need except a bath, but this was something he could easily live without.

A marble shelf with a large, illuminated mirror over it ran along the whole of one wall. A smooth, built-in washbasin was in this shelf, while a toilet was on the opposite wall at the far end.

In the remaining corner, behind the door, was a shower, but this was different from anything he had ever seen before.

It was a corner quadrant shower cubicle, with sliding doors and a touch-control panel on the inside. An instruction manual soon revealed that the shower could be controlled either from within the cubicle or from a small, handheld, remote-control unit. Alex did not wish to read the comprehensive instructions, but by glancing through, he discovered that it had a monsoon shower, handheld shower, high-pressure side body jets and a built-in radio.

The final sophistication was the facility to use the shower as a steam room, even having a built-in seat to relax upon. This really impressed Alex, and he determined to make good use of all the features.

Having checked all areas of the apartment, Alex returned to the kitchen, opened the fridge and looked to see if there was anything to eat. To his surprise, there was milk, margarine, some fresh fruit and vegetables and even frozen pizza and several ready-to-cook meals in the freezer.

Somebody has taken quite a lot of trouble to make me feel comfortable, he thought.

In a cupboard near the fridge, he found a set of four cups, saucers, mugs, plates and dishes, containers of sugar, drinking chocolate, tea and coffee.

A few minutes later, Alex was relaxing in one of the comfortable chairs, drinking a mug of hot chocolate, feeling quite pleased that he now had a decent place to live and a pretty good income from the British and American Governments.

For the rest of the day, he did very little, unpacking his few possessions and watching television. He knew the hard work would start the following day.

A sudden thought crossed Alex's mind. He pressed the numbers on his recently issued mobile phone and was soon connected to the automated bank information line. It had been several months since he had last used this facility, but he managed to remember his password sequence and PIN. His balance was £39,263.15.

It was quite a bit more than he had expected, but, of course, his salary would have been paid in while he was in Afghanistan and Queen Elizabeth Hospital.

It was when he checked the individual credits that he realised how much he had been paid during the last few weeks. This meant that he was already on the payroll in his new employment with the Ministry of Defence. With £7,000 going into his account every month, he was certainly not going to be short of funds.

Even with all his comfort, Alex had difficulty sleeping that night. Everything seemed so strange and unreal, increasing his anxiety level. Why did everything seem so alien? Would he have to live the rest of his life lonely and alone? Was there really any future for him? To his annoyance, his headaches still persisted, and the usual painkillers had absolutely no effect.

When he did eventually fall asleep, he found himself in a weird, troubling dream. His dead friend, Jack, kept reminding him of their thirteen-year friendship. In the dream, both boys were aged about fourteen and, fuelled by their teenage hormones, were seeking female friendship. Karen Simpson had become quite close to Alex, but to his annoyance, Jack managed to entice her away. She was the one girl Alex had fancied while at school, and for a few months he distanced himself from Jack for this selfish action. It was not as though there were no other girls around, but Alex felt that Jack had deliberately stolen her from him to cause annoyance and it had worked. This was the one time their friendship was seriously tested, but after Karen started seeing another boy, Alex and Jack became good friends again.

Alex awoke from his sleep, the dream still fresh in his mind. He had actually forgotten those events eleven years earlier and realised that he and Jack had not always been the best of friends, but as far as he could remember, that had been the only real rift between them. Eventually, he fell back into a more relaxed sleep, this time without any troubling dreams.

Chapter Eleven

Terry said very little during the forty-minute journey and seemed unresponsive to Alex's pleasantries, making Alex wonder if this was Terry's character or because in his line of work, he was supposed to be deferential and remote. The journey was only punctuated by the sound of the windscreen wipers struggling against a particularly heavy downpour. Even with this annoyance and the heavy traffic, Terry never said a word or even uttered a curse against the usual idiotic drivers.

Again, it was a relief when they arrived at the training centre. Terry escorted Alex to the reception area and said that he would return at four-thirty.

The receptionist led Alex to an office where he was introduced to Kate, a pleasant-sounding woman whom Alex guessed from her voice was in her late thirties. He was gradually becoming used to assessing individuals by their style of greeting and the subtle nuances in their voices. What did surprise him was the feel of her hand. For a woman, it was quite large with thick, rough fingers. A vision of a farmer's wife came into his mind.

"Please take a seat, Captain McCloud."

He did as instructed, not knowing what to expect of this very new situation.

"I felt it may be helpful to explain how we are hoping to help you following your loss of sight."

Right, thought Alex. *She doesn't know the true situation.* "That would be helpful," he replied.

"The centre has been provided with a dog that has previously been trained in a military environment. Our job has been to enhance this training to provide the necessary abilities to work as a guide dog."

"What type of dog is it?"

"Ah, Elsa is a beautiful German Shepherd. It's been a delight to work with her over the past few weeks. She's been very well trained already and is a highly intelligent dog."

Alex could tell from the tone of Kate's voice that she had enjoyed training his future guide dog and held some attraction for Elsa.

"Over the next few days, we need to assist you in learning how to control and react to Elsa's movements."

"How long will it take for this training?"

"It's too early to know until we can assess how well the two of you work together. Would you like to meet her?"

"Yes, sure." Alex felt a little nervous at this prospect, but in a way, he wanted to get it over and done with.

"Good! I'll show you the way." Kate took his arm and led him out of the main building and into the kennel area. The smell was unmistakable. Not dirty; more the characteristic odour of several dogs living in close proximity. Alex could hear the scrabbling sound of claws on concrete as Kate approached, each dog hoping to be the one she was seeking.

"Elsa! Come here!"

Alex heard the panting of one dog as it rushed towards them. Kate unfastened the door and quickly slipped a lead over the head of the energetic animal. "Down, Elsa!" Her voice was firm and commanding. Turning to Alex, she said, "Elsa is a really lovely dog. She's been a pleasure to train. Give me your hand, Captain McCloud."

"Please, call me Alex. I'm a civilian now," he lied. As he nervously held out his hand, Kate placed it on the head of what seemed to be a very big animal. Immediately, the dog turned her head upwards and started licking his palm as though she had known him forever. Alex stroked Elsa's head gently, the dog enjoying the new attention. Hot breath could be felt as Elsa again lifted her head, receptive to every stroke he made.

"Take hold of her lead in your left hand and I will guide you to the open training area."

He did as instructed and, trusting his two guides, one on each side, he walked gingerly out of the kennels, Elsa pulling eagerly.

Kate led them to a point in the area where she said, "Okay take the lead off Elsa and instruct her to sit. You must say it firmly and stress the 'S' sound of the word."

He did as instructed and held the lead loosely in his hand. "Sit, Elsa!"

Kate spoke quietly. "You need to say it with more conviction, Alex. She has got to really understand that you are now her master. Be very firm, yet do not shout."

He tried again, extending the 'S' sound. Although he could not tell, Kate said, "She is sitting. Now praise her. Say 'Good girl, Elsa,' and stroke her head."

Again, he followed her instructions. He was surprised that even after only a few minutes, he felt a strangely reassuring attachment to this animal.

"Okay, Alex. Now I want you to tell her to 'Stay'. Again, be firm and repeat the command several times."

"Okay. Stay, Elsa. Stay!"

Kate watched with satisfaction. "Now keep repeating the command while moving further away from her. Try to be casual and don't move too quickly." Kate had already moved a few feet away. "Follow my voice, and remember, keep repeating the command but also praise her at the same time."

Alex followed her instructions precisely and felt that already he had the start of a trusting relationship with this dog.

"Good girl, Elsa! Stay!"

"This should be the easy part. When you're ready, just say 'Come'. Then give her lots of praise." Alex could detect a smile in Kate's voice.

"Come, Elsa!" The dog instantly bounded towards him, almost knocking him over. It was obvious to anybody that Elsa and Alex were going to get on fine. Elsa's tail was wagging vigorously, and she was licking his hands as though she had known him for many years.

"Excellent! Now we should put her on the lead again, and we'll return to my office." Elsa walked at Alex's left side as they returned to the small office. Kate showed Alex the position of the chair. "When you're seated instruct her to lie down."

By now, Elsa was getting used to Alex's vocal commands and immediately lay down near his feet. She was a fairly big dog and occupied quite a large part of the floor area.

After this, Kate went through all the procedures they would be covering over the next few days. For the rest of the day, he received further instruction on how to handle his new 'eyes'. The hardest part was shortly after four o'clock when Elsa had to return to the kennels. It was obvious to Alex that the dog that several hours of working with her new master had come to an end. Alex stroked her head soothingly as he sensed the change in Elsa's demeanour.

When Terry arrived prompt at four-thirty, Alex was equally saddened by their separation and said little throughout the journey.

Back at his flat, Alex's feelings of emptiness and loneliness deepened. Pulling himself out of this morose mood, he picked one of the ready-made meals from the freezer and followed the instructions to heat it up in the microwave. *Got to build up my strength and stamina. I just hope that it will all be worth the effort.*

The silence annoyed him intensely. He turned on the radio, hoping for company, and found Simon Mayo's evening programme on Radio Two, which did help to ease him out of his dark mood. He relaxed, listening to the business news with Rebecca Pike followed shortly by the listeners' humorous confessions. The microwave pinged, bringing him back to reality.

His dinner was a tasty chicken and rice meal, which he followed with fresh fruit. At least his stomach was satisfied even though his soul was not.

At about seven, he picked up his mobile and phoned home. He was pleased when his sister Lucy answered. "Hi, sis! Did you get your results?"

She sounded excited. "Yes. I've got three 'A's. I can go to Cambridge!"

"Fantastic! I'm so pleased for you, Lucy. I'm certain you'll make a fine doctor."

"There's a lot of work before I get that far, but I'm so happy just to get my grades."

Alex knew that his sister had worked really hard and was thrilled by her success. "I have some news for you. I have a new girlfriend, sis."

For a few seconds, there was a stunned silence. "Really? Who is she?"

He could hear the surprise in her voice and had difficulty stopping himself from laughing. "Yes. Her name is Elsa, and she is not some Scandinavian beauty but an eighteen-month-old German shepherd dog!"

"Oh, Alex!" She began giggling and told her mother what her brother had said. "Hold on, I'll put Mum on to speak to you."

For the next fifteen minutes, Alex had to tell Louise the events of that day in every minute detail. His mother had never been keen on dogs, preferring instead pets of the feline variety. Still, she was fascinated by Alex's description of his day.

"You must keep me informed on your training, Alex. I think you are so brave to get on with your life after all that has happened to you over the past years." She sounded so proud, making Alex feel incredibly guilty about concealing the truth from his family.

OVER THE NEXT few days, he and Elsa worked closely together, both being instructed by the ever-capable Kate, who appeared quite impressed by the rapid progress of dog and master alike. It was up to the guide-dog trainer to decide when Elsa should be allowed to stay full-time at Alex's place and, confident in their abilities, she told Terry as he dropped Alex off that day that she would drive him and Elsa to his apartment later in the afternoon.

When they arrived at his place, it came as a surprise to Alex that Kate knew her way around the apartment. She explained that she had been called to assess the premises to determine if they were suitable for a guide dog even before Alex had moved in. In addition, she had organised the construction of a drained concrete run where the dog could urinate and defecate. Alex was thankful that all he had to do was hose the area down daily to flush away all the waste material.

Kate had brought some other items with her. A feeding bowl, water bowl, a large bag of dog food, grooming brush, Elsa's harness with handle and a dog bed were all provided, presumably paid for by donors and the British Government. It was certainly very well organised, but would he be worth the expense and effort?

"Okay, Alex. I think I'm done here. Is there anything you need to know before I leave you?"

"Not that I can think of just now."

"Well if there is anything, just give me a call. When you need more dog food we can get it for you, and if there are any problems with Elsa's health, the vet I recommended will assist you."

"Great! Thanks for all your hard work, Kate." Elsa was at his side as he walked to the main door to his apartment. Alex had wondered if Elsa would want to return to the centre with Kate and was relieved that she stayed close by his side, seemingly accepting Alex as her new master.

As soon as Kate had left the building, Alex again 'switched' on his eyes. "Now, Elsa, I want you to keep this little secret between the two of us. Okay?" He looked at his new partner and was impressed by Elsa's appearance. The dog's coat was predominantly black with contrasting shades of brown, some almost golden in colour, and her long face was mainly brown. As he stared at her, she similarly looked up into his face, her black eyes seeming to acknowledge his secret. There was an obvious intelligence in his new partner. To his surprise, the dog lifted her right paw as if expecting him to take hold. As he grasped it, he knew instinctively that there was a deep understanding between them. The two looked at each other for what seemed like hours yet in fact was probably only about fifteen seconds. It was as though the dog was reading his mind, absorbing all the facts with a newfound knowledge.

Kate had made it quite clear to Alex that keeping regular feeding times was important, and he intended to follow her instructions precisely. At six, he poured the dog food into Elsa's bowl, added water and placed it on the kitchen floor. As soon as he let go of the bowl, Elsa greedily attacked the food. Alex was amazed at how quickly the dog finished her meal, lapping up the food and water and then licking around the bowl to devour every last scrap.

He followed this by taking her out to the run on the lead and was pleased that the dog was happy to relieve itself on the drained area.

That evening seemed very strange to Alex. He was relaxed watching television while Elsa lay on the floor near his feet. Somehow, it felt like they had been together for a long time not just a matter of days.

Alex had read the background of German shepherd dogs purely out of his own interest. As its name implied, the dog was initially bred to help shepherds in the German valleys. They were strong animals with an intelligence that only needed visual signals to follow the shepherd's commands. The breed gained an unfortunate reputation during the Second World War when the Nazis used them to attack and keep control of prisoners in concentration camps. They were given an alternative name of Alsatian in the 1970s to distance the connection to their Nazi training, but several years later, the name of 'German Shepherd' became more acceptable again. They, together with Labrador Retrievers, were favoured by the Guide Dogs Association, as they had the perfect temperament and intelligence to guide and care for their blind owners.

Chapter Twelve

THE NEXT MAJOR hurdle for Alex was to venture outside his apartment with Elsa in harness guiding him through the streets of London. Fortunately, Kate would be accompanying them until she was satisfied that Elsa was proficient enough to leave them on their own. The main problem was that Alex knew little of London streets or, even more importantly, the area in which he now lived. Paul had anticipated this problem and had installed satellite navigation software with speech output on his mobile phone. A particularly useful feature was that as he moved from one location to another, the street name would be announced.

Alex threw himself into the task as though it was a military exercise, and very soon, he had a mental image of quite a large area of London in his mind. Elsa was the perfect partner, negotiating all the obstacles that seemed to fill the pavements of the capital city, preventing him from falling down open manholes and colliding with hazardous roadworks.

Alex had also become accustomed to feeling the dog's movements through the handle on the harness and gradually gained more confidence in the dog's ability to guide him safely.

Within a few days, with Kate following and observing them from a distance, she was confident enough to leave them to manage on their own.

Alex still felt nervous about trusting his safety to a dog irrespective of how intelligent it may be. He did realise that he could leave his eyes switched on, but how soon would it be before a member of the public realised that he could see better than anybody else? It would be more convincing to onlookers if he had the occasional stumble or collision.

He had discovered that within ten minutes' walk from his apartment, there was a supermarket store where he could purchase his weekly shopping. Alex had asked the store manager if one of the assistants could help him find the items he required. "No problem, Sir. Sandra will help you to find just what you need. She has worked here for over eight years and will be happy to assist you."

Sandra, a petite talkative woman in her mid-thirties, escorted Alex up and down the aisles pushing a small trolley while describing what each aisle contained. She always seemed to have plenty to talk about, and he found her ramblings spoken in a high Liverpool accent quite interesting.

Very soon, Alex had a complete mental image of the store, making the experience quite straightforward. At the checkout, Sandra would help to pack his shopping into a backpack, allowing him to carry his shopping while leaving his hands free. This became a regular routine, and it was one Alex quite enjoyed, as it made him feel 'normal' again. He was a man who did not like having to rely on others to carry out the simplest of tasks. His fridge and freezer were now packed with enough food to last for some considerable time.

High-energy foods were also on his shopping list, as he was determined to build up his stamina and body mass to what it had been before his injuries. A lifting frame, weights and a running machine were delivered to his apartment, and he soon had a daily routine of exercises. On top of these, he would have two daily sessions of fifty press-ups. He could feel the difference as his muscles became much stronger and tighter, and he knew that if he had to use physical force, he could easily meet the challenge.

Hmm, not bad, he thought as he looked at his naked body in the full-length mirror in his bedroom. *Not quite Arnold Schwarzenegger, but it will do for me.*

The close bond between Alex and Elsa soon became obvious, and he found the dog really good company. In the evening, Alex would relax watching television, while Elsa lay on the floor at his side. It intrigued him how attentive the dog was, for as soon as he made even the slightest of movements, Elsa would stand up immediately, always eager and ready to follow her master.

With his eyes 'switched on', Alex could see the intelligence in the dog's face, and the cobalt-black eyes seemed to be both penetrating and understanding at the same time. Did she somehow understand why he had to pretend to be blind? Surely, this was impossible, and yet he was convinced that she knew far more than any dog could be expected to know about him.

Now that Alex's bank balance was quite healthy, he did not mind spending some of his wealth, and one day when he was going through his wardrobe, he realised that his choice of clothes was a bit limited. *I could do with a decent suit,* he thought. He could have bought several suits 'off the peg' but instead decided to use some of his newly found wealth to boost his choice of clothes in real style.

Alex, together with Elsa, made the journey to Savile Row by taxi. He had selected what he hoped was his best suit, as he did not wish to appear well below the standard of dress expected by a top-ranking tailor.

"Which company do you want me to drop you off at?" asked the taxi driver.

Alex had searched extensively on the internet when deciding which of the world-famous tailors to use. He was not surprised when he found that he had to make an appointment even for an initial measuring. "Cad and The Dandy, please. It's at number thirteen."

"Good choice," said the driver. "I bring a fair number of clients to that tailor. I just wish I had the money to consider spending so much on a suit myself." In truth, even if he had the money he would rather have a good holiday for the same price as a suit. The cab driver pulled in at number thirteen Savile Row and checked his meter.

Alex paid the fare, allowing for a decent tip, which noticeably pleased the driver. *It's okay to splash a little cash around*, he thought to himself.

The cab driver temporarily left his vehicle and directed Alex to the entrance doorway. Alex pushed the door open and walked upstairs to the first floor. He was surprised that even in these times of austerity, there were still so many expensive tailors to warrant sharing an address on the famous Savile Row.

Elsa's paws clattered noisily on the polished hardwood floor as they entered the premises. There was a dignified yet not intimidating air to this world-class tailor's. "Can I be of assistance, sir?"

"I have an appointment. My name is McCloud."

"Ah, yes. Please come this way, sir. Would you like me to take your hand?"

Alex was pleased that this man knew how best to assist a blind person and relaxed his grip on Elsa's handle, letting it rest on the dog's back.

They walked into a measuring room where the man referred to his notes. "I understand that you would like us to make a two-piece suit for you. Would you prefer machine-stitched, half-machine and hand, or completely hand-stitched?"

It was an extravagance, but Alex had decided that if he was going to have a suit made especially for him, he might as well go for the best. "Hand-stitched, please. I'm looking for a dark-grey suit and would be happy to follow your recommendations on the type of material and style."

The tailor breathed an inaudible sigh of relief. He preferred it when the client left the choice of material up to him, especially considering the problems in leaving the choice to someone who could not appreciate the many different types of material. "Very good, sir. Would you please remove your jacket to allow us to take some measurements?"

"Of course. Lie down, Elsa!" Alex was enjoying this class of service. He observed without it being apparent as the man and his assistant made and recorded all the measurements. He remembered having a suit made to measure several years earlier, but this was far more detailed than he had previously experienced.

About three-quarters of an hour later, Alex was returning by taxi to his apartment. He had ordered a suit, three shirts and two ties, costing him around £2,500. It was a great deal of money, but he felt it would be worth the expense, and providing he did not change his shape too much, the clothes should last him for many years.

He had paid a holding deposit, which did not seem unreasonable, as once the cloth had been cut for him, it would probably be useless for anybody else.

Over the next few weeks, he made several visits to 13 Savile Row for fitting and completion of his purchase, and back in the privacy of his apartment, he admired the sheer quality of the product.

Life had now become more comfortable and 'normal', but with this came a certain degree of boredom, which Alex had never wanted.

However, it was not to last for much longer. On one of his trips back from the supermarket, he was walking past Alexandra Park when he heard a scream. It came from quite close, and he could not just ignore it and walk on as though nothing had happened. It sounded like the scream of a young female, but what sort of person could strike such fear in anyone? He quickly switched on his sight and was just in time to see a man attempting to drag a teenage schoolgirl into the park.

Alex knew he had to intervene and quickly, as there were no other people around. Whatever he did, he must avoid being discovered as a sighted person impersonating a blind man. The girl was still screaming, kicking and struggling, but she was no match for the greater strength of her attacker.

"What's going on?" Alex shouted as he approached the man, who was already dragging the girl through the bushes. Of course, nobody answered him, the man obviously feeling safe with only a blind person nearby. He had muffled the girl's screams with one hand while the other was pulling her roughly into the park. She was putting up a good fight but was soon overpowered by him.

Alex quickly unclipped the dog's handle. "Attack!" As soon as he gave the command, Elsa ran with amazing speed, pouncing on the man and gripping him tightly by the leg with her powerful jaws.

The potential rapist let out a howl of pain, and as he relaxed his grip on the girl, she managed to scramble away to safety.

"Thanks, mister. That dirty old git needs castrating!" she said in obvious relief.

"You're welcome. Get off home quickly before I release him." She took Alex at his word, picked up her schoolbag and rushed away.

The dog's grip on the assailant was enough to incapacitate him but not enough to do any real damage. She was capable of biting much harder and could easily tear into the flesh of his calves, but Alex thought it unnecessary and called to his faithful dog.

"Elsa! Leave! Come!"

Obediently, she loosened her grip and returned to Alex.

"Good girl!" To maintain his guise of a blind person, he deliberately looked just to one side of the man, who was cursing and rubbing his damaged leg. "Clear off before I call the police, you fucking pervert!"

It was with some strange curiosity that Alex noticed the skin colour of the man. It looked somewhat unnatural. Of course, he could have just been unwashed, yet the greyish tone of the man's skin with its slightly blue tinge seemed more than dirt. But what? Alex had a feeling there was some significance in the strange skin colour.

As he pulled himself together, the man similarly stared at Alex in obvious surprise. Alex took advantage of the situation and deftly touched the contacts on his watch to find out if the facial recognition system would come up with anything. The top part of his vision remained frustratingly clear, and Alex was about to cancel the function when details suddenly appeared. George Maxwell was only fifty-one yet looked at least twenty years older. He had a police record, mainly for indecent exposure and sexual assaults. *No change there, then*, he thought.

The man muttered some incoherent curse, and it was a relief when he hobbled away, still holding his injured leg and occasionally looking back at the blind man with his now-passive guide dog.

Alex breathed a sigh of relief. He really did not want this incident to affect his role as a person within the intelligence service, yet the offence could not be ignored. Maxwell was unlikely to tell anyone of his foiled rape attempt, but Alex felt obliged to inform Adrian, who would let the police know of this potentially serious incident.

As for the girl, she might boast to her friends that she had escaped a sexual attack with the assistance of a guide dog, but hopefully, she would be more careful in the future, especially when walking home in the dark.

Alex bent down and clipped the handle on Elsa's harness. "Good girl, Elsa," he repeated. He carried on back to his apartment and thought over the course of the past few weeks.

After Kate had satisfied herself that Alex and Elsa worked together to the standard she expected, Alex had, unknown to Kate, attended further instruction from a military dog handler organised by Adrian King.

This training had been much more difficult and intense than that at the Guide Dog training centre. Many different situations had been simulated where dog and handler would be tested under severe conditions. Tom was a disciplined military guy with twenty-three years' experience of working with dogs in hostile situations. He taught Alex how to respond and how best to exploit the dog's capabilities. Alex never ceased to be amazed by Elsa's intelligence and devotion and thoroughly enjoyed working with her. Now their training had paid off and saved a teenage girl from the clutches of a rapist.

That evening, Alex tried to think about his future. When he had seen the old guy attack the girl, he was sorely tempted to use his own physical strength to teach the rapist a lesson just as he would have done a year earlier. The pretence that he had been asked to follow was difficult to maintain, yet he had not really much choice. Eventually, he accepted that it was better to have superior vision while pretending to have none instead of actually being blind as he was before the prosthetic implants.

He decided to have an early night reading in bed. Even this activity had become complicated. The woman from blind welfare had told Alex that he would be entitled to receive talking books from the Royal National Institute of Blind People, but Alex felt he could not use these resources when he could in reality still see. If he had paperbacks lying around his apartment, it would not take long for anyone to realise that he was concealing his true condition.

As a compromise, he had ordered audiobooks from Amazon. These came in the form of multiple CDs, which could be played in any CD player. He had bought a neat player, which he kept at the side of his bed. Using earphones, he could settle down into a comfortable position and read for an hour or two before going to sleep.

Alex had bought a selection of audiobooks by authors such as Stephen King, James Herbert, Dene Koontz, Lee Child, Tom

Clancy, Nelson Demille and Robert Ludlum, as these horror and action stories fascinated him.

After reading Lee Child's *The Killing Floor*, he had found the character of Jack Reacher, a six-foot-five American ex-military policeman, someone whom he could empathise with. Reacher was a loner who, without trying, managed to get himself involved in desperate situations where some mad, immensely powerful criminal killed without compunction.

In addition to eventually dramatically killing the arch-criminal, Reacher always found time to fall for some beautiful young woman, whom he would leave behind, ready for his next adventure and conquest.

Alex thought of his own situation when Jen had rejected his advances. None of Jack Reacher's women had ever said, *"I'm sorry Jack but I don't think it's a good idea to have sex with you."* Normally, they jumped into bed with him at the earliest possible opportunity.

Alex was now reading the next book in the Jack Reacher series *Die Trying*, which he found equally fascinating and one which was hard to stop reading. Eventually, at midnight, he switched off the player and settled down into an uneasy sleep.

The following morning, he phoned Adrian King.

"Morning, Alex. What can I do for you?"

Alex found Adrian easy to talk to and explained what had happened the previous day. "It was so damn frustrating! I wanted to tear the man off the girl, yet I knew this would compromise my cover."

"Don't worry, Alex. You did the best thing. From what you've told me, you did what any concerned blind person would have done in the same circumstances, and I will inform the police of the incident. I'm sure they'll be paying a visit to Mr. Maxwell. Sounds like Elsa did a good job."

"She is truly amazing. I couldn't have wished for a better dog."

Adrian agreed. "I was going to phone you today. There seems to be a lot of activity in London at the moment, both in terrorism and infighting between criminal gangs. We have a job for you that takes advantage of your visual abilities."

This news came as a great relief to Alex. He had lazed about enough and was hungry for action. "Good! I feel as though I need to get into doing something worthwhile."

For the next fifteen minutes, Adrian detailed everything relevant to this new mission. In addition, he sent an encrypted email to Alex's computer. The Notebook had been supplied by Adrian and had the latest version of JAWS screen-reading software. This meant that Alex could still use the PC as a blind person assisted by the speech synthesiser, which would read any text appearing on the screen and even speak each character or word as it was typed.

Alex decrypted Adrian's email and spent the rest of the day analysing and understanding all the information about his task. It reminded him of his days in the British Army, when he had to read and thoroughly digest the surveillance notes before embarking on a military mission. All the different forms of military intelligence were brought together in one short, concise report, from which it would be his responsibility to determine which course of action should be taken.

Chapter Thirteen

IT WAS A cold, crisp yet dry morning in late October 2011. Georgio Petroski, a twenty-eight-year-old Albanian, strode purposely along Oxford Street. Alex had been tailing him since the Albanian had left his apartment ten minutes earlier. Although noticeable with his guide dog, Alex hoped that Petroski was not aware of being tailed. He did wonder if anybody would ever suspect that they could be followed by a blind person. Hopefully, this would not be the case.

Alex had his sight switched to surveillance mode where the images he scanned were fed back to GCHQ headquarters to check against a huge, computerised bank of known criminals and terrorist images.

Petroski did not seem in any particular hurry. He was heading towards Piccadilly Circus but occasionally would stop under the guise of looking in the shop windows to check for anybody tailing him. Elsa normally walked quite fast, but today, Alex kept coaxing her to move more slowly. Again, she seemed to know the importance of their task and padded along the crowded pavements at a relaxed rate.

Petroski stopped at one of the many stalls at street junctions dotted along Oxford Street. This was one of those dodgy stalls selling blatantly fake fashion products. Alex could not understand why the police still allowed these sellers to carry on plying their illegal trade.

Then he spotted the two men moving towards the stall. They spoke to Petroski for a couple of minutes, and he caught sight of Petroski handing a small package over to one of the strangers.

Nearing the three men and keeping his posture as though he was looking straight ahead, Alex glanced sideways at the strangers, aware that everything he saw would be relayed through GCHQ and from there to MI6.

It was only a side-profile view of the unknown men, and Alex knew that a frontal view would be far more valuable. He reached the edge of the pavement and instructed Elsa to turn left. As they turned, he kept his eyes locked on the group of three men.

He walked slowly down the narrow side street, stopping at a narrow alleyway. There he allowed Elsa to urinate into an open grating. To the casual observer, this would be a natural occurrence for a man with a guide dog. After Elsa had finished, Alex again took hold of her handle and walked back along the street. Now he was facing the three men, who seemed to be in deep conversation. He kept his eyes locked on their faces, zooming in for optimum viewing; to his relief, text began to appear at the top of his field of vision.

It identified the two as Saaid and Mohammad Lalaki, two known Pakistani men with long-established links to terrorist cells. Alex was taken aback when he realised that the skin colour of these three individuals was again bluish-grey, just like George Maxwell the potential rapist. *How strange*, he thought.

He wondered in which direction the men would move after finishing their discussion. Taking a gamble, Alex turned left back onto Oxford Street. He was walking quite slowly, their progress being hampered by the crowds of tourists. It came as a relief when the two Pakistanis overtook Alex and continued in the direction of Piccadilly Circus. Alex picked up speed, hoping to follow them close behind, but was defeated when the two disappeared down the steps of Piccadilly Circus Underground station. It would be impossible to follow them without being noticed.

To his surprise, a message appeared at the top of his vision reading: *Do not follow any further. Other operatives will take over.*

Alex almost felt invaded by this anonymous message. It was now obvious that in addition to the automatic facial-recognition scanner, actual humans were also watching every little detail his eyes perceived. He was both in awe of the technology and affronted by this invasion of his intimate, private world.

Was this the end of this shadowing task? It seemed so brief, yet hopefully, it had proved useful to MI6. Feeling somewhat downcast, he slowly worked his way back to his apartment. Was this to be his future? A brief assignment with others taking over and finishing the job? As long as the mission was successful there was nothing to worry about, so why did he feel so empty and disheartened?

As if to add to his misery, the heavens opened and the rain bounced noisily off the pavements. By the time they reached their apartment, both Alex and Elsa were soaked. As soon as Alex removed Elsa's harness, she shook violently to rid herself of the rain, but in the process, Alex and the walls were peppered with water.

"Oh, thanks for that, Elsa! As if I wasn't wet enough!"

Elsa looked up at him with almost a soulful expression. *Perhaps she didn't like getting soaked either,* thought Alex.

He stripped off, had a warm shower and wrapped himself in a bathrobe. Then he decided to dry Elsa, whose rain-sodden coat was beginning to feel a little matted. Ten minutes later, she looked and presumably felt much better.

After this, Alex phoned Adrian and talked through his mission, although his eyes had silently yet effectively already debriefed him. Adrian was pleased with the information gleaned from the task and did his best to reassure Alex of his usefulness.

Even after this, it felt quite an anticlimax, and once again, he felt lonely and desolate. As a soldier, he'd have had the company of other soldiers within their barracks.

He touched his watch. *"The time is five twenty-three p.m."* Another touch. *"Today is Friday, October twenty-first, 2011."* Brief as it was, the sound of Jen's bright pleasing voice temporarily lifted his spirit. He missed the feeling he had experienced when Jen was working with him. He was still attracted to her and wished she could have been there with him.

That evening, he phoned home and spoke to his mother and Amelia. Lucy was not there, as she was now in her first year studying at Cambridge. Thankfully, this was not too far away, allowing her to spend weekends at home. As usual, his father was at a business meeting and not at home. How his mother had put up with seeing so little of her husband for so many years was beyond him. She had said on many occasions that he was not the easiest person to live with, so the absences may have helped to keep the marriage together.

To add to his frustration, Alex could not tell his family of his newfound career with military intelligence. Fortunately, they asked few questions about his work, accepting that he was assisting the government purely as a military advisor and that he would be unable to reveal much about his daily tasks. The whole family was pleased that even after his great misfortune he was lucky enough to still have a career in the army. If they had a greater knowledge of military matters, they would have realised that Alex was not experienced enough to be accepted as an advisor.

A FEW DAYS later, there was another tailing through the now-familiar streets of London, but sadly, it still did not satisfy his hunger for action.

After this, when he was reporting in to Adrian, Alex asked, "Is there any chance I could speak to Paul Marshall?"

There was a slight pause before Adrian answered. "He's not in the country at the moment but should be back tomorrow. Is there anything I can help with?"

"It's not urgent. I would just like to find out if I can be utilised in a wider choice of assignments." He did not wish to speak to Adrian in any greater depth, preferring instead to raise his issues with probably the only person who could make a difference: the brigadier general.

The tone of Adrian's voice had not changed, and Alex felt that his contact did not mind being asked to refer him to his superior. "No problem. I'll ask him to get in touch with you as soon as possible."

"One other thing, Adrian. I'm not certain the colour sensitivity within my eyes is working correctly. I still keep seeing strange colours on some though not all faces."

Adrian thought about this and said, "Sounds as though some checks need to be made. Leave it with me."

As Alex ended the call, he wondered what he was going to say to the man pulling the strings at MI6. He had at least time to think how he should approach the subject.

For now, he needed to give Elsa some more attention, as her coat was now dry. He had found great relaxation when grooming her and called the dog over. Eagerly, she came close to Alex when she saw him with the grooming brush. Although this brush seemed quite coarse, it did the job of removing loose hairs from her thick coat, and soon the waste bin was quite full of discarded hair. Elsa really seemed to enjoy the experience and stayed relaxed while her master completed her grooming. Her coat felt smooth and silky to the touch by the time Alex had finished the job, and Elsa seemed to appreciate what had been done for her.

Alex mused to himself that instead of giving all his attention to some delightful young female, he was instead sharing his life with a dog, and this was certainly no metaphor for some tired, ugly woman. He supposed that he was lucky that this friendship only cost him dog food and was always appreciated. Still, he was only twenty-five, and hopefully, his love life could only improve. It would certainly be impossible to get any worse, as it was now completely non-existent.

It was two days later when he received a call from Paul Marshall. "Adrian tells me you're looking for a different type of assignment?"

"I'm sorry to sound so ungrateful. Tailing someone for a short while and then handing over to somebody else leaves me feeling so empty and frustrated. I know I'm capable of much more."

The older man laughed more in amusement rather than meaning that this was a ridiculous request. "Do you feel capable of carrying out a different type of work?"

"Yes! I know I can do more if given the chance." Alex felt uneasy that his request may result in the ending of all work for the British Government and in particular MI6 but desperately hoped this would not be the case.

"Come in to the department next Wednesday." Alex breathed a sigh of relief. "We need to assess your full capabilities before we can even think of other types of work."

"Thank you, Sir." Alex slept much better that night and just hoped that he would be up to the task.

SEVEN DAYS LATER, Terry called promptly at nine as the brigadier general had arranged. The twenty-minute journey to MI6 at Vauxhall Cross with this now-familiar escort was still quite economic with conversation, which always gave Alex an uneasy feeling. He found it difficult to decide if it was Terry's character or part of his job description not to converse. Perhaps he was just a sad, miserable unsociable prick?

Adrian met Alex and Elsa at reception and guided them along the maze of corridors and, surprisingly, down several levels in the lift. This building on the South Embankment of the Thames was huge and probably unfairly nicknamed 'LEGOLAND' because of its modular block construction with many different stepped roof levels.

As they left the lift, Adrian opened a door into a comfortable office. A smartly dressed young woman introduced herself as Kelly.

Adrian said, "Kelly will look after Elsa while you're being assessed."

It was with some reluctance that Alex handed the lead over to this stranger. Could he trust this young woman to look after his canine friend adequately? Would the dog think that Alex was abandoning her? Strangely, she seemed to understand, and although a little quiet, she made no move to follow her master.

Adrian and Alex left the office and continued along yet another of the many winding corridors. "You can switch on your sight now, Alex."

Wondering what to expect, he did as instructed. *Nothing special here*, he thought. *Just endless boring corridors.*

He understood fully when they entered the next room. Standing smiling at him was Jen. "Hi, Alex! Good to see you again."

The smile on Alex's face said it all. "Great to see you." He very nearly gave her a hug but realised that in these surroundings and in the presence of Adrian, it would probably be construed as inappropriate. Instead, they shook hands warmly.

"What brings you back to England?"

Jen laughed. "You did! When you asked if you could be assessed for more complex duties, the brigadier general asked if I could fly over to assist in your assessment." After a short pause, she added, "I also need to check the colour palette in the prosthetic eyes after you mentioned possible false colouring."

Now Alex was feeling quite guilty but still more than happy to see Jen again. Alex wished more than ever that he and Jen could have been an item. Dressed in a smart blue trouser suit with crisp white shirt, she looked in great shape and that smile… Such a warm inviting smile that any man who did not fancy her must really have been blind, which in his case was a little ironic.

She continued, "I was tasked to devise tests to fully assess your capabilities in extreme situations. My section leader was not too happy, as I'd only been back a short while, but he understood why it should be me."

True to his lustful mind, Alex thought back to the fictitious Jack Reacher, who somehow always managed to get laid in each story. How he hoped she was going to test his capabilities in bed with her, but this was just wishful thinking. *One day, perhaps.*

"So what have you devised for me?"

Jen handed Alex a pair of ear protectors. "The first is target practice, but you would do well to wear these. Your hearing could be damaged in these enclosed testing areas."

Gratefully, he took the protectors.

"I'm going to stay in this control room but will be in voice contact throughout the tests. Now, start by entering the test area through the doorway in front of you."

Alex adjusted and positioned the ear protectors, which doubled as microphone and headphones for maximum comfort. Warily, he pushed open the door to the testing room.

There was a choice of rifles at the end of a long room used as a firing range. Looking through what weapons were available, he chose an SA80, as this was what he had used in Afghanistan. He set it to semi-automatic mode and told Jen that he was ready. She pressed a few buttons on a control console, and to Alex's surprise, a cloud of smoke entered the room through grilles positioned around the perimeter of the floor.

"Don't worry, Alex. It's quite harmless yet very effective at obscuring the targets. Are you ready?"

Alex realised this would be a good test of his ability to see clearly in low-visibility situations. "Okay, Jen. I'm ready."

By now, the room was full of this strange mist. Alex looked through his sights at the far wall. As he watched, a figure began moving across the wall, slowly at first but gradually speeding up. He fired two shots and then noticed other targets moving into his visual field. One by one, he pumped the rifle until he was certain that all had been hit. Even with his ear protectors, the noise seemed extremely loud. In contrast, the sound of the electric pressure motors working hard was quite muted.

"How did I do?" he asked as the mist began to clear.

There was a slight pause. "I'm checking. You can come back in here now."

He replaced the rifle, pulled off his ear protectors and walked back through the heavily built door.

Jen was looking through data on a screen. All the hits were electronically calibrated, and the results were displayed in tabular form.

"There were twelve targets, and all received two hits in the head. Twelve kills! Congratulations, Alex!"

"What was the mist about?"

"We were testing your ability to see in low-light situations. The mist simulates a five per cent visibility level, and you still managed to hit all targets accurately. Under the same circumstances, a normally sighted person would have been lucky to hit one."

"Good! I still don't see why the lights could not have been switched off or at least dimmed instead."

"It would have been unfair to expect you to carry out the test in complete darkness, and the mist is useful to replicate actual combat conditions. This test is used for other combatants but not usually down to five per cent visibility. Okay?"

"Yes, fine. Is that it?"

"No, not yet. I want you to take a pistol and go into the next room. The obscuring mist is being pumped in there." She looked at her console to check the visibility level. "Okay, it's ready for you. Keep on your toes. In this room, the targets can pop up from anywhere. Just be as quick and accurate as you can."

He was about to enter the room when Jen added, "Oh, by the way, the red figures are enemies while the black are friendly. Try to avoid shooting our friends!" She smiled coyly at Alex after making his task even more complicated.

He grinned. "Thanks for that. Okay, I'm ready."

He pushed the door open and slipped through, closing it firmly after him. This room was full of low building facades and shells of vehicles. He scanned the room for any signs of movement. Sweeping around, he spotted a red figure in a doorway and fired into it. The figure disappeared, and then other figures began to appear from all over the large room. He walked fast through the maze of objects, picking up any enemy targets he spotted as he moved to the far end of the area.

After a few minutes, a siren sounded and the mist was sucked out of vents, leaving it clear once more. He walked back into the control room where Jen was again studying the results on a console.

She smiled. "One hundred per cent accuracy with a five per cent visibility factor." Then she added, "And not a single friend hit!"

"Have I passed then?"

"With flying colours, Alex. There's no doubt that your bionic eyes have proved highly efficient and successful. In fact, far more successful than we had ever imagined."

Alex knew his extensive training in the British Army and his experience on the battlefield had proved invaluable in the accurate use of weapons.

"So what now?" Alex asked, wondering if she had any more tests for him. He was actually enjoying not only her company but also the difficult exercises she had devised for him.

"I'm going to hand you over to our in-house psychologist, Susan Masters. She needs to determine if you're capable of handling greater stress. Oh, and after that, we'll do a colour-calibration test on your eyes. It could be that your colour palette has become misaligned."

A few minutes later, Alex was in the office of Susan Masters. Jen had taken him to her room and then left the couple to their privacy. The psychologist was in her late forties, had shoulder-length black hair and looked remarkably fit.

"Please lie down and make yourself comfortable Alex."

He wondered just how she would assess his psychological profile. As he lay back on the sofa, she began to ask him to describe what he felt to be the major turning points in his life, even going back to being an infant.

She stopped him at many points, asking him to elaborate on particular stages where she felt it would help to assess him in more depth. After ninety minutes of these deeply probing, sometimes personal questions, she had a pretty good assessment of his past and moved on to more recent events.

"How do you feel about the Taliban bombing that injured you and killed your comrades?"

"Pissed off and bloody angry! Is that so surprising?"

She replied quite calmly, "No it's not surprising at all. But do you feel you're handling it adequately? Is the anger as strong now as it was when you were admitted to hospital?"

He had to think about this. "How do you measure anger?"

"You can't! But you probably can tell whether the anger is as strong now as it used to be."

"I suppose I feel just as angry now as I ever did, and I honestly can't see that changing."

"What about your broken relationship with Helen? Tell me how you feel about it.

Alex took a sharp intake of breath at this most personal of questions. "Thoroughly pissed off! I can't ever forgive her." His forthright answer was made without any apology. "If her feelings for me were dependent on me staying fit and healthy then it could never have been true love."

The psychologist did not comment, merely making notes on a pad. "Okay, Alex. I've finished my assessment. I'll call Major Sherlock to return here for you." Within a couple of minutes of her speaking on the phone, Jen returned. From there, the couple walked to a laboratory for the next test.

"This one is very simple," said Jen. She asked Alex to sit in front of a computer monitor. "All you need to do is look straight at the screen and avoid blinking as much as you can."

Alex did as requested. What he saw was what appeared to be a blank screen but whose colour changed rapidly, running through the whole of the visible spectrum and then back again.

Jen explained, "The computer is comparing the colours on the monitor with the perceived colours transmitted from your eyes and through your wristwatch." She paused to study a report appearing on a separate monitor. "Good! This shows that the implants' perceived colours match precisely those presented on the monitor."

"So where does that leave us?" Alex could not think why these results were so significant.

"It indicates the implants are performing precisely as intended, and if you perceive any difference as you did in the terrorist's facial colour, then it is your brain that is modifying the palette."

That made no sense to Alex. "But how can that be? And why?"

Jen took a deep breath, realising that his question was not easy to answer. "Scientists know a great deal about the human brain, but it still holds many mysteries. Some studies suggest that people without sight have greater activity in the part of the right side of the brain that deals with intuition."

"So you feel that my brain now has the capacity to change the perceived skin colour of an individual depending on whether he or she is good or not?"

Jen nodded. "That's about it. I know it sounds a bit far-fetched and cannot be scientifically proven, but that's my personal interpretation. Of course, I could be completely wrong, but frankly, I can't think of a better explanation."

Alex pondered on this remarkable observation. "There is a danger if this is what's happening. What if a person has a naturally darker colour of skin? Or if they are unwashed? Could I mistake a good person for an evil one?"

Jen did not seem to be thrown by this question. "Just think. How many faces have you seen with your new eyes, yet only these few individuals had an observable difference?"

He could not argue with her logic, yet the concept of being able to identify potential criminals or terrorists filled him both with awe and dread.

Jen realised that this revelation was causing him some anxiety. "Don't worry about it, Alex! Just think how valuable you would be to the British and American Governments."

He shrugged. "It's a hell of a responsibility, and I may just be used as a filter without seeing any real action."

Jen now fully understood his anxiety. "Come on. Let's go and report to Adrian, then get Elsa and go somewhere for a meal."

His face lightened. "Okay. That sounds great to me."

Adrian had a smile on his face when they entered his office. The section leader had been looking through the printed results of the shooting range tests. "Great work Alex. Your ocular implants appear to be working superbly. As far as I am concerned your eyesight is unparalleled in the whole of the human race."

"Does that mean that I can be used on more dangerous missions?"

"It means, Captain McCloud, that if more difficult missions are presented, you will be one of several individuals to be considered for the task. I am also able to issue you with a Heckler and Koch MP5 carbine handgun with the compliments of the British Government."

Adrian stepped over to a cupboard in his room, unlocked it and took out the weapon together with shoulder holster and spare clips. "I just need your signature to acknowledge receipt of this weapon before you can take it."

"No problem." Alex signed the paper offered by Adrian. He took hold of the weapon, feeling the weight in his hand. "That feels good." He removed his jacket, fastened the holster in place and inserted the gun. "I feel fully dressed again. Nice choice of weapon."

"Only the best for our soldiers. Just take good care of yourself and only use the weapon in extreme circumstances."

"Understood!"

Alex and Jen walked back to where his dog was being looked after. He need not have worried about Elsa. She was fast asleep in Kelly's office, paws twitching as she perhaps chased some imaginary cat.

When Alex touched her back, the dog, like many humans in similar circumstances, recovered from her slumbers slowly and then shook her head as if trying to clear it. By the time Alex had clipped on her handle, she was fully alert and ready to guide her master yet again.

Chapter Fourteen

T HE FRESH CHILLY air of the November day was welcoming after the air-conditioned offices of MI6. Jen knew the area better than Alex, and together, they took a taxi to a restaurant favoured by Jen.

Within twenty minutes, they were sitting opposite each other in the very busy Scott's Restaurant on Mount Street in Mayfair with Elsa curled up under the table at Alex's feet. Fortunately for them, there had been a cancellation or they wouldn't have found a place.

Jen was recognised by both the bowler-hatted doorman and head waiter. She had used this renowned restaurant on several previous occasions while working in London. She read the menu to Alex, who chose roast Cornish lamb while she opted for roast Gressingham duck with crispy bacon and port wine sauce. Alex cheated by switching on his sight during their meal together, as he was still worried about making a fool of himself in this stylish restaurant by knocking his food off the plate or, worse still, spilling his glass of Gran Coronas Cabernet Sauvignon wine over the crisp white tablecloth.

Not wanting to be emotionally rebuffed again by Jen, he kept the conversation light and polite, hopefully without being boring.

Jen was just about to take a sip of wine when she stopped as if frozen.

"What's wrong?" Alex asked.

"That guy! He looks familiar."

Alex looked in the direction Jen had indicated without making it too obvious. The man was quite tall, probably of similar height to Alex, and had gingery, slightly greying hair and wore a patterned shirt and velour jacket. There was a good-looking brunette on his arm, and from the way the head waiter was fussing around them, he was quite well-known.

"He does look familiar," agreed Alex. He gently touched the display on his watch, and within seconds, a message appeared in the top of his vision.

> Name: Christopher James Evans
> Nationality: British
> Date of Birth: April 1, 1966
> Marital status: Married
> Occupation: Radio and television presenter.

Alex was constantly impressed by the facial-recognition software available through the watch. "That's Chris Evans and his wife, Natasha," Alex whispered. "It must be some kind of celebration. Perhaps a birthday or anniversary."

"Oh, I remember where I've seen him now. Sometimes when I was in the hotel before your operation, I would watch *The One Show* on TV. I'm sure he was on every Friday."

"Yes, I watch that programme myself. Chris has quite an extrovert, almost challenging manner, which sometimes gets him into deep trouble. I wonder who's looking after Noah?"

"They seem like a nice couple," commented Jen.

Chris and Natasha were escorted to their table, where the head waiter continued to take good care of them.

"This is what I like about London," said Jen. "It's one of the few places where you can rub shoulders with the rich and famous."

Chapter Fifteen

November 2011

E VEN FOR LONDON, it was a bitterly cold evening with a biting icy wind as they left the restaurant together. Jen looked for a cab. "I'll find a taxi for you. My hotel is within walking distance, but it's quite a way to your place from here." They walked along Mount Street looking for a taxi, unaware they were being observed.

The man had followed them from MI6 to the restaurant and had patiently waited without making it too obvious until they had left Scott's. Who was this tall guy with the guide dog? There was no time to request new instructions, and he was now entirely on his own.

At last after a few minutes' walk, Jen spotted a taxi driving on the other side of the road and waved her arm towards the driver. Luckily, he spotted her and, through a brief gap in the traffic, did a smart U-turn and pulled up in front of the couple.

Jen leaned in through the open front window. "My friend needs a cab to his flat about twenty minutes' drive from here." She gestured towards Alex.

"No problem. Does he need any help?" The cab driver had noticed Elsa and understood his handicap. In London, it was not unusual for the driver to ferry blind passengers through the crowded city, but blind passengers with guide dogs were not quite as common.

"No, that's okay. I'll give him a hand myself." Jen opened the taxi door and guided Alex into the cab. As he took a seat, Jen leaned in to speak to him, meaning to arrange when they would meet again.

"Jen! Quick get down!"

To her surprise and shock, Alex grabbed the upper part of her body and pulled her roughly downwards towards him. She was horrified and angered, about to ask him what the hell he was playing at when she heard the shot. Elsa gave a single bark; with her thorough training, she knew how the sound of gunfire represented a dangerous situation for her master.

The top of the cab's doorframe splintered as the bullet hit it. A second or two earlier, the back of Jen's head would have been in line with the door trim.

"What the hell?" The driver was obviously not used to having his cab shot at.

Alex spoke with great urgency. "Jen! Get in quick!" She was half in and half out of the cab, sprawled without dignity, partly on Alex and the seat, but her legs were still outside. He used his strong arms to assist her. With his help, she managed to regain her balance and slammed the door shut. Alex swiftly touched his watch and stared out of the window, scanning the dark pavements where the shot had originated from.

"Drive! Quickly!"

The driver was visibly shocked. "Where to?" His question was automatic, the same as he would have asked any of his thousands of usual fares, but there was nothing vaguely routine about this pickup. The driver wished he had taken a leak before this job, as he now felt an urgent need to urinate.

"Hell, anywhere! Just get us away from this area!" The tension in Alex's voice was very apparent. The driver wasted no time engaging the gears and pressing his foot hard on the accelerator. In his desperation, he nearly collided with the back of a bus, which was just pulling up at a stop.

Taking hold of the situation, Alex spoke again to the driver, giving him his home address and directions. "As quick as you can, please." He held Jen close. She was trembling with emotion, having come so close to a very grisly death.

Nothing was said during the journey, both sitting in shocked silence. It was a relief when they arrived at the apartment. Alex paid his fare including a generous tip, and although his cab had been damaged, the driver did not ask for any compensation. Thankfully, the damage to the doorframe was quite minor and could have been far worse, especially if Jen had been hit by the bullet.

Alex, Jen and Elsa wasted no time in entering his apartment. As soon as they were in the privacy of his living room, Jen asked almost in anger, "How the hell did you know that a sniper was aiming for my head?"

During the journey, Alex had been pondering on this very question, knowing that it would be the first one Jen asked. "I really don't know. I had a sudden feeling like a heavy pressure within my head, but I can't explain how I knew to pull you out of the sniper's sights."

Jen looked at him, not certain if she believed him. Then the emotion overcame her, and she put her arms around Alex, pulling herself close to him and resting her head on his chest. The normally calm and controlled Major Jennifer Sherlock had disappeared, and a warm, feminine, vulnerable woman had replaced her. She said nothing, satisfied with just holding Alex close.

He could sense the change in Jen's demeanour. This was a strong woman who had risen to the rank of major, and yet the person gently sobbing on his chest seemed so young, vulnerable and frightened.

"Even though I can't explain how I knew, I'm thankful you escaped injury or possible death."

Elsa sat quietly looking up with some curiosity at the embracing couple. It was as though she sensed the change in her master's situation.

Jen lifted her head. "Thank you so much for saving my life, Alex. I'm so grateful." Then she kissed him full on the lips, lingering for what seemed like an eternity. Eventually, she pulled her mouth away but still held on to him. Her normally pale golden skin was now suffused with a pinkish hue as she became more aroused.

Struggling to regain her composure, she said quietly, "I must phone Adrian and report this incident." Her voice, initially shaky, was now more controlled and calmer.

"Yes, of course."

Jen still held him close as though finding it difficult to separate herself from the man she had not really wished to have a relationship with and yet he had just saved her life. Eventually, she loosened her hold on Alex and took her mobile out of her pocket.

As soon as Adrian answered, she quickly yet precisely described all the details of her near-assassination.

"Whatever you do, don't go back to your hotel tonight. Whoever it was may know where you were staying. Tomorrow, go back and check out. Find another place not too close, and keep a low profile." Adrian sounded concerned for the American agent.

"I'd like to have a word with Adrian," Alex said.

Jen handed the phone to him.

"Hi, Adrian. Listen, I scanned the area where the sniper must have been. If you review the recordings around eight forty-five tonight, it may give you some useful information." Now always aware that his vision was being recorded, Alex knew that it would also prove to be a very useful tool.

"Thanks, Alex. We'll check it out. Take care, you two." Adrian ended the call. Alex handed the phone back to Jen.

"Do you mind if I stay here tonight? Adrian thinks it may be dangerous to go back to my hotel?"

"Of course not. You're welcome to stay as long as you want." Without a second thought, he added, "You can have my bed and I'll sleep on the sofa."

How gallant this Englishman was, but aware that she did not really want to be on her own, Jen replied with a coy smile, "Your bed will be fine for both of us. That is if you don't mind sharing it with me?" As if reading his thoughts about when she told him she did not want a long-distance relationship she continued, "Tonight's experience was a stark reminder that if I keep putting things off, I might never realise my dreams. I've always been too driven by my career, but I think it may be time to look a bit beyond my role within the CIA."

Was he really a part of her dreams? Alex's smile said it all. It was not anything triumphant but one of tenderness and understanding. "That's fine by me, as long as this is really what you want."

"I think that may depend upon you." The excited look on her face made Alex feel better than he had for a long time. "But for now, I'd like to freshen up. Can I use your bathroom?"

"Of course. There's no bath, but I do have a fantastic shower. The high-pressure side jets can be quite invigorating." He smiled at Jen, whom he now saw in a completely different light. Then a sudden thought struck him. "Jen? Is there a way of stopping Adrian monitoring everything I see?"

At first, she seemed puzzled and then, with a sudden realisation, laughed. "I can see why you asked the question. It could be quite embarrassing for both of us."

"I could imagine Adrian and his colleagues crowding around the monitor as unseen voyeurs watching our every intimate moment. So what can we do to foil them?"

Jen held out her hand. "Give me your watch."

He slid the stylish watch off his wrist and dropped it into her open hand. Jen opened the battery compartment on the rear of the watch and took out the tiny lithium cell.

"There! That will stop a peeping Adrian!" After a moment's thought, she added, "Though he will know that you're up to something when he realises you've disabled the internet connection."

She handed the watch and battery back to a smiling Alex. "Just don't forget to replace it when you're on surveillance work. There's a smaller battery for the time setting and other functions, so you won't need to reset it every time you remove the main battery."

Alex laughed. "I should have realised that the solution would be a simple one." He took the watch and battery, placing them carefully in a drawer. Jen had already gone through to the bathroom, and within a few minutes, Alex could hear the jets of water splashing noisily in the shower unit.

Alex took the opportunity to feed Elsa her nightly bowl of dog food, and not wanting to be disturbed by a desperate dog during what may happen in the immediate future, he took her outside to relieve herself on the concrete run.

This duty done, he settled down in one of the chairs in the living room with Elsa curled at his feet. Alex was deep in thought as he stroked the dog's head. What would the next few hours bring? Was his life about to change?

When Jen appeared in the doorway, Alex was stunned into silence. "I hope you don't mind me borrowing this?"

She was wearing one of Alex's T-shirts, and although it was far too big for her, it certainly looked far better on her than it had ever done on him. The bottom edge of the shirt was only a few centimetres below 'C-level', displaying her long, firm, shapely legs. Jen was smiling invitingly. Her eyes sparkled with the anticipation of what was to come.

Is this the point where Lee Child's Jack Reacher gets the girl? Alex mused. He walked over to where Jen was patiently waiting. Putting his arms around her, he drew her close and kissed her lips with a passion and tenderness which noticeably aroused Jen, as it did himself.

They parted briefly and hurried towards the bedroom. Elsa stared after them, puzzled by this strange human behaviour, never to understand the pleasure derived from the act of coupling, as the unfortunate dog had been neutered while still a puppy.

In the bedroom, Jen looked at the steadily increasing bulge in Alex's trousers and tugged at his belt, loosening it and unzipping the fly. Desperate for him, she unfastened the buttons on his shirt and pulled it up, assisted by Alex. He stepped out of his pants, kicking them sideways, and then with one swift movement, he pulled his T-shirt off this beautiful, raunchy woman.

Jen had already pulled the covers back and nimbly jumped on the bed where she lay on her back, inviting Alex, who wasted no time in joining her. She spread her legs, allowing Alex's huge erect member to enter her already-moist vagina. She gave a little gasp as he thrust himself deep into her. Her hands were on his buttocks, pulling him even harder and deeper inside her. Their tongues searched each other's mouths, deriving every possible pleasure from this so intimate of kisses.

At first, he moved in long, slow, tantalising movements, but gradually the pace quickened as their senses sought sexual climax. When it came, both their bodies moved convulsively and in unison, extracting every possible second of mutual pleasure from their orgasmic ecstasy.

Sleep came very quickly to the exhausted couple. It was one of sweet, satisfied love-making, and they held each other close in their exhausted state.

He did not know how much later it was when Alex woke with a start. Something cold and wet touched his bare buttocks. No need to switch on the light to find out what it was: Elsa's nose had burrowed through the covers and prodded him again. He put out his hand and stroked her head.

He pressed the button on his bedside light and looked at the clock. It was six-thirty. Alex could not remember having such a deep, restful, untroubled sleep and was thankful to Jen for such superb sleep therapy.

She was still fast asleep as Alex climbed out of bed and followed the dog to the kitchen. Alex smiled to himself, thinking that he had the typical, slightly twisted Jack Reacher smile after getting off with the girl.

The dog padded in front, eager to lead him towards the kitchen. "Poor Elsa! Are you desperate for a pee?" He unfastened the door and let her outside. She soon returned, happier now she had expelled the contents of her bladder.

Alex checked the bedroom to find Jen still fast asleep. He grabbed some clothes and closed the door quietly so as not to disturb her. He shaved, showered and dressed and then moved into the kitchen and began preparation of breakfast.

His spirit was certainly better than normal. Within a twenty-four-hour period, his life had taken a new turn with the attack on Jen, and it now seemed to have a purpose, but would it last? Was he in the right place at the right time for Jen, or did she have genuine feelings for him?

As if to answer this question, Jen appeared in the doorway. "Good morning, love. Mmmm… That smells great. I feel quite hungry."

"Good! Will scrambled eggs and coffee help?"

"Yes, that's fine. Can I help?"

"The eggs are almost done, and the coffee maker is on. All we need is cutlery." He pointed to the drawer where she could find knives and forks. Unlike Jack Reacher, Alex preferred milk in his coffee.

During breakfast, conversation was easy, and they both felt comfortable with their new intimate situation. What was perplexing to both of them was the question about the reason for Alex's heightened perception. Even this was not a great description, as a perception is usually observed after the incident not before. Whichever way they looked at it, no explanations were possible.

Jen needed to return to her hotel to get her case and check out. She believed it would be safe for her to make this journey on her own, but Alex felt that he should stay with her in case there was a further threat. She did not put up much resistance, and by ten-thirty, they were in a black cab driving towards Jen's hotel. Alex had decided they would be less obtrusive if Elsa remained at the flat. Poor Elsa was noticeably sad at the separation and remained in the living room, keeping a watchful eye on the door as she waited for her master to return.

Mindful of the situation the night before, Jen and Alex asked the taxi driver to drop them off a couple of streets away from the hotel. Now Jen had to act as his eyes, as Alex was determined to keep the 'blind person' persona at all times outside his apartment.

She took his arm and walked swiftly towards the hotel. They avoided using the main entrance, choosing instead a little-used doorway that led into the reception hall where they took a lift to the fifth floor.

Jen inserted her card in the slot at room 527 and gently pushed the door open, half-expecting to find some sinister figure inside. Everything looked normal to her, and thankfully, the room was empty. She swiftly moved to the bathroom and pushed the door open wide. Nobody there either.

Jen looked around the room, picturing it in her mind as it had been the day before. Again, nothing seemed disturbed or out of place. The bed was made presumably by the chambermaids the day before.

Swiftly, Jen gathered up her few possessions and threw them into her suitcase. She travelled quite light and did not take long to pack.

Alex had switched on his eyes and watched, interested but without comment, as Jen finished her packing. He had a feeling, though he knew that it may be nothing. Just a strange incomprehensible feeling that something was wrong. If Jen had this same apprehension, she did not show it now and seemed quite relaxed.

It was then that Alex spotted it. A light was flashing on the bedside phone, indicating that there were messages. Jen spotted Alex looking at it. "A message for me?"

She was about to press the button to replay the message when Alex shouted, "No, Jen! Don't touch it!"

She looked puzzled. "Why? It's only a phone."

Instead of answering, he asked her a question. "How does Adrian contact you?"

"On my cell phone. Why?"

Again another question. "Does anybody else know you were staying here? Your parents or other relatives, for example?"

"Why, no. But what should it matter?"

Patiently, Alex explained, "The fact is that the chance of somebody calling you on the hotel's phone line is quite remote. You said yourself that Adrian contacts you by mobile, so why would anybody contact you on the room phone? I had a feeling that something was wrong as soon as we entered the room, but I couldn't put my finger on it until now."

She now understood. "You think there are explosives in the phone?"

He nodded. "Come on, let's get out of here." He opened the door, letting Jen pass through, and then grabbed the do-not-disturb sign from the back of the door and placed it on the handle outside.

The wide, carpeted corridor was empty. Alex stopped. "Jen, can you phone Adrian from here and ask him to get the bomb squad to check your room? We don't want the next guest to find the surprise in your phone."

Jen paused and looked at Alex. "How certain are you about the phone?"

He did not hesitate. "Absolutely! One hundred per cent certain! At first, I couldn't place the smell. Then I realised it was similar to the bombs in Afghanistan. That's why they use dogs to sniff out areas of likely danger. I think that, like my other senses, my sense of smell is heightened."

Now convinced, Jen phoned Adrian and explained the situation to him.

"Leave it to me. You two get out of there before the squad comes. I don't want any awkward questions."

Jen and Alex decided to walk down the stairs to the ground floor, leaving by the same doors as they had used when entering the hotel. Jen explained that she did not have to check out, as the details from her credit card were taken on registration a few days earlier.

They did not leave unnoticed. The man followed them at a distance, Alex's build and stature assisting his task of following the couple. When they hailed a taxi, he did so too, determined to find their new destination. He was surprised when the taxi dropped the couple off outside Harrods store in Knightsbridge. He did the same but knew this location made his task that much more difficult.

Chapter Sixteen

JEN LEANED AGAINST Alex, cuddling up to him as they relaxed on the sofa in his living room. "That's the first time I've been to Harrods. Interesting place, but I was puzzled when you told the taxi driver to take us there."

Alex smiled. "It's a good place to lose a tail. I had a feeling that we were being followed so decided to lose them."

"Your sensory perception is truly amazing. I never even realised we were being tailed until you told me, and how on earth did you smell the explosives in the phone?"

He shrugged. "It amazes me as well. I really don't know why my senses are so acute, but I'm grateful if only to save your life."

Alex then remembered the words of the neurologist, Peter Jacques. *"Individuals with higher activity than normal in this area tend to be more aware, more perceptive and, in some cases, have an unusual talent such as increased memory retention or the ability to mentally calculate complex mathematical calculations."* Alex felt certain that his heightened senses were a direct result of the impact on his skull in Afghanistan. *Behind every cloud, there may well be a silver lining.*

"Hello? Can you come down from outer space please?"

With the thoughts churning through his mind, Alex had not noticed the curious smile on Jen's face. "Sorry. I didn't mean to ignore you. I was reflecting on something somebody once said to me."

"That's all right. I was suggesting that we could do with a drink. Nothing strong, just coffee!"

"Yes, that's a good idea." This 'new' Jen seemed very different from the formal, militaristic Major Jennifer Sherlock he had been introduced to only four months earlier. So much more seductive and extremely attractive.

While Jen made coffee in the kitchen, Alex was brought back to the real world by the sound of his mobile. It was Adrian. "I've had a look at the recordings from your vision as you suggested. There is definitely a hazy figure that could have fired at Jen, but I'm afraid it's not clear enough to make a positive identification." As if it was an afterthought, he added, "Not even with software enhancement."

"That's a pity. Especially since they seem quite determined to try and kill her. Somebody followed us from Jen's hotel, but we managed to lose them."

Adrian sounded concerned. "Best if Jen can stay at your place for the time being."

"No problem at all." There was nothing he would like better than to have Jen move in with him, but it would only be a short time before she felt she had to return to the States.

"I have asked the hotel for a copy of the recordings from their security cameras and should get those later today. As soon as we have them, we'll do everything to identify the person who tampered with the phone in room 527."

"Good! Let me know as soon as you get an ID on this guy, assuming he's in the database." Alex ended the call. As Jen brought mugs of coffee into the living room, he explained to her what Adrian had told him. "Can you think of anybody who would want you dead?"

"None that immediately come to mind, but after nearly seven years in the military, it's quite possible."

Chapter Seventeen

D ANNY JACKSON AND Paddy Conroy shuffled uneasily as they reported their failure to kill the American woman. They had messed up and big time. Even more worrying was the fact that they had been instructed to meet their employer in person rather than using a coded phone message as usual. To actually meet the 'big man' gave them a distinctly uncomfortable feeling. Danny noticed how dry his mouth felt but knew they were unlikely to be offered a drink by their demanding and currently furious employer. This man reminded Danny of the business tycoon Alan Sugar but with a distinct Italian flavour.

The two criminals had worked together for the past thirteen years and so far had managed to look after themselves without being caught. They met as troublesome teenagers and with similar backgrounds found it profitable to work together. Most of their work came from contract killings, and to date, they had been quite successful. They had already completed several killings for Gianni, making this failure even more compromising.

They knew not to ask questions, just to carry out the jobs cleanly and efficiently. The money was good, allowing them to indulge in their passion for travel. Another few weeks and the two were due for a holiday in Thailand, something they were both looking forward to. Good, hot climate, great food, cheap drinks and a few days of fun with sexy, young Thai girls all added to the attraction. Danny had been thinking about this when he was suddenly brought back to the real world.

"This job should have been so easy, so how come you two idiots screwed up and managed to leave the fucking bitch alive?"

"Sorry, Boss." Beads of perspiration ran down Danny's face. He glanced briefly at Paddy, who was, in Danny's mind, equally responsible for leaving the woman alive. Both men knew what could happen to those who failed Gianni. "The woman got lucky. She was in my sights and must have moved a fraction of a second before my shot would have hit her." He still found it incredible that she had moved just in time to avoid certain death. *My bad luck*, he thought.

Gianni Lamancusa did not believe in luck, neither good nor bad, and could never have been described as a patient man. He looked stone-faced at the two men who had been given the role of ending Jennifer Sherlock's life. "Once was bad enough, but you two goons somehow managed to screw up twice. Don't I pay you guys enough?"

It was Paddy who answered. Looking as uncomfortable as Danny, he replied, "Sure you do, Boss. We'll get her next time."

Gianni's normally placid face creased into a smile, which was unusual for this powerful, dangerous man. "Next time? You want another chance to fuck up? You don't even know where the bitch is!"

"Don't worry, we'll find her. She won't survive our next hit." Both men felt uneasy and wished they'd gone for a leak before meeting Gianni.

"Relax, guys. Don't look so worried. I'm not going to hurt you. Just get out of my sight before I do something you may regret."

The relief on their faces was instantly noticeable. They headed for the door, Danny opening it, eager to escape. His eyes grew wide as he was confronted by the muscular, black torso of a huge man, whose body seemed to completely fill the door opening. Gigantic hands reached towards their necks. They were lifted completely off the floor, and this giant of a man began to squeeze all life out of the unfortunate pair even before they had chance to say another word.

The unconcerned Gianni, still smiling, spoke quietly. "I kept my promise, boys. I said that I was not going to hurt you, and I always keep my word, but our friend Sam is going to do the job for me. Goodbye, boys!"

Sam, a giant of a man at six foot eleven, had picked up the two men by their necks and was steadily squeezing all life out of the now ex-employees of Gianni. Black-skinned Sam, his polished, shaven head glistening with the close proximity of the ceiling lights, held up the unfortunate men. Their eyes were bulging, bones cracking and blood pouring out of their mouths. They never stood a chance. Sam dropped the two men on the floor where they landed unceremoniously like a child's discarded broken dolls.

There would be two empty seats on the Etihad flight to Thailand, and those young Thai girls would never benefit financially from sex with the two British men.

Gianni's serious look returned. In an irritated tone, he said, "Get rid of them, Sam."

Sam's deep baritone voice resonated around the room. "Sure, Boss. Do you have anywhere in mind?"

"The Thames is probably a fitting resting place for anybody stupid enough to disappoint Gianni Lamancusa."

Obediently, Sam dragged the corpses away as easily as if they were a couple of small suitcases.

Gianni leaned back in his comfortable chair, feeling resigned and depressed. He watched as Sam dragged the corpses away. He had to admire the strength of the huge man; nothing seemed to faze him.

Sam had been Gianni's 'muscle' for over eight years after his life had been saved by the Italian mobster. Sam had upset another gang when he prevented them from robbing a bank where he was one of the customers. The big man was surprisingly quick for his size and prevented the gang from completing their raid. They still managed to escape before the police arrived, but a price was put on Sam's head. When Gianni heard of what had happened, he offered him a job, and very quietly, members of the opposing gang gradually disappeared. Their bodies were never found.

Gianni picked up a strange-looking phone, pressed a few buttons and spoke. "Danny and Paddy have gone for a long swim. No sign of our friend, but we're still looking."

The person on the other end of the phone clearly understood the message.

"We will find her eventually." He ended the call, annoyed yet determined. He had clearly emphasised the word 'will' and meant it in honour of his family.

He had the absolute belief that if it was not for the interference by American Intelligence Services and Jennifer Sherlock in particular, over three hundred of his family and compatriots would not now be languishing in high-security Italian prisons. He and about forty of his direct family members had managed to evade capture, but it meant that they'd had to go underground in another country.

The United Kingdom had not been their first choice, but the fact that it was physically apart from the other main European countries gave it a distinct advantage.

The 'stealth' submarine had been expensive and far more sophisticated than the one found in Colombia by the authorities. The submarine had proved to be a valuable investment, as most of his immediate family had evaded capture by using this method of transportation. That was when they had left Calabria in Southern Italy for London. It was a bold move but hopefully one the authorities would never have expected.

Valuable contacts in the UK had provided information about possible locations for the family. Locations in which they could continue their luxurious lifestyle yet remain hidden and undisturbed by the authorities. After all the necessary modifications had been completed, the 'workers' had also mysteriously disappeared.

In Italy, the phrase 'Silence of the Lamancusa' had been used to describe the collection of numerous family members. One tended not to hear much from the family, but anyone found to have crossed them or leaked information would have their life terminated in a particularly gruesome way.

Gianni returned the phone to its cradle on his desk. There was no need to worry about his conversation being overheard. His phone was not connected to any conventional telephone network. Instead, it was a dedicated radio phone with all transmissions deeply encrypted. After the arrests of many of his 'Ndrangheta members in 2010, he had realised that even encrypted emails and mobile-phone conversations were vulnerable to the sophisticated analytical methods employed by the CIA and, in the UK, GCHQ.

Gianni relaxed, unconcerned that the lives of two men had just been cut brutally short. Those two contract killers, who had proved useful in the past, would not be missed.

Chapter Eighteen

BOTH JEN AND Alex awoke at the same moment to the insistent sound of the musical tones from Alex's mobile phone. Sleepily, he reached for the source of the noise. Through heavy eyes, he glanced at the screen and realised it was Adrian calling him.

"Morning, Adrian. Any news?"

"We certainly have." Adrian sounded excited. "The video from the hotel has revealed the two guys who planted the explosives in Jen's phone."

"Great! Any idea who they are?" Alex was wide awake now, and Jen was cuddling close to him trying to hear Adrian's words.

"Thankfully, they're on our database. The first is Daniel Jackson, a thirty-three-year-old dangerous criminal from London, and the other is Patrick Conroy, thirty-two years old. He's Irish-American."

Alex smiled and gave Jen a wink. "Have you managed to pick them up yet?"

"Not yet. We have alerts out for them, but so far, there's no sign of them."

"But why would they want to kill Jen?"

"That's a very good question and one for which we as yet do not have an answer. For now, you two had better keep out of sight until we've caught these guys."

Alex agreed. "Adrian, can you send us their mugshots?"

"Sure. I'll send them in the next few minutes. In the meantime, just take good care of yourselves."

Alex returned the phone to his bedside cabinet and lay back on the pillow. "What I don't understand is why these goons wanted you dead. Once could be a mistake, but twice is hardly likely. Too much of a coincidence?"

"Excuse me, Alex. I need the bathroom." As she climbed over him and walked naked to the door, he did not see the troubled expression on her face, too busy admiring her long, powerful legs topped by a perfectly formed, pert butt. Now that he knew her more intimately, he also realised that her blonde hair was absolutely genuine and not from a bottle.

He checked the time as she left the room and was amazed to find that it was ten forty-five. Their love-making of the previous evening had lasted at least two hours, after which they had collapsed into a heavy, undisturbed sleep.

He lay there quite relaxed, thinking of his newfound relationship with Jen and compared this with his three-year romance with Helen. The two women were quite different. Helen had been loving, tender and, until that day in the hospital, dependable. He could imagine that had they married, she would have been a superb, reliable wife, well-organised around the home and a very good mother to their children.

Jen, on the other hand, had vitality, an energy that really blew him away, especially while making love. As for what sort of wife she would make, he had not known her long enough to predict what she would become. He knew that he must be patient and not expect too much of her, as they had only been intimate for a couple of days. But what was his future with her? He hoped it would prove more long-term than Helen. It was difficult for Alex to admit, but he still had genuine warm feelings for Helen even after her change of heart.

Alex suddenly sat up. "Elsa!" He had forgotten about the dog, who by now must be crossing all four legs. The German shepherd had stayed in the living room overnight, as her presence in the bedroom disturbed Jen during their sexual antics.

Alex jumped out of bed and walked quickly to the living room. The dog had been sitting patiently near the doorway waiting for her master to appear. He checked to see if there were any wet patches on the carpet but thankfully found none.

"Poor Elsa. Sorry for leaving you this late. Come on."

She padded behind him as he entered the kitchen. As soon as the external door was opened, she ran with some urgency towards the concrete run. Knowing he could not be seen, Alex stood quite naked in the doorway, undisturbed by the chill November day. The dog returned, and he made a fuss of her, still feeling guilty for leaving her so long.

Within thirty minutes, Jen and Alex were sitting at the table enjoying their breakfast, or should that perhaps have been an early lunch? They looked at the pictures of the two criminals sent by Adrian. Alex had printed them, making the images much easier to see than on the phone's small screen.

"I'm sure that I've seen this guy before." She was pointing at Conroy. "But where?" Alex was silently urging her to remember.

Jen did have a near-perfect photographic memory for faces. "I know! He was near the restaurant the night when they tried to shoot me."

"Are you sure? I don't remember him."

Jen looked again at the picture. "I think so. I thought he looked a bit out of place in Mayfair standing near Scott's when the two of us left the restaurant."

"Really? But I can't understand why." Then he noticed her troubled expression. "Do you know something you're not telling me?"

Jen blushed slightly but still maintained that she had no idea why she had been targeted. Alex felt uneasy, aware she was not telling him the whole truth, but decided to let it go for now.

Jen then phoned Adrian to let him know that she had spotted Conroy outside the restaurant the previous day, but even after ending the call, she still looked uncomfortable, avoiding Alex's gaze. Changing the subject, she said, "I could do with phoning my parents." She checked the time. "My father gets up early, so now is probably a good time to call." She scrolled through the list of contacts on her mobile and touched the highlighted number.

"Hi, Pop! I'm just calling to say I'm going to be in England for a while longer. No, I don't know when I'll be back, as I've got quite a bit more to do here." She chatted for a few minutes, asking her father to let his wife know that Jen was missing them both. "Love you, Pop. Bye."

For the rest of the day, the couple enjoyed each other's company, mainly in the bedroom. Even so, Alex had an uneasy feeling that Jen was concealing some important facts.

It was two days later before they heard from Adrian again. "We found them," said Adrian with a cautious tone in his voice.

"Great! Where were they hiding?"

"Not really hiding. Their weighted corpses were recovered from the Thames this morning."

Alex was stunned by Adrian's response. "You're certain it's the same guys?"

"No doubt about it. We have a positive ID on both of them, and they were killed within the last seventy-two hours, probably in retribution for failing to kill Jen even after two attempts."

Alex thought for a moment and even though he knew the likely answer asked, "I don't suppose they drowned while having a casual swim?"

Adrian laughed. "No." His voice adopted a more serious tone. "They were dead before they entered the water. Their necks were broken. It looks as though someone with very powerful hands strangled both of them. And they were themselves quite big guys."

Alex shuddered. Even after seeing what the Taliban was capable of in Afghanistan, this retaliatory killing in the heart of London sickened him.

Adrian again emphasised that both Alex and Jen should stay in his apartment for the time being.

Alex admitted to Jen, "I don't think the threat is over just because those two killers are dead. Whoever told them to kill you is obviously pissed off you're still alive."

Jen agreed. "They do seem pretty determined."

Alex held his gaze steady on Jen's face as he asked, "Do you know why these people are out to kill you?"

Her look was one of frustration. "I…I don't know."

Alex ran his hand through his hair in an unsettled gesture. For the first time since they had met, he was angry with her and couldn't hold it in. "Come off it, Jen. You're not a very good liar! I know you're hiding something, and I want to know what it is."

Her face reddened as she bowed her head in obvious distress. "I'm sorry for getting you into this awful mess, Alex. Are you certain that you really want to know?"

"Of course I am. We're both in deep shit, and if I am going to die, I need to know why!" The silence emphasised the tension in the room. "How the hell can I help you if you don't tell me all the fucking facts?" He did feel sorry for her but decided that he had to be firm. "Come on, love. No more bullshit!" He put his arm around her shoulder as she trembled with emotion.

Could she really tell Alex what she suspected? She knew it would not be fair to keep the truth from him much longer, especially now that they were beginning a much closer relationship. Taking a deep breath, she asked, "Have you ever heard of the 'Ndrangheta?"

"No. I can honestly say I've never heard of it. What is it? Some kind of STD?"

She gave a weak smile. "No, much worse. Like the Sicilian Mafia, it's a family-run crime syndicate based in Calabria, Southern Italy. The word comes from the Greek, meaning courage or loyalty, and even goes as far back as 1412 to a gambling organisation—The Garduna—based in Toledo, Spain. It's been in Italy since the 1850s, but in the 1990s, it became the most powerful criminal organisation in Italy, even beating the Sicilian Cosa Nostra Neapolitan Camorra and Apulian Sacra Corona Unita."

Apart from the Mafia, Alex had never even heard of any of these criminal organisations, but he noticed the names tripped off Jen's tongue as if she was a native Italian. He guessed he was about to learn of the secret part of Jen's life before Moorfields.

"Income from drugs, prostitution, intimidation and money laundering for the 'Ndrangheta amounted to over three per cent of the Italian GDP, making them both immensely wealthy and dangerously powerful. Around 2008, the Italian Government decided they had to do something to curb the powers of the 'Ndrangheta, which would prove to be very difficult, as they had many judges and politicians on their payroll. The US was asked to assist in this task called Operation Crimine, and since I had majored both in IT and Italian at high school followed by internet studies at Stamford Research Institute, I was part of the team assigned to the job."

This was certainly a new side to Jen. Intrigued, Alex asked, "So exactly how did you assist?"

Jen looked extremely anxious and played nervously with her hair. "Working for the CIA, I was on a team monitoring phone calls and emails between members of the families within the 'Ndrangheta."

Alex's face indicated great surprise at Jen's admission. "I thought it was illegal to monitor phones and emails."

Jen laughed, although a little nervously. "Most governments monitor electronic traffic. They just don't talk much about it." Seeing the disbelief on Alex's face, she added, "The British Government intercepts far more electronic communications than any other government. GCHQ runs an eavesdropping operation called Tempora, and it's proving very successful in combating terrorism." As an afterthought, she added, "The NSA even monitors the cell phones of most European leaders, but keep that under your hat!"

Alex supposed he should have known these facts but was still surprised by her revelation about his own country and America's security agencies. "So did your intercepts prove useful?"

She smiled triumphantly. "Oh, yes. The operation was very successful, and by July last year, over three hundred 'Ndrangheta members were arrested."

"Good! So why is somebody within this Italian organisation still trying to kill you?"

To his surprise, Jen continued to play nervously with her hair, which was completely out of character. "Unfortunately, they had a mole in the CIA who discovered the people involved. They were out for revenge."

Alex now understood and asked with some trepidation, "Have any CIA staff been injured or killed because of the mole?"

An expression of great sadness filled Jen's face. Quietly, she replied, "Jason Barriman was my partner in the CIA, but more than that, we were in a close relationship." She had been uncertain about revealing her past lovers but wanted to be absolutely honest with Alex. She owed him that much.

Surprised and uncertain that he really wanted to hear the answer, Alex asked, "What happened to him?"

Large tears began to flow slowly down Jen's cheeks. "He received a call saying that his mother was ill, so he took leave to visit his parents in Fairfield, just over fifty miles away. It was a trap." She paused, finding it difficult to continue.

Alex put a comforting arm around her shoulder. "I'm sorry, Jen. You don't need to tell me any more."

"I must. You need to know just how ruthless members of the 'Ndrangheta are. When he did not contact me within a day, I informed my section head, and a team was sent to Fairfield. I insisted on going with them, even though my leader did not want me there." She paused to take a deep breath. "Jason and his parents had been brutally executed. Their bodies were tied to dining chairs around the table." Jen's voice was very shaky and almost a whisper. "Their heads had been hacked off and placed on dinner plates in front of each body. The table had been set with knives and forks as though they were about to eat their own heads. But all the blood and the look of absolute horror in their eyes was enough to break me, and I was dragged out screaming. It was the worst thing I have ever seen, and it still to this day gives me nightmares."

She burst into tears and clung on tightly to Alex. He now realised just what she had been through and sympathised. "I'm so sorry, Jen."

Still sobbing, she wiped her eyes with a tissue. "I had a breakdown after that. The Government gave me and my family protection, and after three months, I moved to the Augmented Reality Unit within the CIA. I hoped it would be a less conspicuous position and that the 'Ndrangheta would forget about me, but it seems that there is a cell even here in England, and they're determined to kill me. Although most of the Italian family was arrested, their rackets continue in over thirty countries, and their income amounts to many billions of dollars."

Alex had a sudden thought. "Does Adrian know about your background?"

She shook her head. "He doesn't know about my involvement with the 'Ndrangheta. That information is highly classified. All he knows is my involvement in Augmented Reality at the CIA. I think Brigadier General Marshall probably knows."

Alex saw Jen in a completely new light and was now not surprised by her initial rejection. She was probably trying to protect him from a terrible fate similar to Jason's. The dreadful scene Jen had described was now firmly imprinted into Alex's brain, and it was unlikely that he would ever forget it.

Whether she liked it or not, he was now deeply involved and in equal danger of losing his life. "I think we need to tell Adrian so he knows exactly what we're dealing with. My feeling is that we're both in deep shit!"

Chapter Nineteen

WHEN ADRIAN HEARD of Jen's past, he understood why she was being targeted.

"These criminals will be looking for her at the airports, so I think she had better stay in the UK for now. I don't want either of you to come here since everybody knows exactly where MI6 is, and these guys probably have lookouts for her."

Alex could understand the serious situation they were in but countered, "We can't stay hidden forever. I'd much sooner do something to find them and neutralise the threat."

Adrian had a hint of impatience in his voice. "Alex, this is not Afghanistan. The 'Ndrangheta are even more difficult to locate than the Taliban. You don't even know where to start looking."

"We've fucking well got to do something!" Alex felt so impotent and just wanted somewhere to start.

"Okay." Adrian thought fast, anxious to help these two, whose lives were now in extreme danger. "First, you need different identities. I'll give you an address where this can be done without the need to come here."

"Okay. We'll need as much information about the 'Ndrangheta as possible. More than we could find just on the internet." Alex was thinking like a soldier again.

"That's no problem. With Kristin's assistance, I can get all the data we need and send you files on them, which will tell you everything there is to know except their location in the UK."

"Great!" Alex had a sudden thought. "What about Elsa? She identifies me better than any ID."

"That's true. It's up to you really. If you wish, I can ask Kate to take her back for a few weeks. How would you feel about that?"

What Adrian had said made good sense, but Alex would feel guilty about sending her back. "Let me think about that." He looked down at Elsa. She seemed to be listening to every word of his conversation. He decided it would be unfair on the dog; somehow, they were going to have to work with her even through this present danger. Alex did know that when necessary, he could leave Elsa in the apartment without any problem.

THE FOLLOWING DAY, Alex and Jen travelled by taxi to the address Adrian had given them. Alex thought it might make life easier if he went there as a sighted person.

Strangely, the place in Adrian's directions appeared to be a small greeting card shop, but when they asked for Pauline as instructed, the person behind the counter escorted them into a backroom.

Pauline was a small, dark-haired, middle-aged woman who welcomed them enthusiastically. "So pleased to meet you both." As she spoke, she was already studying them, assessing how she could give them plausible new identities.

Her colleague Rich was given the task of assisting Alex with his new profile while Pauline looked after Jen.

"We'll leave the girls in here and use the spare room." Rich seemed friendly enough, though Alex could not stand men who shortened 'Richard' to 'Rich'. It was almost a statement of pretentiousness. Shrugging off this uncomfortable feeling, Alex followed the strange, tall guy with spiky, blonde hair into a separate room.

"Right! Let's have a look at you." It was an uncomfortable feeling being studied by Rich. "You have some variations in your skin colour on your face and neck. Are they from burns?"

Alex longed for the day when people did not notice the damage he'd received from the explosion but had to accept there would always be tonal differences.

"Yes, burns," he confirmed.

"It's not a problem. I can provide you with a natural-looking skin tone that will cover the marks. A black hair colour would also make a big difference. I could colour your eyebrows as well, and with a small moustache, your appearance would be completely different."

Alex was not particularly thrilled at the thought of changing his hair colour but accepted that the 'Ndrangheta already knew what he looked like. In truth, he was a sitting target for any assassin.

His mid-brown hair had grown quite a bit since his operation and probably could do with thinning and reshaping, hopefully disguising his appearance to some extent.

He allowed Rich to add colour to his hair, which took about twenty minutes to permeate throughout his thick hair. This was followed by a shampoo and rinse and finally a haircut. Rich stood back and looked at Alex in a way that one may look at a famous work of art in some national museum. "I think you need to move away from the military-style cut. Let your hair grow longer and thicker. You'd be surprised at what a change it would make to your appearance."

By the time Rich had finished, Alex was amazed at the difference his new hairstyle and skin make-up had made to his appearance. As a finishing touch, Rich opened several small drawers inside a cabinet searching until triumphantly he produced a small, neat false moustache the same colour as Alex's new hair. Rich held it in place on Alex's face. "What do you think?"

"To be quite honest, Rich, I don't like moustaches or beards. I think I'll take the risk of not using it."

Rich looked a little hurt. "Suit yourself. My brief is to change your appearance as much as possible, but it's your call."

Alex stood his ground. "How else can I change my appearance?" As he looked at Rich, he realised that his initial thought that this strange man was in his thirties was incorrect and he was more likely in his fifties. He felt certain that his face had undergone quite extensive plastic surgery in an attempt to make him look younger. Unfortunately, it did not work.

"Your clothes. You give the impression of a neat, tidy guy. You need to look a little more relaxed. Perhaps by wearing more casual, less close-fitting clothes." Rich disappeared behind a curtain, and after a few minutes of mild cursing, he reappeared holding a couple of hangers of jackets and trousers. Rich had a triumphant look on his face. "Yes! This is what I was looking for." He pulled back another curtain and switched on the light in the changing cubicle. "Try these on and see what you think."

Alex was relieved that he did not need to strip off in front of this strange guy and took the clothes into the cubicle. When he looked at himself in the mirror, he had to admit that his change of hairstyle and colour together with the more casual clothes had managed to make him look completely different. He tried on both sets of jackets and trousers and after a few minutes chose one and stepped out of the cubicle. "What do you think?"

Rich had been relaxing in one of the chairs reading a P. D. James paperback and quickly stood to inspect Alex's new persona. "Oh, fantastic darling! Even your own mother wouldn't recognise you."

Alex cringed at the guy's choice of expression but tried to ignore it. "Yes, I think this will do fine."

"Right! Now we need to take your photo for your new IDs. I suggest that you either wear a pair of ordinary spectacles instead of the dark glasses or preferably no glasses at all."

Alex had a sudden thought. *My eyes! I need to change the colour.* "I could do with having a quick word with Jen. Is she ready?"

"We'll soon find out." Rich went to the adjoining door, knocked and opened it slightly. "Alex would like a word with you, Jen, if you're ready."

She was. Alex couldn't help but be amazed by the change in Jen's appearance. She was now a convincing brunette with long, stylish hair. Like Alex, she had lost her formal, efficient appearance and was now far more casual-looking. For a few seconds, they stared at each other almost in disbelief and then both burst out laughing.

"Do you mind if Jen and I talk in private, Rich?"

"Not at all. You two stay in here and I'll go and annoy Pauline."

That may not be far from the truth, thought Alex and then quickly explained to Jen his idea to change his eye colour. "Can I wear contact lenses?"

A smile lit her face. "No need. Pass me your watch, Alex."

He did as instructed, and Jen touched the display several times. Satisfied that she had entered the correct option, she asked, "What colour would you like your eyes to be?"

"You can change my colour as easy as that?" He was surprised and impressed at yet another function within his prosthetic eyes that he had never even considered. "Perhaps a dark shade of brown or black?"

"No problem. Look in the mirror while I go through the palette."

As he watched, she stepped through the many shades of brown, waiting for Alex's response. It was fascinating.

"Can you go back a couple of steps?" She did as requested. "Stop! No, I think a darker shade may be better. Take it slowly and move darker again, please. Yes! That's the one."

"Right, that's set now. It's very easy to switch between the original blue iris and your new choice of dark brown."

"You are truly amazing, Jen! To be able to programme the eye colour so easily is a touch of genius."

"It's mainly down to Professor Goldman. My input is purely the interface electronics and software."

Alex replaced his watch, checked his image for one last time in the mirror, and the two walked into the other room where Pauline and Rich were relaxing, deep in conversation.

Rich looked up as they entered and immediately noticed Alex's change of eye colour. "Ten minutes ago, you had blue eyes and now they're very dark brown. How on earth did you do that?"

Alex cursed to himself and wished this man had not been so observant. Jen came to the rescue.

"I had some coloured contact lenses that suited Alex's new hair colour."

Neither of them knew if Rich believed this explanation, but they had to maintain secrecy about his artificial eyes.

Pauline interrupted. "Right! Let's get your new IDs sorted."

It took about forty minutes after having their photographs taken before their new ID cards and passports were ready.

Alex looked at his and then Jen's new passport. "Stephen Bancroft and Charlotte Ferguson. Where do you get these names from?"

Pauline hesitated a little but decided it would not hurt to let them know. "They're legitimate names, but both are from individuals who died in childhood."

This came as no surprise, as both had heard of this method being used by the Secret Service in the past.

"I think we should go back separately, as we're less likely to be recognised even with our new appearances," Alex suggested.

Jen agreed and left Pauline and Rich about ten minutes after Alex.

Chapter Twenty

December 2011

IT WAS A sumptuously decorated room. Several tan-coloured leather chairs and sofas were arranged carefully around the perimeter. The lighting was subdued, yet the many elaborate obviously expensive paintings that adorned the walls were easily visible each with their own dedicated illumination. The floor was a rich, mahogany timber, and a large, hand-woven rug filled the space between the furniture.

Gianni looked quite relaxed sitting in one of the large chairs. He had helped himself to a measure of single malt whisky from the well-stocked cocktail bar and sipped at his drink.

"No sign of the American woman, but we're still looking. It was sheer luck when she was spotted by Agostino in Woolpit at the cannabis farm we had to abandon. We lost track of her two years ago when she and Jason Barriman meddled in our operation."

The man he was talking to made no comment but listened intently to what he had to say.

Gianni took another sip of whisky and continued, "Although we'd really like to eliminate Miss Sherlock, I have to balance this against possible leaks about our organisation here in the UK. I must admit, I don't want to bring in any more outside agents who could lead back to us."

The other man simply nodded in agreement.

Gianni continued, used to this strange, one-way method of communicating with his father, the Capocrimine. It was not always a one-sided conversation, but the older man could be very moody, probably as a result of his confinement, and on many occasions just resorted to a slight nod of the head. Gianni knew better than to expect more of the very experienced, battle-worn leader of his family. The old man had a gold ring with a large, inset diamond on one of his fingers, signifying that he was an 'Illuminati', which denoted that he was a leader rather than one of the henchmen.

"For now, I feel that it's best to leave her alone and concentrate on our core businesses. We have done quite well considering that the UK operation has only been going for a couple of years, but there is always room for improvement."

Again, a brief nod of the head assured Gianni that his judgement was accepted. That was enough for him, and after downing the last of his whisky, he returned to his quarters.

Chapter Twenty-One

December 2011

E LSA HAD NO difficulty recognising the changed Alex. As usual, she nearly knocked him off his feet greeting him with many licks, her tail wagging excitedly. *I can't send her back to the training centre*, Alex thought. He knew it would not be fair on his canine friend to abandon her even for a short time.

Jen arrived a few minutes later and was similarly greeted by Elsa, who was getting used to her master's new friend. All were by now hungry. Fortunately, Alex was well prepared and had plenty of food stored in the freezer fridge and cupboards. The couple decided on pork steaks with potato wedges and vegetables to satisfy their appetites. Elsa was equally hungry but had to settle for her usual dog biscuits and water. The way she devoured the contents of her dish was enough to indicate to anyone that she enjoyed her regular diet.

During their meal, Alex contemplated all the difficulties they would face with their new identities and appearances. "I can't go to the supermarket now I've changed my appearance. It looks as if we'll have to use home deliveries for our shopping from now on."

Jen and Alex looked at each other with some amusement, their appearances now completely different, particularly Jen with her long, brunette wig.

Jen smiled coyly. "I was amazed what a difference a change of hairstyle and colour could make. How about you?"

"I just hope none of my family and friends turn up unexpectedly. I'm not sure I could explain the change, especially the eye colour."

Jen had a sudden thought. "I didn't bring many clothes with me, as I thought I would only be here for a few days. I could do with buying some."

"That shouldn't be a problem unless you want me to go out and buy them for you."

"Would you like to choose some new underwear for me, sweetheart?" Jen had a mischievous look in her eyes.

"Only if you want me to get the wrong size. I'd probably get them far too small."

She laughed. "I can imagine you'd enjoy yourself in the bra and panties section at Victoria's Secret in New Bond Street, but there's a simpler way. We just order online for a home delivery."

Alex was relieved but also a little excited by the thought of choosing Jen's underwear. "Good idea. Do you want to go on the website now?"

"Might as well." For the next hour, the two of them looked through the numerous choices of lingerie on the website, both of them feeling quite aroused by the experience. At last, they had chosen what to buy and clicked on the shopping basket, ready to finalise their order.

It was then that they realised that their credit cards were still in their real names. After all the time they had spent on the website, they had to exit without placing the order.

"Never mind," said Jen, disappointed. "I'll have to manage with what I have for now."

Alex realised he would also need a replacement credit card in the name of his new identity, Stephen Bancroft. He would have to think it out, carefully withdrawing cash from his old account and depositing it in the newly opened account to prevent a paper trail leading back to him.

When Alex checked his emails, he found a message from Adrian. There was a huge attachment, which hopefully would give the couple all they needed to know about the 'Ndrangheta. Alex read through the document, rereading it several times to absorb the vast amount of information it contained. Jen had been sent the same files to her mobile phone and, like Alex, was studying the contents thoroughly.

By the time they went to bed in the early hours of the next morning, their heads were buzzing from the wealth of information about the Italian mob. What remained of the 'Ndrangheta after the police raid in 2010 had seemingly disappeared. However, the racketeering, money laundering and drug smuggling continued unabated. They were obviously still operating, but from where?

Too tired to read any more, both Alex and Jen agreed that they should try and get some rest. Alex was even too sleepy to shower and within minutes was in bed next to yet not cuddling up to Jen and then nothing. It was like a mutual crash-out where the second the lights turned out, both were completely immersed in a deep, bottomless slumber.

Then there was light! Alex thought he had woken up, but when he looked around him, he was certainly not in his bed nor even in his apartment. The space seemed very confined, the light dim and the floor, walls, even the ceiling, appeared to be made of metal. He could almost feel the coldness of it on his bare feet as he stood naked in one corner of the cramped room. Stacks of strong plastic bags were arranged along one wall, leaving the narrowest of passages.

Alex jumped with surprise as a man entered the room. He was sure he had spotted, but when the man walked over his foot without any sense of pain, Alex realised that, like a ghost, he could not be seen.

The man checked the packages, looking at labels and counting. He shouted something incomprehensible to someone else. Although Alex could not tell what had been said, it was unmistakably Italian.

A reply came back. There was some urgency in his voice, perhaps even a hint of excitement.

Picking up courage, Alex walked straight through the man and into the other room. This was a control room of some sort, and after seeing all the instruments dials and controls, he realised that he was inside some kind of submarine.

The man in the control room was studying several screens and instruments, making small movements of the control levers.

Alex noticed that most of the monitors displayed images around the submarine, but the view through the curved observation window was so spectacular, Alex found it difficult to look elsewhere.

The water was fairly dark and murky, suggesting the craft was at a considerable depth, and many colourful types of marine life glided effortlessly past the craft.

The guy looked very relaxed as he used the fingertip controls to guide this mini-submarine. There were two leather multi-position seats, and both looked as though they could double as very comfortable beds.

The guy who had been checking the bags returned and took his seat. Again, some incomprehensible conversation. They both laughed; Alex wondered what the joke was. Hopefully, not his naked torso. If only Jen was in this 'dream' with him, she could have translated. A few minutes passed, with the helmsman making even more delicate movements of his controls. Another glance at the window showed Alex that where initially they were in open water, they now appeared to be in a narrow passage where precise control of the craft was essential.

Several more minutes passed, and to Alex's surprise, the view outside indicated that the submarine had broken through the surface of the water. Soon after, the craft had docked and a hatch automatically opened, allowing the escape of the pressurised air within the submarine.

Shouts were exchanged with at least one other person at the dockside. Eager to see what lay beyond, Alex ventured through the hatch, although he felt certain that he could just have easily passed through the submarine's hull. It was very weird trying to move. Not like walking. More like gliding, and he could pass easily from one area to another, and best of all, he was completely unseen.

Alex was now on the dockside watching the men unload the many bags of what must have been millions of pounds worth of cocaine.

Looking around, he realised that it was underground. This was a highly organised method of smuggling drugs, and after what Alex had been reading before bed must have been organised by the immensely wealthy 'Ndrangheta. The submarine itself had to have cost millions, the whole operation perhaps even tens of millions. This was certainly a wealthy organisation.

There were four men in total. All were now on the dockside, and the submarine had been tethered to bollards. Nearby there was a floating hull of what looked like a canal narrowboat. The superstructure was suspended at least ten feet above the hull.

All four men were busy transferring the many bags of drugs from the submarine to the floating hull. They had obviously done this many times, as they precisely arranged the bags within contoured pockets around the base of the hull. At last, every bag was in place. One of the men seemed to be in charge and closely inspected the final placement.

Satisfied that everything was correct, he controlled an electric winch to lower the superstructure back into position. Once done, all four men moved around the craft firmly securing the superstructure to the hull.

Incredibly ingenious, thought Alex. To outward appearances, it was just another canal boat, the superstructure even appearing to be old and weather-worn.

The four Italians seemed cheerful, exchanging what, to Alex, appeared to be pleasantries. The original two returned to the submarine while the others loosened the moorings. Alex could not decide whether to return to the submarine or stay with the narrowboat. Which would provide more useful information? In the event, he did not have the choice, as he seemed to be suddenly flying through a maelstrom of incredibly powerful wind. He shut his eyes, and when he finally opened them again, he was in his bed. Jen was sound asleep, her gentle breathing being the only noise. Had this been a vivid dream, or had he really witnessed the criminal activities of the 'Ndrangheta?

He checked the time. It was three-thirty, and he realised how incredibly tired he felt. It seemed only seconds before he was asleep again, and this time, there were no dreams or visions.

Chapter Twenty-Two

WHEN ALEX TOLD Jen over breakfast the next morning of his strange, dream-like experience, her first thought was that it must have been his vivid imagination. Alex remembered every detail and went over it many times in his mind.

"After reading all that information last night, it's not surprising that you would dream about it. Even the submarine! Don't you remember how the authorities found a 'narcosa' submarine in Colombia? That could have triggered your imagination."

Alex had to admit that he had read that part of the report, but he still insisted that it was definitely no dream. "Perhaps it was a 'remote viewing' like Uri Geller? The Americans and the Russians both accept such possibilities."

Jen agreed but countered, "Those 'viewings' were never as detailed as you described. If it's really true then you are absolutely unique."

"Ever since losing my eyesight, I have somehow been far more perceptive. I don't know why, but it could prove extremely useful to the Intelligence Services."

"It could also make you a perfect sitting target for terrorist assassination!" was her blunt reply. She looked nervous and genuinely worried for this man who now meant everything to her. She did not wish to find his headless corpse one day, as she had with her previous partner. "You said that they spoke Italian. Can you remember any words? Anything at all?"

Alex tried his best to recall anything useful but shook his head. "I could only pick out a few words here and there, but without the context of the whole conversation, they were meaningless. They spoke very fast."

After breakfast, Alex phoned Adrian. He was even more pessimistic than Jen and had never been convinced about remote viewing. "Was there anything in the dream to locate this underground harbour?"

Alex had been thinking about that see he woke up and wished there had been something to locate it. The narrowboat was typical of many he had seen in the United Kingdom, but further than that, he had to admit that he had no idea where it could have been.

"What colour was the main superstructure?"

Alex pondered on this question. "The lighting was not very strong, but I would guess it was a greyish blue."

"That should narrow it down a bit," said Adrian sarcastically.

"Listen, Adrian, I'm sorry I don't have a fucking recording to play back to you, but I still believe it was an actual real-time viewing of their activities."

Adrian backed down a little. "Sorry, Alex. I'm just used to dealing with facts, not visions seen during sleep. We don't even know if what you saw was in real-time or a past event." Alex had not considered that possibility. "Apart from the two corpses in the Thames, we have precisely nothing. Our intelligence concluded that there was insufficient evidence to indicate the existence of a cell in the UK."

"Well, at least we know that the assumption was incorrect," countered Alex.

"Okay. But next time you have a vision, leave the fucking battery in your watch, and then we might even manage to monitor your 'vision' and do something useful about it."

Alex cursed himself for not thinking of that. Would it have worked? Could his visual cortex actually have transmitted the images from his 'viewing'? He blushed slightly as he thought of the reason why they had removed the battery. "Okay, I'll leave it in tonight."

Adrian sounded cool. "Keep in touch, and don't do anything stupid."

Jen, only hearing one side of the conversation, still knew that it had not been a particularly good communication. She put her arms around Alex and pulled him close, kissing him softly on the lips. "Don't look so worried, darling. Adrian can be short-tempered and a bit of an asshole sometimes, but he'll get over it."

"You're probably right, but I still feel as though I let him down. I've got to be more observant, but I'm still not letting him snoop on our sexual activities."

"Perhaps he's jealous of you." Again, she smiled coyly, an idea obviously forming in her mind. "Don't put the battery back in your watch just yet. We can make love in the shower."

"Mmmm, that sounds like a very good idea."

"I must modify the software to add a 'switch-off snoopers' function." The two started hurriedly undressing each other, dropping their clothes in small bundles all the way to the shower.

They had just stepped inside the cubicle when Alex's mobile rang. "Go play with yourself, Adrian! This is for my eyes only."

"That's almost a good title for a film," joked Jen. Alex turned on the powerful side jets. The water temperature was warm yet not too hot. They held each other while moving around to allow the fine water jets to play on their buttocks, backs, breasts and genitals. Jen gently pushed Alex so that he was sitting on the cubicle seat his strong erection being assisted by Jen's caressing hands. She straddled him, using the shower handrail to give her some leverage. She rode him vigorously, water jets still spraying the couple's torsos and splashing water in all directions.

It did not take long to reach a climax, and their bodies writhed in a pleasurable union. Jen dismounted and soaped both their bodies with shower gel. A final rinse with each using the hand-jet on the other made it a superb, exhilarating experience. The water was turned off and they stepped out of the cubicle.

As they dried, Alex noticed how happy Jen looked even though her life was in extreme danger.

After drying off and pulling on bathrobes, they once again read through the 'Ndrangheta reports. A new one had been sent early that morning to add to the already extensive folders.

"No wonder Adrian was grumpy. He sent this new folder at seven thirty-two this morning."

"Have you not noticed that he answers our calls whether they are early morning or late evening? All work and no play make Adrian a dull boy."

Alex laughed at Jen's observation. "I take it that he isn't married?"

"Adrian? You're joking! I can't imagine any woman who would put up with him." When Alex looked surprised, she continued, "Don't get me wrong. Technically, he's brilliant and one of the sharpest minds in British Intelligence, but socially, he's totally inept and still feels that women are a completely different race."

Jokingly, Alex raised his eyebrows. "You mean they're not?" He saw the sudden flash of revenge in her eyes and quickly jumped up to get out of her way.

She chased him around the apartment, Elsa looking with some puzzlement at the crazy couple's antics. "I'll get you, Alex McCloud!"

They were both just wearing bathrobes, and as Jen reached him, she grabbed him by the testicles, squeezing gently.

"Okay, okay! I take it back!" Alex laughed.

"You see?" Jen said triumphantly. "It's not the man with his finger on the button who rules the world. It's the woman holding the balls of the man with his finger on the button!"

"Accepted!" The couple collapsed into laughter and then began again to kiss with increasing passion. Dropping their bathrobes on the floor, they returned to the bedroom where once again they made wild, exciting love.

Sleep came very quickly after reaching their climax. The young lovers were holding each other close as Alex's sleep turned once again into what seemed to be another dimension. He was on the narrowboat. Two of the men from his previous vision were sitting towards the rear of the craft. One of them was steering, and the steady *chug-chug* of the engine made it seem like a leisure cruise. The man who was not in control of the boat was relaxing, looking very comfortable and reading a book. Nobody would imagine that millions of pounds of drugs were secreted in the bowels of this seemingly innocent method of transport.

Alex moved as near the men as he could and studied them closely. The one who was reading was perhaps in his early thirties and had thick black hair. He was of medium build, and his casual T-shirt revealed strong muscular arms. Interestingly, the book he was reading was Dan Brown's *Deception Point*. *A good book and a very apt title*, thought Alex. *It's not one of Dan Brown's most recent books, though, so that does not help with a timeline.*

The other man seemed to be slightly older, perhaps in his late thirties. There was a physical resemblance, indicating that they were probably brothers.

Although the two were silent, Alex could hear a man's disembodied voice. It sounded familiar. Then he had it! The voice was from a portable radio, and it was Ken Bruce on Radio Two. The *Popmaster* quiz was almost finished, and a woman had just beaten her male challenger with a score of thirty-three points to his fifteen.

"And now for a beautiful BBC Radio Two DAB radio, I want you to give me, within ten seconds, three hit singles by…" There was an obligatory pause as the countdown timer started. "Glen Campbell!"

As the countdown advanced, the woman contestant said, "'Wichita Lineman', 'Rhinestone Cowboy' and…" She paused, struggling to think of a third. Just before the pips sounded, she quickly added, "'By the Time I Get to Phoenix'!"

"Yes! You just managed it!" Ken Bruce sounded genuinely excited and pleased for the lucky contestant, and the recorded applause ended the item. As the woman started to name her friends and relatives, Alex pondered what he had just heard. *So it is about a quarter to eleven, but on which date? I can find that out.*

Next, Alex began to look at the countryside they were passing through. It yielded no obvious clues other than that the land was fairly flat. Few other craft sailed on this stretch of water. He peered into the distance and could see another boat, but it may have been travelling in the same direction.

Direction! Alex had nearly forgotten the basic principle of observation. *Locate the course of the canal by observing shadows.* He looked at the two men, trying to observe which way their shadows were falling. Before he could determine anything useful, a large, grey cloud overshadowed the craft. *Damn! Come on, sunshine!* He was willing the sun to reappear, and then it did.

From the shadows cast by the men and the time of the day, the boat was heading in a slightly west-of-north direction. The guy who was reading had a swig from a bottle of Coke and offered it to the other man. He took the bottle, had a large gulp, belched noisily and handed it back, saying something in Italian.

Alex jumped in surprise when a loud *honk* sounded. It was from another canal boat coming in the opposite direction, a colourful craft, which looked as though it could have been one used by a family on holiday.

This was reinforced by the appearance of two small children waving at them. A man and presumably his wife were in the rear, controlling the craft. The man shouted in the direction of the Italians. "Be careful at your next lock. The turnscrews are extremely tight, and the gates are a bit worn!"

To Alex's amazement, the older Italian shouted back in what seemed to be a perfect East-End accent, "Thanks a lot, mate.

We'll look out for that." He waved back at the children, who were now disappearing from view.

Before the entire craft was out of sight, Alex realised that a clue may lie on the other boat. As well as being highly decorated, there was on the side of the superstructure a large picture of the head of a white cat with a red bow. Underneath the picture were the words *Hello Kitty*.

Even as he looked at the quickly disappearing craft, the image began to break up into tiny fragments, and then there was nothing but blackness.

As soon as Alex awoke, he climbed out of bed, careful not to disturb Jen, who looked serenely peaceful. Pulling on his clothes, he went into the living room and switched on the computer. "Damn! Why is it that it seems to take longer to start up when you're in a hurry?" Eventually, the familiar Windows 7 desktop appeared. He clicked on 'internet' and opened the BBC Radio Two website. Jeremy Vine's programme was playing. He looked at his watch. It was one-fifteen, and he cursed himself for not waking a bit sooner.

Anxiously, he selected the 'Listen Again' option for the Ken Bruce show and moved the timer to ten thirty-five. As he listened, he began to smile; the same contestants were playing as in his 'vision'. By the time the winner had finished the 'Three in Ten' item, there was no doubt in his mind. What he had seen in his vision was definitely in real-time.

Next, he had to identify the location. He searched for British canals and not surprisingly found far more than was helpful. Even when he looked at photographs of many canal routes, there was a great deal of similarity in them. Of course, the land had to be fairly flat for canal waterways to work. He had wasted enough time and phoned Adrian.

His contact, always to the point, reminded Alex that his watch was still not transmitting.

"Damn! Sorry, Adrian, but I've had another vision.

"Another? During the daytime? What is it you don't want me to see, Alex?" As on the previous occasion, Adrian sounded annoyed, but before Alex could think of an excuse, Adrian remarked, "I take it you're screwing the delightful Major Sherlock and don't wish to share the experience?"

"Something like that," mumbled an embarrassed Alex. *God! Why did it have to be so fucking obvious?* "Let me tell you about this vision. It's definitely in real-time, and I have an identification of another canal boat." He described the whole scene in great detail to the attentive Adrian.

"If we're quick enough, we may find this boat with the kitten on the side, but all it will give is a general direction. Do you know how many canals there are in the UK?"

"I know it's a long shot, but it's all we have."

"Okay! Leave it with me."

As Alex ended his call, he noticed Jen had wandered in from the bedroom. Still quite naked and looking superb, she sat next to Alex. He recounted the vision to her and saw the glimmer of hope in her eyes. Or could it have been maybe lust for his body yet again?

When he explained that his visions were definitely in real-time, Jen, with a smile, said, "It's a pity these visions are not *ahead* of time. Just imagine how you could make a fortune by knowing the Lotto numbers in advance!"

Alex laughed more out of resignation than amusement. "I never thought of that, but I've never been lucky financially. I gave up doing the lottery ages ago, as I never won a thing! Not even a measly ten pounds."

Chapter Twenty-Three

Franco was not complacent about the dangers of moving such a huge quantity of drugs as was stowed in the hull of his narrow craft. His younger brother Georgio was a little too relaxed and assumed that they were smarter than the intelligence services seeking out contraband drugs. *That's how mistakes are made*, Franco thought. They were making good progress and had been cruising along the waterways for about thirteen hours. It would take another couple of days to reach their eventual unloading point, after which he could finally relax.

His phone began to play the start of 'Popeye the Sailor Man', a ringtone that he had felt with a certain amount of amusement was fitting to his role.

"Yes?"

He listened carefully to the coded message and frowned in annoyance. No response was necessary. He ended the call and replaced the phone in his pocket.

Georgio was asleep. This stretch of canal had no locks, and after taking the helm for three hours, he decided to rest. "Wake up, Georgio!" He shook his brother in an attempt to disturb him.

The younger man woke with a start. The tone in Franco's voice told him something was wrong. "What is it?"

"There's a change of plan. We're unloading our cargo earlier than originally intended."

Rubbing the sleep from his eyes, Georgio asked, "Why?"

"A message from headquarters. They want to get this load distributed more quickly, so we have to do the change at the earlier transfer point."

"Shit! You know we won't get as good a price if we unload early."

"It won't make any difference. We'll just have to drive the cargo a bit further than usual, but all the stuff will still get to the centre of the city a day earlier."

"Good! That's okay then," Georgio conceded.

"And it's a damn sight more comfortable in the van than in this tub," Franco added, feeling quite unenthusiastic about these long boring journeys. "See how much further it is to our new transfer point."

Obediently, Georgio pulled out a map from a waterproof pocket at the rear of the boat. He used a scale to calculate the distance. "About fifteen miles—perhaps another three hours or so. At least it'll save us from going through over sixty locks."

Both men found the routine of changing level through the use of locks quite tiresome and wondered why canal cruising for leisure was so popular in the UK.

"Good," Franco said. "Let's see if we can do it less than that. It may make all the difference." He pushed the throttle lever fully forward, the *chug-chug* becoming a little more urgent and intense in its tone.

The noise of the engine drowned out the music from the portable radio, but neither Georgio nor Franco was concerned as they concentrated on their new mission.

Chapter Twenty-Four

WHEN ALEX HAD described his vision, Adrian decided for the time being to believe there may be some truth to what Alex had experienced. He contacted the BBC and asked for an alert to be announced. Now he was about to hear the result of his call.

Harvey Cook, the newsreader on Radio Two, which had the UK's largest listening audience, began his report. *"Police are asking the owners of a canal narrowboat with a picture of a kitten on the side and the words 'Hello Kitty' to contact them. It is believed that they may have important information of interest to the police. It is understood that there is a man, woman and two children on this boat, and they are asked to contact the police urgently on the following number."*

It was five twenty, and the announcement had interrupted Simon Mayo's evening programme. Simon made some comedic comment about having a picture of a kitten on the side of a boat, but Adrian had already stopped listening and just hoped there would not be too many hoax calls.

As expected, there were some cranks, usually from lonely people who sought any excuse to speak to a police officer. He smiled to himself when a woman told him that she had a beautiful 'pussy' on her boat and couldn't wait to show it to an officer. *Sad lonely cow! She probably doesn't even have a boat or a cat.*

After a few fruitless calls, one came through that attracted his attention. "My narrowboat has a picture of a kitten on the side and the words 'Hello Kitty' underneath it."

"Okay." So far, what the guy had said was what had been announced on the radio item, but somehow, Adrian felt this may be more promising. "Can I have your name, sir?"

"Sure, it's Paul Rogerson." The man sounded a little nervous and uncertain as to why his boat was of such interest.

"Were you on a canal waterway at about ten forty-five this morning?"

"Yes, definitely. We were cruising most of the morning until we stopped at a hotel for lunch."

"Isn't it a bit cold for canal cruising in December?" The idea of freezing on Britain's canals certainly did not appeal to Adrian.

"It can be a bit cold, but there's less traffic at this time of the year. We don't sail as much but enjoy the occasional cruise on the canals."

"Do you recall speaking to a couple of men on another boat around that time?"

The man had to think about this and then exclaimed, "Oh, yes. We were going in the opposite direction and warned them about a particularly difficult lock, which they would come across about ten minutes later."

This is definitely the one, thought Adrian. *Perhaps Alex really does possess some inexplicable viewing power after all.*

He had paused too long, and the man thought he had been cut off. "Hello?"

"Oh, sorry, Mr. Rogerson. I was just checking some of our facts. Now, this is very important. Can you recall where this encounter was? And where do you think the other boat might have been heading?"

"Let me think. It must've been somewhere well north of Brentford, closer to Braunston. The Grand Union Canal is a bit wider around that area, but further north, it's only wide enough for one boat. As for where it could have been heading, well, it could have been anywhere north of Braunston Junction. As its name implies, there are many different waterways branching out in that area."

Not a lot of help, Adrian thought. "But it still may get us a bit closer to what's going on. What about the boat, Mr. Rogerson? And the men in it?"

Paul had to admit that there was nothing really distinctive about the boat and the men. "A grey hull and a greyish-blue superstructure. It had a rear well for steering and was one of the more recent designs similar to a river cruiser like ours. As for the men, all I noticed was that both had black hair."

"Did either of them speak? Did they have an accent?"

"Oh, yes. One man shouted, 'Thanks for the warning.' It was only a few words, but I think it sounded like an East End accent."

That fitted in exactly with Alex's report. "Thank you so much, Mr. Rogerson. Can I take your number in case I need to get back to you?" He noted the number. "If there's anything else you think of, please get back to me as soon as possible."

Clearly puzzled, the man asked, "What is this about? Were those two men criminals?"

"We are as yet uncertain. Just following up on some information. Thanks again for your help."

Adrian relaxed. He called the switchboard and asked them not to put any more calls through unless it was Paul Rogerson. "I've had my fill of crank calls today."

He requested detailed maps of the canal network in the area Rogerson had mentioned. The subject of narrowboats was a new one to him, and he used his internet search engine to gain as much information as possible. "How fast could they travel and just where could the boat be now? It was six-thirty, and if they were quick enough and had a certain amount of luck, they may find the boat. If it could not be found soon, the chances of finding it at all were minimal.

Chapter Twenty-Five

A T SIX THIRTY-FIVE that evening, the boat glided slowly into the docking area of a large yet unimposing metal-framed building. Doors had closed automatically after the boat had passed through into the building and away from the normal canal routes.

Wasting no time, Georgio jumped deftly onto the quayside and moored the boat to the bollards. Once secured, he returned to the boat and, together with Franco, moved around the vessel in an organised, well-practised fashion, loosening the many retaining bolts. Two other men had appeared and began to position the mobile crane to raise the superstructure. As soon as it was locked in position and a good ten feet above the hull, all four men jumped into the boat and began the routine task of removing the many plastic bags of drugs. The men spoke little, the transfer process requiring their full attention.

Once the hull was empty, the superstructure was slowly lowered into position and the bolts tightened. Again, as if it was a well-practised routine, they next began to peel what could best be described as a 'skin' off the superstructure. What had before been a drab, greyish-blue exterior was slowly transformed into a smart, bright-yellow-and-green appearance. It truly was a floating chameleon.

The 'peeled' skin was then separated into smaller areas before being carefully laid in shallow baths of acid, reducing the plastic to an unrecognisable piece of waste. The pulp would be dumped many miles away from the warehouse, all possible links being carefully thought out. No evidence could be left to incriminate the group of drug dealers. This was certainly a well-planned exercise, but it was not yet complete.

The forty-five-kilo bags of drugs had been placed on trolleys. These were moved to another area within the warehouse where ten gleaming-white Hotpoint washing machines were lined up. The ballast weights normally used to provide some stability as the machines were working had already been taken out. The back of each machine had been removed, allowing the men to insert the drugs, four bags per machine, into specially prepared mouldings attached to the chassis.

Franco reminded the others to take extreme care not to catch the plastic bags on anything sharp within the machines. They were all aware of the vast wealth in the pure Asian cocaine they were handling so routinely. These four men again exchanged few words as they carried out the task of concealing the drugs within their new hosts. When all the backs were replaced, the men again used the trolleys to put them into a white van. The whole military-like operation of transferring the drugs from the canal boat into the washing machine delivery van had taken just forty-five minutes to complete.

Franco and Georgio now exchanged places with their cousins, Alfonso and Pedro, who entered the cabin of the canal boat to rest for the night.

The other brothers would have to wait a while for their rest. They had ten addresses in the Birmingham area where they had to deliver the washing machines. They might manage to deliver perhaps one or two this night and the remainder on the following day. After all, who would want to take delivery of a washing machine after nine o'clock in the evening? Everything they did had to be above suspicion, and their task was to blend in with everyday life. It only needed one little mistake for their whole operation to be compromised.

Franco started the engine, the electric sliding doors raised just long enough to allow the van to pass through. Georgio was already entering the first delivery address into the sat nav, and once again they were ready to deliver another shipment.

Within forty-five minutes, they had arrived at their first address.

JIMMY WARBURTON WAS not surprised to see the delivery van arrive at his apartment in East Birmingham. It had been due in two days' time, but he had received a call telling him that the delivery had been rescheduled earlier than expected.

A forty-one-year-old, stocky, muscular man, Jimmy had been a drug dealer in this part of Birmingham for over fifteen years and had made a comfortable living out of the business, never once being foolish enough to take the drugs himself. His supplies had been uncertain until about two years earlier when this new gang offered him a steady supply. He knew little about them apart from that he knew not to cross them unless he wanted severe repercussions against him and his family.

He smiled as the two delivery men wheeled the smart new washing machine from the van into his ground-floor apartment. The men returned to their van and came back carrying a couple of boxes supposedly containing all the accessories for the new machine. Once everything was inside his kitchen, the two men, saying little, unscrewed the rear panel off the machine and carefully slid the four plastic bags temporarily used as ballast. These were replaced with the real manufacturer's ballast from the cardboard boxes, and the panel was replaced.

Jimmy's thoughts were on the vast amount he could charge for the twenty kilos of high-quality cocaine in these four inconspicuous bags. No negotiations were necessary, as he had already agreed the price well in advance of shipment. He had numerous business contacts and had put most of his money into offshore accounts; when the time came, he would retire either to Portugal or Spain where he could spend the rest of his life with his wife Jacquie and their children in reasonable comfort and in a climate far superior to that of Britain.

"Can I offer you two a drink of tea coffee or something a little stronger?" Jimmy's Birmingham accent was unmistakable.

"Thanks but no. We have many deliveries to make, but it's good of you to offer refreshments." Franco preferred to say little to their customers. "Bank transfer as soon as possible Jimmy."

"Of course. I'll do it tomorrow first thing." Jimmy knew not to play games with these people. Before they came along, he had dealt with other drug importers who had not been quite as well organised or efficient. When he learned of the grisly demise of his usual supplier at the hands of this new organisation, he realised that they really meant business.

He shuddered as he remembered how the bodies of the drug importers had turned up in a huge industrial mincing machine within a slaughterhouse. Police had never been able to discover the truth behind the killings, but it was a poignant reminder that he always needed to toe the line. He did not even know who was behind the organisation; it was safer not to ask too many questions. He was aware that there was an Italian connection, but that was as much as he wanted or dared to know. Jimmy was a family man, and the thought of his wife or children being slaughtered was all he needed to keep his mouth firmly shut.

Chapter Twenty-Six

A LEX AND JEN had heard the message broadcast on the radio and wondered if anything would come of it. It came as a great relief when Adrian phoned and told of his conversation with Paul Rogerson. To have his 'vision' validated so precisely gave Alex a feeling of at least being of some use again. It was also satisfying that Adrian now believed in his vivid dreams, which were in reality accurate visions.

Jen, meanwhile, had been taking the time to read the vast volumes of information about the 'Ndrangheta. Sadly, it reopened many old wounds to think once again of Jason's terrible death. She remembered all the times they had spent together, both of them analysing the 'Ndrangheta's electronic traffic but also some of their more intimate moments. She was already comparing Jason and Alex and had to admit that she was falling deeply in love with Alex. True, the sex was superb and she could never get enough, but there was also a much deeper emotional bond with him that she knew was absolutely genuine.

She, like, Alex wanted to do everything they could to bring down the hated Italian family of criminals.

Of one thing Alex was absolutely certain. He was going to have to learn Italian and without further delay. He downloaded a translation course and, with Jen's assistance, began to pick up the language quickly. Jen was amazed at how fast a learner he was. Again, Alex felt that the blow to his head and the increased cortical activity had improved his ability to absorb new information. Within this first day, he was able to speak and understand simple sentences in a dialogue between him and Jen, who told him that in normal circumstances it could take several weeks to reach this same level of competence.

That night, Alex followed Adrian's request and left his eyesight switched on to test if his 'visions' could be transmitted to Adrian's computer. It proved far more difficult than he had thought to avoid looking at Jen as they prepared for bed, but he had not revealed anything that may have caused her any embarrassment.

They refrained from making love that night, but much to Alex's annoyance and frustration, he awoke the following morning well-rested with no recall of dreaming. What determined if a vision would appear while he slept? Was the fact that they had made love on both occasions essential? Perhaps coitus lifted his awareness to a level which allowed him to see activity from a distance?

Since it was now obvious that the visions occurred in real-time, Alex realised it would be far more useful to experience them during the day rather than at night when the Italians were themselves probably sleeping. For this reason, he did his best to tire himself by strenuous exercise during the morning and after lunch went to bed for a short, hopefully fruitful sleep.

He asked Jen to try to stay awake and observe him during sleep, as this may also prove to be useful. She noticed that at first, he seemed quite restless, turning several times. There followed a restful stage, during which he was probably experiencing normal dreams. Watching Alex sleeping and recording times of the different stages was making Jen tired too, but she persisted, occasionally sipping water to keep awake. Alex was lying on his back his breathing deep and regular. *Sleeping like a baby.*

What happened next nearly caused Jen to spill her drink. His eyes had suddenly snapped wide open and seemed to be staring at the ceiling. She moved her hand over his eyes. He showed no indication of having seen it. Quickly, Jen made a note of the time. He stayed absolutely motionless, in this trance-like state for just thirteen minutes, after which his eyelids slowly closed and his body seemed to relax. It was a relief when he awoke an hour and a half later.

"Did you have another vision?" Jen asked eagerly.

Still a little groggy, he replied, "Yes. A very strange one."

Jen explained how his eyes had opened presumably during his vision. "Tell me what you saw." She was curious and impatient to learn of his new experience.

Alex put a hand to his head and groaned a little. "I don't know if it's because I'm having these visions, but I've noticed that when I wake up I have a splitting headache."

Jen was quite concerned by that. "Would you like something to relieve the pain?"

"No thanks, love. Once you start taking painkillers, it's very easy to get into the habit, and I don't want to get hooked on them."

Jen nodded in agreement. She remembered the cocktail of drugs she had been prescribed when she suffered depression after Jason's death. Thankfully, that was now all behind her. "Take your time, sweetheart."

Alex's memory of his vision was completely intact, and he knew that once he had recounted it to Jen, it would be even easier to retain. He closed his eyes and tried to completely immerse himself back into the vision.

THE TWO GUYS from the canal boat were in what looked like a Ford Transit van. The one who had been steering the boat was driving while the other was giving him directions by using a portable sat nav. It was obvious the driver was unfamiliar with the area. Alex looked through the windscreen at the roads ahead. There was a great deal of traffic, and somehow the busy roads seemed familiar. There were many junctions off this complex network of roads. At last, the driver found his way out of the confusion and headed down what was still a busy road but at least it seemed to be heading in some positive direction, which satisfied the man at the wheel. The repetitive rhythm of the windscreen wipers was hypnotic as they worked hard to improve vision. Driving conditions were indeed difficult on this stormy December day.

The driver glanced at his watch, cursed and put his foot harder on the accelerator.

Suddenly, the guy in the passenger seat shouted to the driver to turn left at the next road junction, but he had left it too late. The driver panicked and turned sharp left without noticing that a cyclist was on the nearside of the van. The female cyclist hit the side of the vehicle with great force and was thrown heavily to the ground, her tangled bike falling on top of the unfortunate young woman.

With a look of panic, the driver realised what had happened, but instead of stopping to assist her, he accelerated down the road. The two men started arguing, and this time there was not a hint of an East End accent. They were speaking in fluent Italian, and Alex could understand some although not all of their heated conversation. They seemed to be frantically looking for a way to escape; one of them spotted a narrower road off to the left and pointed to it. The driver turned sharply into the road, looking for somewhere to abandon the vehicle. A passageway between two buildings offered a solution to their problem. The driver turned smartly, drove about fifty metres into the passage and braked sharply. The two remaining washing machines rocked unsteadily with the shock but somehow managed to remain upright.

Both men quickly gathered all personal belongings from the vehicle to prevent any identification. They moved swiftly and strangely coordinated in their actions as though the possibility of an accident had at some time been considered and subsequent actions decided in advance. Next, they took off their jackets, turned them inside out and put them on again. This simple action had significantly altered their appearance.

Satisfied that they had left nothing of use to the police, they locked the front doors and with some caution climbed out of the back. Before locking the doors after them, one took something out of his bag and attached it to the inside of the rear door.

They walked away trying to put on a casual air.

Alex had watched this in shock. He wanted to rush back to where the woman had been knocked off her bicycle but decided to follow these two men if only to provide Adrian with as much helpful information as possible. To his surprise, Alex watched as each man took a different route—a clever ruse should the police be on the lookout for two men.

Now who do I follow? Alex decided to tail the older man on the chance that he may reveal more information. It was strange trying to control his movements. It was neither walking nor flying but more like ice-skating but with far less control of his limbs. He found it extremely difficult to keep up with the man but concentrated all his effort on staying as close as possible. The man took a cap out of his pocket and placed it on his head, making identification even more difficult.

Alex nearly collided with the Italian but instinctively knew that he would just have passed straight through the man's body like a ghost. Alex was close enough to hear a mobile phone conversation.

"Had to abandon delivery. Two machines left but alternative plans are in place." Alex realised that the device on the rear door must have been a bomb timed to detonate when the criminals were well clear. "Will organise transport to return to base." With that, he ended his brief, seemingly innocent call.

Alex thought how professional and organised these men were. He was hoping that he could follow this man and discover where his base was located, but then the sound of a huge explosion reached his ears, and with that, his vision abruptly ended.

HE WAS DISAPPOINTED when Jen told him how long he had been asleep and, more importantly, how long it had been since his vision had ended. "They could be miles away by now. I must phone Adrian."

The intelligence officer answered his call quickly on seeing Alex's name appear on the display of his phone. "Do you have any more information?"

"Yes!" Alex was excited and told Adrian of the events in his vision earlier that afternoon.

Adrian listened with interest then asked, "Do you have any idea where all this happened?"

Alex thought carefully. "I recognised the road network but where?" He turned the images over and over in his mind and then exclaimed, "It must be Birmingham! No wonder they were lost. That complicated road network could only have been Birmingham's Spaghetti Junction!"

"Great! Hold on while I check news reports for Birmingham." The forty seconds or so that it took Adrian to find the news item on the internet seemed much longer to Alex. "Yes! I found it." He read it to the fascinated Alex. "At two-forty this afternoon, thirty-two-year-old mother of two Jessica Turner was knocked off her bicycle as a van turned sharply off the A456 near Birmingham's city centre. Mrs. Turner is in Intensive Care in Birmingham Hospital, suffering from severe abdominal and chest injuries. It is understood that she is four months pregnant. The two men driving the van have disappeared, and the van, believed to be a white Ford Transit, was destroyed in an explosion. As yet, the police have not established the cause of the explosion, but it is thought that it may have been a deliberate act to destroy evidence."

"That fits exactly with what I saw in my vision. Poor woman." Alex now wished he had returned to the scene of the accident, wondering if he could have done something to help the woman and her unborn child, even though he knew it would have been physically impossible.

Alex had a thought. "Adrian, did the monitor show my vision?"

"Not a thing. I've already replayed the monitor recordings for this afternoon, and for the whole time you were asleep, there was absolutely nothing!"

Alex felt both relieved and disappointed by this news. A video of his visions would have been extremely useful in determining the absolute facts, and yet somehow, it would have felt like an even greater intrusion into his privacy.

Alex was still replaying the vision in his own mind, trying to think of anything which could be of assistance. "We do know that these two guys were in all three visions, and although they spoke in an East End accent for most of the time, they were obviously Italians."

Adrian agreed. "Yes. Which brings us back to the 'Ndrangheta. My guess is that the drugs from the submarine were transferred into the canal boat and later into the washing machines for delivery in the van. Since there were only two machines left, the question is how many other machines had already been delivered and where to?"

"These guys were unfamiliar with that part of Birmingham, which may mean that this is not where the drugs were originally intended to be delivered. Either that or this was their first time in Birmingham." Alex remembered the conversation between the two men while in the van. "One of them had mentioned a change of instructions, complaining about this on their route towards the Midlands. That could be why they ended up in unfamiliar territory.

"This is all fitting together like a jigsaw, but we're still missing many of the pieces. I've been looking at the canal system, and it's quite fascinating. The Grand Union Canal starts at Brentford north of London. At Braunston Junction, the canal system heads towards Birmingham and even runs under Birmingham's Spaghetti Junction.

From there, there are many branches which could have taken them anywhere within a seventy-mile radius."

"So Birmingham could still have been their ultimate destination even with the change of plan," Alex speculated.

Adrian agreed with this supposition. "We've carried out a search for the canal boat, and it seems to have completely disappeared, but keep on having these dreams, Alex, and we may yet manage to put all the pieces together."

Jen had been listening to this conversation with interest, and as Alex ended the call, she said, "I think you may be better off sleeping during the day if only to get more useful visions."

With a feigned look of innocence, he asked, "But what can we possibly do during the night?"

Jen's eyes sparkled with excitement, a smile lighting her beautiful face. "I know exactly what you have in mind, Alex McCloud, and I think it's a great idea."

"At least we now know Adrian can't monitor my visions, so we can just remove the battery when we don't want him to see us together."

Chapter Twenty-Seven

December 2011

A T FIFTY-EIGHT, GIANNI Lamancusa had never been a patient man, and the news of the partially aborted drug run to Birmingham had angered him far more than the usual petty irritations he encountered in his line of business. "Six fucking million lost through this stupid mistake. It's bad enough when fixers outside the family fuck up, but when it's your own family, it's even worse!" He coughed, a deep throaty retching cough made worse by smoking heavily.

"Don't worry so much, Tesoro. Your blood pressure is already too high! Please try and calm yourself." Gianni's long-suffering wife Carina knew the pressure her husband was feeling, and since their flight from Italy, it had increased significantly thanks to their unusual way of life. *What is the point of all this luxury if one's health is compromised?* This was a question she often asked herself.

His stomach ulcers could be treated with medication, but his blood pressure was, on occasion, dangerously high despite taking daily tablets to supposedly help keep it to an acceptable level.

Even getting hold of proper medication had proved to be difficult. As fugitives, they did not have the luxury of a GP to monitor their health and prescribe medication. Of course, with money, anything could be bought, but it was becoming ever more difficult to live in this underworld, and she was tired of permanently hiding from the authorities. The worst aspect of their life was the boredom of living unseen, scurrying away like rats in a sewer, even though it was a somewhat more comfortable one at that.

This life was not what she had expected when, thirty-eight years earlier, she had married her cousin twice removed as was the custom within the 'Ndrangheta. Gianni had been tall, ruggedly handsome and physically strong, and Carina had welcomed their union. She had known even at the tender age of eleven that they were destined to marry, their parents carefully planning the long-term future of the family. Life had been much different then, as they could carry out their illegal activities unhindered by authorities, thanks to the bribes paid to a few select senior officials.

"Where are Franco and Georgio?" Carina was concerned that two of her four children were in danger of being caught by the authorities.

Gianni looked downcast, sharing his wife's concern. "They are on their way back. Franco is on the InterCity train from Birmingham to London, and Georgio is coming back by coach."

Knowing that neither of them would feel at ease until their sons had returned safely, Carina tried to engross herself in her book, a biographical work describing the turbulent relationship between film stars Richard Burton and Elizabeth Taylor.

What Carina did not realise was that her husband was not only suffering from these current problems but was also missing the relative freedom they had enjoyed back in Italy. Although not risk-free, those were happier times when everybody showed them some form of respect even if it was fear-inspired.

The door opened, and an energetic, attractive woman in her early thirties briskly entered the room. "What's the matter? Why are you two looking so glum?" It was Francesca, the fourth of their children and their only daughter.

Carina explained the problem in the Birmingham drug run and how they were worried about the safety of their sons.

"Don't worry! They'll be okay. They can handle themselves, and at least they are brave enough to do the run." It was plainly obvious that Francesca admired her brothers.

Gianni found his daughter's irreverence annoying and bluntly asked, "What do you want Francesca?"

She looked taken aback by her father's brusqueness. "Nothing! I just came to let you know that the casino had a record evening last night. Since you let me take control eighteen months ago, profits have trebled." She had been tired of having nothing to do and had begged her father to let her do something worthwhile. It had been with some reluctance that Gianni conceded that she could look after the casino operations. He had not yet joined the ranks of enlightened males, who believed their female counterparts deserved some form of equal opportunities. Like many Italian men, Gianni felt that women were much better having babies and carrying out domestic duties, leaving the men to do the 'hard' work. It was unlikely that would change within Gianni's lifetime.

Carina gave her husband a disapproving look, which without words said, "Don't be too hard on our daughter."

Seeing this, he softened a little. A smile crossed his lips, yet his eyes gave no impression of softening. "Good. How did you manage to improve profits?"

Francesca knew that her father was not normally interested in detail as long as the money came in, yet she humoured him. "In two ways. In all seven casinos, we have reduced the size of the lounge area, making room for more tables. Secondly, we're keeping a greater check on crooked staff. We've sacked seven croupiers over the last six months for taking bribes to help players win." It was quite ironic that probably what was the most unscrupulous gambling organisation in the UK considered these greedy croupiers to be 'crooked'. Still, Francesca felt proud of her achievements and contributed as much to the family as any of the men around her.

"Keep a watch on those who have been sacked. We don't want any comeback because of staff with a grievance." Back in Italy, if Gianni had caught anybody cheating on him, they would not be sacked. They would literally disappear without trace. Building sites with deep concrete foundations had always proved to be very useful. It annoyed him that here in England, he did not have the resources nor the numerous corrupt officials he could depend on as it was in Italy. He did hope that this situation would improve in time, as he spent a great deal of effort identifying corruptible officials in all political parties, police and the civil service.

What Francesca did not tell her father was that she had her own method of ensuring the silence of those who had been sacked. The threat of violence against someone close—parents, husband, wife or even children—was more than enough to keep their mouths firmly shut. She was indeed her father's daughter.

Chapter Twenty-Eight

ALEX FELT ELATED that his visions were far from that. It was as though he was a cameraman able to capture a scene where the criminals were in the act of carrying out their crime. The worst aspect was that he had absolutely no control over what he could observe. He had to take whatever was given, but he now had a hunger for more detailed information. If somehow he could fine-tune this newfound ability, it could prove to be essential to the intelligence services, making his existence far more worthwhile.

He and Jen had lengthy discussions where they both tried to work out how best to utilise his visions to improve his usefulness. The worst aspect was that it meant sleeping during daytimes and evenings to gain any useful information.

What they agreed on was that they could try to adjust their sleep patterns to start about two in the afternoon until roughly midnight, followed by vision analysis if any had been experienced. This would be followed by taking Elsa for exercise at about three in the morning when the streets were quite empty.

There was no point in Jen staying awake while Alex slept, as she could only record the times he was having visions, and now they knew they were in real-time, there was little point. It was already after five o'clock, so for today, they would have dinner and then an early night. When Alex awoke at two-thirty in the morning he felt that he had had enough sleep, but this time, there had been no visions. Jen had slept badly and was already awake. Alex looked outside. It was a cool, clear December morning, and Alex yearned for some exercise.

"Do you feel like a walk this fine morning?"

Jen was tired from her uneasy sleep and was not certain that a walk would improve how she felt. Still, she realised that both of them needed exercise after being confined to the apartment. "As long as you promise not to walk too fast."

Alex laughed. Although Jen was quite tall, she had on the few occasions they had all been out together, found difficulty walking at Alex's pace. "Do you hear that, Elsa? Can you slow down for our new friend?"

The dog, on hearing her name, looked up with curiosity at the two of them, turned over and put her head down, ready for another sleep.

As soon as Jen and Alex had showered and dressed, they, together with Elsa, ventured out of the apartment where they had spent most of their time over the past few days. The roads in the area were quiet apart from an occasional taxi. Alex kept Elsa to a manageable speed for Jen's benefit, and the three walked for about an hour, taking a route that would follow a circular path bringing them back to the apartment. They talked little, finding it intriguing to just listen to the sounds of London at a time when most people were fast asleep in their beds.

All three felt better for the exercise and fresh air, but once Alex had relaxed in his chair, his eyes became heavier, and he fell into a light slumber.

Jen returned from the bathroom to find Alex asleep and gently snoring. *This won't help with our new sleep regime if he's dozing already,* she thought. She looked at her watch. It was four ten, and dawn was still a few hours away.

Elsa was lying down, her eyes following Jen and Alex. "Elsa! Come on and wake up your master!" Jen encouraged the dog to come closer to Alex, who was sitting with his legs slightly parted, the steady breathing noises indicating that he was quite settled.

"Get him, Elsa! Come on get him!" Jen's words did the trick, as the powerful dog pushed her long snout firmly into Alex's crotch, causing him to wake up with a start.

"What the…"

Jen laughed. "Good girl, Elsa! Sorry, Alex, but you need to keep awake until this afternoon. It's no use sleeping now when you need to stay awake."

"I suppose you're right." He stroked Elsa's head. The excited dog licked him vigorously.

"I'll make us coffee and toast. That will help to keep you awake."

"Okay. Good idea. It's going to take some time for me to get used to my new sleeping routine."

THE MORNING DRAGGED along slowly, but the couple kept busy, mixing domestic chores with necessary paperwork. Alex phoned Adrian, but neither of them had anything new to report. Alex told Adrian of his new sleep pattern and his hope that it may provide many more visions. It was also a reminder that Adrian needed to phone them in the morning rather than the afternoon.

By one-thirty, both Jen and Alex felt ready for sleep but this time remembered to let Elsa out for relief beforehand so she wouldn't interrupt them.

As the couple relaxed in bed, they were both hoping that this afternoon would prove fruitful in having another glimpse into the murky world of the 'Ndrangheta. So far, these visions had proved to be completely unpredictable without any obvious pattern.

Alex had been asleep for several hours when his mind latched on to a new vision. He was standing in a shop of some sort. It seemed to be a general store. Looking at the shelves, Alex spotted packets of cereal, chocolate bars, sweets and other confectionary. Another group of shelves had numerous types of vegetables and fruits. Muted displays of packets of cigarettes were along most of the wall behind the counter.

There was just one customer who was buying a bottle of vodka, which Alex noticed the person serving had pulled out from under the counter. *Probably not a legitimate manufacturer*, Alex thought.

The customer seemed unconcerned that he may be purchasing a dangerous vodka substitute and, with shaky hands, passed over the money.

Clutching his purchase, the man pulled the door open. Before he could escape, two men pushed their way in, almost knocking him over as though he did not even exist. Seeing the grim look on their faces, the customer escaped as quickly as his legs would carry him while still clutching his precious vodka.

One of the two men closed the shop door and turned the sign to indicate that the store was now closed. The shopkeeper, a small Asian man in his fifties, appeared to know the men. He seemed to shrink on seeing them and wore a very nervous expression as they approached the counter.

One of the men, a tall, bear-like, stocky guy, held out his paw, inviting the shopkeeper to hand over cash. Alex at first thought they were attempting to steal the man's takings, but it was the fact that he recognised them that led Alex to the only possible conclusion. They were demanding protection money.

With shaky hands, the shopkeeper opened his till and extracted a small bundle of notes.

The guy who had held out his hand greedily grabbed the notes and swiftly counted them. A broad smile lit the face his face. "That's a good boy, Masseud. Same time next week."

What surprised Alex was the fact that this guy spoke with a strong Scottish accent, probably Glaswegian. This puzzled him, as he felt that these tough guys were not connected to the 'Ndrangheta, so why was he having a vision about them? Some accents were easier to copy than others, but in addition to the accent, these men did actually look as though they could be from Glasgow.

Pocketing the money, the guy turned around and headed for the door, closely followed by the other. Masseud looked relieved to see the back of them.

What happened next took them all by surprise, including Alex. The door burst open, and two men suddenly appeared in the doorway. *Police?* wondered Alex. He could not have been further from the truth. These two were holding small weapons, yet they were not revolvers. Each fired at the two Scottish criminals. There was no explosive sound from the weapons, more like the whoosh of compressed air. A small dart appeared in the neck of each of the two targets and, with looks of surprise, they collapsed to the floor in obvious pain and struggling to breathe.

The two men, seemingly unconcerned, retrieved the darts from their victims' necks, placing them into small containers, which they pocketed. Next, they rifled through the pockets of the men on the floor, removing any money, credit cards and even driving licences. It was obvious to Alex that any identifying documents were being deliberately removed. But why?

Masseud, meanwhile, was frozen to the spot, finding it difficult to comprehend what was happening in front of his eyes.

One of the men approached the terrified shopkeeper. "You have seen nothing, understood?"

Masseud nodded his head vigorously. "I see nothing at all." A forced smile appeared on the terrified shopkeeper's face.

"You won't be troubled by these guys anymore."

Masseud had a feeling that this was no cause for celebration and nervously asked, "Who are you? Why did…?" He looked down at the prone figures on the floor.

"We will take good care of you from now on. How much did you pay these guys?"

"A hundred and fifty every week."

The man almost dismissively said, "Is that all? From now on, you will pay two hundred and fifty every week. Cost-of-living increase, okay?"

Meekly, Masseud replied, "I don't earn much from this place. Are you trying to put me out of business?"

"No, not at all, my friend. We are here to look after you, and we know you can afford it, especially from the dodgy spirits you sell." Although these men were smaller than the two Glaswegians, they appeared to be far more sinister and worrying to the Asian man. It had not been difficult for Alex to detect an Italian accent in the man's words, and he now understood. This must be the connection.

"It seems I have no choice." Masseud worried about his and his family's future. He was married with three children, and on many occasions, his wife had begged him to find another, less precarious occupation. Faced with attacks by petty criminals and extortion by the crime syndicates, he had also thought of closing his business, perhaps becoming a postman or delivery-van driver.

He may have to reconsider his options again if the demands made it impossible for him to earn a decent living from his store.

"I'll let you off this week, thanks to the money I found on him." He pointed to the prone figure of the bigger of the two unconscious men.

"What about those two? Are you going to leave their bodies here?"

The man smiled. "Oh, they're not dead yet. Go to the other room and give us ten minutes. When you come out again we will all have gone." As if with an afterthought, he added, "Just do not tell anyone of what you have seen today, or you will live to regret it. We will return next week, okay?"

Masseud gave a little nod, a sad defeated expression overpowering his normally impassive features. As instructed, he opened the door to the room behind the shop and quickly disappeared, pulling the door shut tightly behind him.

As soon as he had left the room, the two intruders acted without hesitation. Each pulled a hypodermic syringe out of their pockets and skilfully injected the contents into a vein in the arms of the two men. One of the figures on the floor began to moan and attempted to lift his head. Gradually, the sedation began to ease, and both figures sat up, looking glassy-eyed, unaware of what was happening to them. The two intruders helped them to their feet.

Alex watched in horrified fascination. Was this an elaborate set-up? If that was the case, why take the money and documents from their pockets? Slowly, he realised that the Glaswegians had vacant glassy looks on their faces. It was a strange sight, seeing the intruders assisting the more heavily built Scottish men walking like zombies out of the shop. Not wanting to lose them, Alex moved to follow the four men, but to his annoyance and frustration, the vision melted away into nothing, and he returned to normal sleep back in his own bed.

Chapter Twenty-Nine

EVEN THOUGH ALEX was unable to continue with his vision, the incident at the shop continued. Tom and Barry McTaggart had a tough reputation in this part of London, especially for their strong-arm tactics in their protection racket, but in their present subdued state, they were unrecognisable as the same two men. Their captors led them towards a car parked nearby. Obediently, they took a seat in the back of the Vauxhall, the two Italians taking the front seats.

The driver wasted no time, and after turning on the ignition, he put his foot hard on the accelerator, in a hurry to escape the area. The car sped off in the direction of the North Circular Road at South Woodford, heading towards the M11, which continued northwards towards Cambridge.

The front passenger kept turning to look at the two guys in the back but was satisfied that the drugs they had used were powerful enough to stop them from becoming a problem. Had they become difficult, he had a spray which, if directed towards their faces, would have been inhaled, deepening their drugged state.

They drove about eight miles on the motorway and, making certain they were not in an area covered by cameras, pulled onto the hard shoulder.

The driver put on his hazard lights and stayed there while his partner climbed out and opened the rear-nearside door. "Come on, you two. It's time to go for a little walk."

Again obediently and without argument, they left the car, looking quite confused as the traffic sped past, many headlights illuminating the area.

Once he was satisfied that he had done his job correctly, the Italian slammed the door shut and hurriedly took his seat in the front. Even before he had chance to fasten his seat belt fully, the driver put his foot down hard on the accelerator, and they sped off towards the next junction, from where they could return to London and dump the stolen Vauxhall. No forensic evidence would be left, as the car would be torched, allowing the two Italians to escape.

Meanwhile, the two abandoned men, still drugged and confused, cowered on the hard shoulder watching almost spellbound as cars and heavy vehicles thundered past with monotonous regularity. Gradually, they began to wander somewhat aimlessly onto the traffic lanes, seemingly oblivious to the danger.

The brakes on the forty-four-ton articulated truck were well maintained and efficient but still did not manage to stop the huge vehicle in time to avoid a disastrous collision with the men. The impact crushed many bones and sent their bodies flying high like spinning toys into the other lanes, where they were hit many times by several other fast-moving vehicles. By the time the police and emergency services had arrived to discover a multiple pile-up, the bodies of the two Scottish men were broken, battered and completely unrecognisable. The small shop owners who had been paying for protection would, from now on, have new Italian protectors.

Chapter Thirty

WHEN ALEX WOKE up, it was ten past midnight. Jen was sleeping, her gentle, rhythmic breathing comforting to the still-sleepy Alex. He remembered his vision and went through it several times in his mind in the hope of remembering all the details. While doing this, he fell asleep again, cuddling up close to Jen, and it was after two o'clock before he awoke fully.

Excitedly, he recounted his latest vision to Jen, who listened, fascinated.

"Your previous visions covered drug distribution by the 'Ndrangheta, but this seems to be about their protection rackets. I wonder what the Scottish guys were injected with."

Alex had been thinking about this. "It was the way he said that they were 'not dead yet'. So either the drug would eventually kill them or they would be killed in some other way when the drugs wore off."

Jen agreed. "I wonder if it is the injection that eventually kills them. If it was a stimulant just to bring them around, they would have been pretty angry, but you said that they went 'like zombies' with the Italians. Perhaps something which attacks the nervous system."

What she had said made good sense, and Alex agreed with her, but the big question was where was the shop and, more importantly, the two Scottish guys?

As soon as he thought Adrian would be in his office, Alex phoned and detailed his latest vision. It was frustrating that his vision had not given enough information to locate the shop, but Adrian said he would keep a check for any information that may link the incidents.

It took three hours and a great deal of searching before Adrian phoned back. "Alex! I think I've found a news item related to your latest vision." Alex listened with interest. "I checked for anything that happened in the London area early in the evening yesterday. There was quite a big incident on the M11 at seven twenty-five. There was a multiple pile-up, and fortunately, there were only minor injuries amongst the people within the cars."

"So what's the connection?"

"I'm coming to that! There were the bodies of two men who appeared to have been wandering on the motorway. The driver of a heavy artic saw them, but it was too late to stop. He's in shock and finding it difficult to get the images of the men out of his mind. He distinctly remembers that the men looked lost and puzzled as they stared at him."

"That must be what the two Italians planned for these guys! Was there any identification?"

"Not a thing! Which fits what you saw. The two guys were quite big, probably about six feet tall, and well-built. Can you remember what they were wearing?"

Alex thought back. "I'm pretty certain they were wearing long, dark-grey coats. I remember how alike they looked and dressed."

There was excitement in Adrian's voice. "That matches what the police report stated. I think these are the Scottish guys."

"It would be interesting to know what the post-mortem finds in their bodies. The chemicals must have been quite powerful."

Adrian agreed. "I'll keep a check on the PM results. These Italians seem quite resourceful with their extortion rackets."

"Dangerously so," Alex said, part in admiration yet so revolted by their actions. "How about mugshots of these guys to show around likely areas of London?"

Adrian gave an audible sigh. "I wish that were possible. There's not much left to recognise after a forty-four-ton truck and several fast-moving vehicles collided with and ran over them. I don't think the artic driver would be able to describe them either. The only chance would be from an artist's impression from your description."

"I'll try, but it's not going to be easy when you consider how little I saw of them and the fact that it all happened in a vision."

Adrian knew this but hoped Alex's military training would assist in the process of accurately describing their features. "Presumably, these two guys also had family, so sooner or later somebody is going to miss them."

Alex felt that this would probably be more fruitful than his descriptions, however, Adrian said he would organise an artist to visit Alex that same day.

"I didn't get much of a look at the second man. I was mainly concentrating on what the main guy was doing, but my guess is that they were related."

"That's all right. We'll just concentrate on him. Just keep me updated on anything new."

Their discussion ended, the call was disconnected, and for a while, Alex and Jen carried out domestic chores as if they were a married couple, which, to Alex's mind, was quite comforting.

"I don't know what I would do without you, Jen. Everything between us feels great."

She smiled again with that flirty yet coy look. "Same here. I never thought I could fall in love with anybody again after what happened to Jason, but I'm so happy with you. And on top of everything else, you've twice saved me from certain death."

As they held each other close, Jen noticed a look of pain on Alex's face. "What's wrong, sweetheart?"

He gave her a tender kiss, saying, "Nothing to worry about. Just one of these damn headaches."

Alex did not know if it was the strain of these increasingly disturbing visions, but he was suffering daily headaches, and Jen was concerned about him. She insisted that he take pain relief.

Reluctantly, he agreed and had just taken a couple of paracetamol when the artist arrived.

Samantha Parkinson was an attractive twenty-six-year-old with long, black hair that almost reached her nicely shaped backside. To Alex's mind, she actually did look the 'arty' type. Taking the seat offered to her, she removed a sketchpad from her bag and arranged several pencils ready for use. "Now, Mr. McCloud, can you briefly describe the man you saw?" Adrian had decided it would be better to avoid telling the artist how Alex had seen the man in his vision, as the fewer who knew the real situation the better.

"I'm guessing he was in his late forties about six feet tall, perhaps even as much as six feet two. Weight would be about seventeen or eighteen stone. I would definitely describe him as overweight. Hair colour is black, quite thick yet shortly trimmed. His ears are quite large, and his face is a bit fleshy. Heavy-jowled, quite large mouth and nose."

"Good description." She reflected on his words for a moment and asked, "Could you say what colour his eyes are? Or any distinguishing marks?"

Alex thought before answering. "I couldn't really tell what colour his eyes were, but my impression was dark. Probably black, but that's a guess. As for marks, I think he had a small scar above his right eye. Oh, and I think his nose may have been broken at some time."

Samantha smiled. "That's quite a useful detail." She wasted no time and began sketching. Within minutes, she had a rough outline. "How does this look?" She turned the pad to face Alex, who studied it carefully.

"Close. Perhaps a little less depth in the forehead, and the jowls need to be a bit heavier." Alex laughed. "He gave me the impression of a bit like a slobbering bulldog."

Samantha quickly modified the sketch and again showed it to Alex.

"That's pretty damn close. Yes, I think you've perfectly captured the image in my mind." He admired Samantha's talent as an artist, something he had never been particularly good at when at school.

"Excellent! I'll take this to Mr. King."

Jen offered Samantha coffee, which she gratefully accepted, and for about thirty minutes, they chatted, bringing an air of normality to Alex's strange new life.

Shortly after Samantha had left, Alex's mobile rang. Jen had to admit that she did not like his ringtone, as it sounded too sinister. The start of Gustav Holtz's 'Mars' from the Planet Suite was certainly striking and for Alex a suitable tone noticeably different from all the rest. He did not get many calls but was pleased to see the caller display indicated his sister Lucy.

"Hi, sis! How's university?"

"Great! The first week or two was difficult, but now I'm getting quite used to university life and I've made lots of new friends. Anyway, I phoned to see how you are. I was going to phone tonight but had an early finish in lectures so thought I'd give you a call. How are you coping?"

Alex smiled to himself, as he could hear the concern in his sister's voice. How he wished he could tell her the truth. "Absolutely fine. Elsa my guide dog is terrific and helps me to be quite mobile. On top of that, the army is keeping me really busy."

Jen, realising that Alex would not want her presence to be known, had kept quiet but at that instant found it impossible to restrain a loud sneeze.

Lucy heard it and somehow knew it was not from her brother. "Sorry, Alex. I didn't realise you had company."

"It's all right. A business colleague has called to discuss some work with me," he lied, hoping his words would be accepted.

Lucy, however, was a perceptive young woman and realised that the sneeze had sounded distinctly feminine if that was possible. She smiled, convinced her older brother had a girlfriend living with him. In truth, she was relieved, knowing how depressed he had been following the breaking off of their engagement by Helen.

She thought about congratulating him but instead told him about the medical course she was studying at Cambridge University. "I'm managing not to vomit when being shown gory bits of the body specimens. I'm looking forward to finishing for the Christmas break when I can stay at home for a couple of weeks and hopefully see you there. Anyway, I'd better go and let you get on with your 'work.'"

As she ended the call, Lucy was wondering whether she should tell Amelia and her mother about Alex's so-called business colleague. There had been a time when she could extort money from her older brother just to keep quiet about his indiscretions. In the event, she decided to keep this information to herself and perhaps share it with her university friends instead.

As Alex disconnected the call, Jen said, "Sorry about the sneeze, sweetheart. I just couldn't stop myself. Do you think she realised I was here?"

"I don't know, but don't worry about it, love. If I know my sister, she won't say anything anyway. To be quite honest, I wish I could come clean about everything, but I won't."

Chapter Thirty-One

December 2011

IT WAS ABOUT four in the afternoon before Alex and Jen could settle down for bed after their somewhat unusual day, especially the call from Lucy. When they awoke around two in the morning, Alex realised that he had not only slept a comfortable dreamless sleep but that he had also not experienced another vision. On top of this, his headache was gone. He felt good but wondered if the visions had ended, and if so, why, and would they ever come back?

Later on that morning, he received a call from Adrian. The identity sketch had been shown on the television news the previous evening, and to Adrian's relief, there had been a response. "Sixty-eight-year-old Margaret McTaggart, a Scottish woman living in London, saw the news and realised that the two dead men were her sons, forty-four-year-old Tom and forty-one-year-old Barry. This morning, she identified the bodies mainly from their clothing, having been spared from seeing their battered and crushed faces. She's in shock from their deaths but expected them to be caught either by the police or deadly competition at some time in their lives." Adrian sounded pleased that thanks to Alex's vision the identities of the two Scottish men had been revealed without undue delay.

"What do the police know about the McTaggart brothers?"

Adrian was enthusiastic about the identification. "They have a long track record for violence and extortion in London and have been in prison three times over the past fifteen years. They were without doubt the guys from your vision, and the world is probably better off without them."

Alex was surprised by Adrian's insensitive comment. "I don't know about you, but I would not want to die in that way, and I wouldn't wish that on anybody else." He paused, thinking of what it must be like to be killed in the horrific road accident described so vividly by Adrian. "And that still doesn't get us near the Italian family."

"No, perhaps not," admitted Adrian. "But as long as you're still having visions, the chances of identifying where they are hiding are improving. Anything in your sleep yesterday?"

How he wished he had more revelations, but Alex had to admit that he had no new visions. He would let Adrian know as soon as he had any valuable information.

FOLLOWING ANOTHER INTENSIVE Italian language lesson, Alex and Jen did not get to bed until almost seven p.m., and within a few minutes, Alex was fast asleep. Jen was still awake, and after about another fifteen minutes, she felt Alex's body go quite rigid. Unfortunately for her, there was only one part of his body she liked to feel stiffening, and that part was quite relaxed. She realised he was having another vision but knew that with it there would be a painful headache for the man who now meant so very much to her.

For Alex, the scene before him appeared to be different from what he had seen in his other visions. He could not decide if the female he was now watching was a girl or a woman. She was sitting on the edge of a bed and was quite good-looking with long, black hair framing delicate, typically Eastern European features. She seemed almost anorexic with her unusually thin limbs. The black dress did not leave much to the imagination, but the main impression was one of abject terror. She had been crying and kept dabbing her eyes with a tissue, an anguished expression spoiling her naturally beautiful features.

She stood, shakily walked towards a window and gently pulled the curtains back. It looked like any other bedroom window except that the lower part had been boarded up, leaving a narrow strip of glazing only visible at a high level. Standing on her toes, she could just about see out of what was left of the window and gazed longingly through it. Alex stood beside her, following her gaze. It was dark outside, but lights from various shops illuminated the scene. Alex was much taller than the girl, which he had now decided she must be. Probably only about fifteen or sixteen years old. With the advantage of his height, he could clearly see the group of shops on the opposite side of the road. Then it suddenly hit him! He recognised the location. Checking the order of the five or six shops visible, he knew exactly where he was. On the days he had been shopping at the supermarket, he had passed along this very road and had, on occasion, left his eyes working to see what lay along this route.

Tearing her gaze from the window, the girl with sudden resolve walked to the door. Opening it slightly, she listened for any sounds and then crept slowly and purposefully onto a landing and began to descend the stairs. Trying to keep her in his sight, Alex moved to follow her; as he had discovered from previous visions, it was not easy.

The girl had almost reached the bottom of the stairs when even with her slight build the step creaked. A door flew open, and a man emerged, looking with stern features up at the terrified girl. She turned and tried to clamber her way back to the bedroom. The man was quick and grabbed her roughly as she tried to escape. He pushed her back up the last few steps, and once inside the room, he slapped her hard across the face, the force of his blow sending her reeling backwards onto the bed.

"What the fuck are you trying to do? Why do you want to escape? Do we not look after you?"

Alex's impotent frustration boiled over. "Leave her alone, you bastard!" His shouts, of course, went unheard. His fists directed towards this brute simply met no resistance as they punched the air.

Tears ran down the girl's face. She held her hand against the area where she had been hit so violently. "Please let me go back to Romania to my family. You promised me work when I came here."

Roughly, he dragged her to a standing position and shouted, "Go and clean yourself. If you're a good girl, you can eat well after tonight's clients.

Alex heard the emphasis on the word 'clients' and wondered just how many perverts were going to screw the unfortunate girl this evening.

With a resigned look, she walked, defeated, into the tiny bathroom. She rinsed her face with cool water and then dried it gently. The expression in the mirror was that of a broken person. The man had returned downstairs, secure in the knowledge that his sex slave would not attempt to escape again.

The girl used the toilet, ran a comb through her long, silky hair and then returned to the sparsely furnished bedroom. The bed, bedside cabinet and a couple of flimsy chairs were the only furnishings. Then Alex noticed a clock radio on the bedside cabinet. He peered at the display and saw it was seven twenty-five. At least he had a positive time for this particular vision.

Within a few minutes, the man came back up the stairs, followed by another person. This man was about five feet nine and noticeably overweight. He was sweating in spite of the cold night, and Alex knew that it was the excitement and anticipation of sexual relief with this underage girl. It made Alex so angry he felt as though he was going to explode from the sheer frustration of not being able to intervene.

The girl's pimp spoke excitedly, "This is Jacqueline. She will look after you." He then left the room, closing the door after him.

Alex was trying to determine if the pimp was Italian and thinking of how he had spoken to the girl rather than the client, he felt certain of the connection. This was yet another branch of the 'Ndrangheta. Drugs, protection and now forced prostitution. There had to be some way of stopping them.

Staring at Jacqueline with obvious lust in his eyes, the client took off his jacket, put it on the back of a chair and unfastened his trousers. He almost seemed embarrassed as he removed the rest of his clothes. The girl watched the man with dread in her eyes. She looked at his erection and knew that she was soon going to have that awful thing inside her.

Nervously, the man said, "Come on, er, Jacqueline. Take your clothes off." With a half-smile, he looked the kind of guy who could soon turn nasty and perhaps even violent.

She stared at him with a pleading look in her tear-filled eyes. With sudden, resignation she unzipped her dress and let it drop to the floor. She wore no bra, just a brief pair of panties, which she dropped on the top of her dress. Her breasts were quite small, adding to the skeletal appearance of this young girl.

She climbed onto the bed and lay ready with her legs apart.

The client looked wide-eyed at her youthful body and climbed on top of her, not even bothering to use a condom. The pain was etched on her face as he pushed himself inside her. As he began to move, Alex felt sick and wondered why he had to watch this act of depravity. As if in response to his revulsion, the scene faded and he returned once again to a restful sleep.

Chapter Thirty-Two

It was several hours before Alex awoke, and as before, Jen was still fast asleep. Snuggling up to her warm body, he tried to avoid disturbing her.

When she did eventually wake up, he quickly related his latest vision to her. She was equally revolted. "Are you certain that you know where this place is?"

"I think so. As soon as I can phone Adrian, I'll see what we can do for that poor girl."

Later that morning, Adrian listened with interest as Alex recounted his latest vision. "Can you pick me up so we can check the address of this place?"

"Are you certain you can recognise the road?" asked a sceptical Adrian.

"I think so. It reminds me of the shops on my journey to the supermarket."

Within an hour, a smart vehicle with blacked-out windows pulled up outside Alex's apartment. Jen had wanted to join them, but Alex was worried that she may be seen by members of the 'Ndrangheta and insisted she remain at the apartment for her own safety. Reluctantly, she agreed to stay with Elsa, giving Alex a hug of encouragement before he left.

As Adrian drove along the route he had described, Alex peered through the windows at the shops. "Yes! It looks different than it did at night with all the lights on, but I'm certain these are the shops I saw through the bedroom window. There's a coffee bar, fast-food place and a betting shop all next to each other."

216

They pulled up to the kerb in front of the shops, allowing Alex to look across the road. He scanned the first floor until he spotted the partially boarded-up windows. "There! That must be the window I was looking through!" He pointed it out to Adrian, who had a register of the various properties along the road listed on his notebook computer.

"That belongs to number two hundred and seventeen." He laughed. "It's supposed to be the premises and showroom for a taxidermist.

Alex laughed too. "I'm certain there's a great deal of stuffing going on in there but not of dead animals! From what I saw, that poor girl is a sex slave."

"You'd be surprised how many sex slaves there are in the UK." Adrian seemed quite knowledgeable on the subject. "Gangs have been bringing in young girls for many years, usually from Eastern Europe. They con the girls, sometimes pretending to be their boyfriends, and once they're here, their passports are taken away and they're locked in seedy rooms and forced to do what their masters tell them. In many cases, the girls are doped full of heroin to make them more submissive."

Alex shuddered at the thought that Jacqueline was only one of many and wished he could do something to help these unfortunate victims. "Well, it would be a start if we could help some of them."

"We can't even help here until we have a search warrant." Adrian made a call on his mobile, requesting a warrant to be issued immediately. "We're a bit conspicuous sitting here. I think we'll drive around for a while." He gave instructions to the driver, who pulled into the traffic and drove away from the area.

Within thirty minutes, a motorcyclist drew alongside their car. Both vehicles parked up as soon as they could considering the heavy traffic. The cyclist dismounted and took an envelope out of his carrier. Adrian pressed the control to lower the passenger window and was handed the envelope by the cyclist. No pleasantries exchanged, the cyclist returned to his machine; seconds later, he had disappeared back into the heavy traffic.

Adrian opened the envelope and carefully read the official-looking document. "Good! This is what we need to get into that brothel without breaking any laws." He gave instructions to the driver, who skilfully manoeuvred the large vehicle, returning to the address where hopefully Jacqueline was still imprisoned. Adrian turned to face Alex. "I know this may seem hard, but I want you to stay in this car while we go in."

Alex opened his mouth to protest but, seeing the serious expression on Adrian's face, changed his mind and said quietly, "If I must. But how will you identify Jacqueline?"

"I don't want to take the chance that any of these criminals see you, as it'll put you in even more danger." Adrian touched a screen in the car, and immediately, an image of Alex appeared on the display. "Don't worry. What you're seeing is the feed from a camera in my jacket. I'll keep in voice contact with you so you can tell me if you spot this Jacqueline on the screen."

"I'm impressed," Alex admitted. "Very high-tech."

"It would have been even more helpful if we could have monitored your visions in a similar way, but that's probably asking a bit too much." Adrian turned around and looked through the rear window. Alex followed his gaze and could see that another similarly blacked-out car had pulled up behind them. Adrian pulled open the door and stepped out. He approached the other car, and a moment later four, men piled out, following Adrian.

He led the way to the door and tried it, but as expected, it was locked. One of the men produced a silenced gun and shot at the lock. The men rushed through the opening with Adrian following. Alex turned to look at the screen in the car and could see the mass of men quickly forcing their way through the building, weapons at the ready. There was a great deal of shouting and confusion, with doors crashing open revealing surprised men. One scene reminded

Alex of his vision as he saw a naked man being given a blow-job by a young woman. As the two realised what was happening, the half-naked girl, obviously frightened by the intrusion, bit hard on the man's penis. He let out a howl of pain, blood spurting from his organ, and was about to slap the girl when Adrian pointed a gun at him.

"I wouldn't do that if I were you! Get your clothes on!"

The man scowled and did as directed, hastily stuffing tissues into his underwear to soak up the blood.

Alex looked at the girl. It wasn't Jacqueline although she did appear to be of similar age and ethnicity.

"That's not her, Adrian. It looks as though she's not on her own."

Adrian left one of the men to keep control in this room while he moved to another. It looked at first as though there was nobody at all in this room, but when Adrian pushed the bathroom door wide open, Alex saw a terrified Jacqueline trying to get as far away as possible, almost as though she could somehow squeeze her emaciated frame through the solid wall.

"That's her!" he said, relieved they had not caught her in the middle of providing sexual favours for a customer.

Picking up the prompt, Adrian asked, "Are you Jacqueline?"

Still terrified, she stared at the gun in his hand and nodded, tears streaming down her face. She must thought this was the end of her short life, killed by an unknown assassin.

Now certain that there were no men in the room, Adrian put the gun away. "Don't worry, Jacqueline. You're safe now. Have you a coat? It's quite cold outside."

The girl's face lightened. "You are here to help me? No more sex?"

"No more sex." Adrian smiled down at what looked to be nothing more than a child. "How old are you, Jacqueline?"

"Fourteen two weeks ago." The fact her birthday was so recent understandably did not give her cause for any happiness. Her large sad eyes said it all.

"What about the other girl? How old is your friend?"

"The same as me. Fourteen."

Adrian shook his head in disbelief that anybody could take advantage of girls so young. "The men who controlled you are under arrest. You are now free." Alex was quite impressed by Adrian's calmness. "Come on. Bring your possessions."

Jacqueline moved towards Adrian and hugged him. "Thank you. I dreamed of this day for so long."

"It's over now, but I'm not the person you should thank. You will meet him in a few minutes. Come on now."

With a renewed energy, she retrieved a small bag from under the bed, opened the zipper and pulled out a coat. It was only thin and more like a cheap plastic raincoat, but it was all she had. She put this on, picked up the bag and followed Adrian. At last, there was a hint of a smile on her young, proud face.

As they went downstairs, the guy with the damaged manhood was angrily demanding his money back and even some compensation for his injury. "What am I going to tell my wife when she sees teeth marks?" He sounded worried.

One of the Secret Service men lost his patience. "Listen, I don't give a fuck what you say to your wife, but the people here are under arrest, and if I were you, I wouldn't make a fuss, or we may just take you along as well."

Adrian interrupted. "The girl you were with is only fourteen. Having sex with an underage girl is a criminal offence, so we have enough against you to make an arrest. Quite honestly, I think you should have your dick cut off for what you've done. Would you like to explain that to your wife?"

That was enough for the middle-aged man, who hastily fastened his blood-spattered clothes as he left through the still-open doorway.

Through Adrian's camera, Alex could see another young girl and two handcuffed men. He recognised one of the men. "Adrian! The man with the short black hair is the one who slapped Jacqueline. I think he may be Italian."

Adrian turned to this man. "What's your name?"

He glowered at Adrian but refused to say anything.

"Suit yourself. We'll identify both of you, no matter how long it takes, so it makes no difference to me. You're both under arrest." Adrian read them their rights, and three intelligence officers took them out to their car. One officer remained, still checking for any other evidence. He took his time, making certain there were no concealed areas within the old building. Cupboards were searched thoroughly, and if there were any signs of loose floorboards, these were also investigated. Eventually satisfied that nothing had been overlooked, he carried a bag with the few items he had found and secured the outside door to prevent drunks and vagrants from taking over the building.

The two girls followed Adrian out of the place in which they had been imprisoned and into the cold December day. Some people, aware that there had been a raid on the building, were watching with a mixed curiosity. Thankfully, there was no press yet; all Adrian wanted to do was get these girls away from this place as quickly as possible. He opened the door of the car where Alex was waiting. "Please, have a seat, Jacqueline, and … ?"

The other girl spoke. "My name is Rosita. Are you certain we are really safe?"

"Absolutely. This is the man who helped. I would prefer not to reveal his name, but I can assure you that without his help, we would not be here now."

Alex felt quite embarrassed by Adrian's praise and spoke quietly. "I'm so pleased that we could help you both. How long have you been trapped in that place?"

The car was quite spacious, and the two girls simultaneously hugged Alex.

"It is hard to keep track of time, but I think it will be about eight months." It was Jacqueline who answered. "How did you know about us?"

Alex did not know how to respond. They would never believe him if he told them of his visions. Even he found it incredible that he had developed this ability since the disaster in Afghanistan.

Again, Adrian came to the rescue. "I'm sorry, girls. That information is classified, but I can guarantee that without this man's help, you could have been trapped in that hellhole for years."

Jacqueline wondered if there had been hidden cameras in their rooms, and if so, had this man been watching them perform all sorts of sex acts for their clients? Even if this was the case, she would not have been ashamed, as she felt she could trust him, and he would have been far more preferable to some of the weird creeps she had endured over the past months. Jacqueline felt strangely comforted by this tall, good-looking man.

She blushed at these intimate possibilities. In this though, she was not far from the truth, but she would never discover how Alex had learned of their activities.

Trying to take the pressure off him, Alex asked, "Were those men violent towards you both?"

This time, it was Rosita who answered. "Oh, yes. If we did not do what Barry and Phil said, they would hit us. We have both been raped many times by both of them." These thoughts brought fresh tears to her eyes. "I still cannot believe we are really free."

"Listen, girls. We're going to take you somewhere you can rest, clean yourselves up and have a good sleep. Then after that, help will be given to start the process of getting you back with your families. Please take a seat and fasten your belts." Adrian certainly sounded reassuring, and Alex hoped the nightmare was over for these two young Romanians. They followed his instructions, and very soon, the car was moving through the heavy traffic.

Jacqueline and Rosita leaned back, one on either side of Alex. No words were necessary. The fact that their ordeal was over was enough.

Jacqueline's thoughts returned to the poor area of Bucharest in Romania where she and her cousin Rosita, the only girls in a male-dominated family, had been born in 1997. The two girls had been very close for most of their lives and were equally determined to break out of their background of poverty and hunger. Both had learned to speak English, convinced that one day it would prove useful.

When the advert for junior secretarial staff based in London appeared in the local paper, it seemed like a dream come true to the girls. Together, they replied to the advert and were amazed to be invited for an interview. Even more surprising, they both passed the interviews and were told that transport to London and accommodation would be provided as part of the contract. Their parents were delighted and looked forward to the money their daughters would be able to send for family support. They were even given financial help to acquire their passports by the agency that supposedly was to provide their future employment.

They and six other teenage girls were transported by minibus over the mainland from Romania to France and from there by ferry to the United Kingdom. The level of excitement was high amongst all the girls, who had quite willingly handed over their passports to the two men, Barry and Phil, who had organised the journey.

It was only when they reached their final destination that the truth dawned on them. Their passports were withheld, they were locked in and forced to work as prostitutes. The secretarial work had been a ruse to get the girls into England, and the pimps found plenty of clients to earn them a profitable income.

Of course, the girls saw nothing of the financial benefits. These two men, who initially seemed friendly and caring, turned out to be sadistic beasts looking on the girls as their property just like domestic pets. Any sign of dissent was dealt with harshly, with violence against the girls being carried out in a way that would not leave any bruising to frighten off potential clients.

The other six girls had been 'sold' to other pimps while Jacqueline and Rosita were retained because of their exceptional looks by the two Italians.

After eight months of absolute hell, all the two girls wanted was to return home to their families.

Adrian had made a call requesting medical and social workers to be on hand to look after these two damaged teenage girls and had given directions to the driver.

Meanwhile, Alex was talking to Jacqueline and Rosita, being careful not to ask too many probing questions, as they would soon be asked the same questions by the professionals. "What are you both looking forward to?"

Without hesitation, they both replied, "A good meal!" Apparently, they had been given the minimum amount of food during their captivity. "I would really like a Big Mac with lots of fries."

"And lots of sticky-toffee pudding with thick fresh cream," added Rosita. Both girls looked as if they were in heaven at the mere thought of good nutritious food.

Alex laughed. "I'm sure you will get plenty to eat when we get you to a safe place. I'm not surprised by your choice of food. You're making me feel hungry for a Big Mac myself!"

He could almost see the girls salivating and noted that both were now laughing at his admission.

Rosita looked thoughtful and said, "I suppose I really don't mind what I eat as long as I can get some food inside me. We are so hungry."

Alex was in no doubt that these two girls, who resembled prisoners in Hitler's death camps, would soon improve with adequate supplies of good nutritious food.

Eventually, they arrived at the centre Adrian had chosen as the closest source of assistance. "Okay, girls, I'm afraid our friend here will not be able to accompany you." He was pointing to Alex. "I'll take you inside to introduce you to these people, who are going to look after you, and then I will leave you in their care."

Once again, they both hugged Alex, Jacqueline even giving Alex a kiss on his cheek. "Thank you so much, mystery man." The smiles on the faces of their faces made Alex feel very proud of what had been achieved today.

Alex laughed. "I will ask for a progress report on getting you both back to your families. Take care, girls."

Adrian escorted them into the care centre, and ten minutes later, he returned to the car.

"Right, Alex. I'll take you back to your apartment. It's been a good day's work."

Within thirty minutes, they had arrived back.

"You will keep me informed won't you, Adrian?"

"Of course. Don't worry. We'll do everything possible for those two young girls."

Jen and Elsa were equally pleased to see Alex. He was feeling quite hungry, and together, he and Jen prepared a meal while he explained what had happened as a result of his vision. At last, they had succeeded in foiling the 'Ndrangheta's crime syndicate at least in a small way.

Chapter Thirty-Three

December 2011

G IANNI WAS FURIOUS and in a foul mood when he heard of the arrest of two of the younger members of the family clan. "How the fuck did Brando and Carlino let themselves get caught? I thought they could handle themselves! I'll have to speak to the Capocrimine about this. Our line may have been compromised. Let everybody know that the security code needs re-scrambling." He threw the phone on the desk in disgust.

Events did not seem to be going their way recently. The failure to kill the CIA woman, the loss of forty kilos of cocaine, and now this. Gianni did not really believe in luck whether good or bad, but he was not used to losing three times in a row and fumed inwardly. He sat at his desk for a few minutes as if in deep contemplation. Finally, he rose and walked out of his room, along the corridor to the door at the far end.

He knocked and a voice said simply, "Enter." It was the voice of an older man and someone of obvious authority.

Gianni pushed the door open and walked into the luxuriously furnished room.

"Take a seat, Gianni. You look troubled." Gian Battista was in his late seventies and still had a good head of hair, although the black had now turned a silvery-grey. His black eyes were as sharp as those of a much younger man, but the lines on his weathered face belied this.

"We have a problem, Papà. Carlino and Brando have been arrested at one of our East End brothels."

"So what went wrong?"

Gianni shrugged. "They were raided late morning, but from what I understand it wasn't a police raid. Brando seemed to think they were Secret Service officers."

Gian Battista raised his eyebrows in surprise. "Do you think we have a leak?"

Gianni pondered on this question and then shook his head. "I don't think so. If the Secret Service knew of this place, we'd have been raided before now. Must be because of some recent intelligence."

"I hope you're correct. There is a great deal at stake here, and I have no intention of giving up without a fight. The location of this place must remain a secret." Gian Battista had not reached the fine age of seventy-eight only to be caught by the authorities and imprisoned, as had happened to many members of his family two years earlier. He would fight with his life should there be any threat on his empire, of that Gianni was certain.

"Is it worth putting a bit of pressure on our friends in high places?"

The old man frowned. "I need to think about that. It would be a last resort, but if I feel it necessary then it will be done. Just make sure Brando and Carlino are comfortable while in custody. When it comes to the court case, the barristers on our payroll should manage to get them a lighter sentence. In the meantime, remind everyone to stay alert and do nothing to compromise the family in any way."

Gianni took heed of his father's words. He had seen how, over many years, his father had ruthlessly crushed any opposition. He was a formidable opponent and deserved the title of 'Capocrimine'.

After a thoughtful silence, Gian Battista added, "Of course, if something were to stop them ever getting to court, that could solve many problems."

A sly smile appeared on Gianni's face. "I'll see what can be done."

Chapter Thirty-Four

December 2011

B Y NOW, ALEX had a good working knowledge of Italian and, eager to master it, asked Jen to converse with him in this beautifully expressive language. She was amazed at how proficient he had become in such a short time but had accepted that his brain had switched into super-absorbency mode. Alex was determined that should he have any more visions involving the 'Ndrangheta, he would be capable of fully understanding what they were saying.

He was also concentrating on getting his body in shape and had had a running machine delivered a few weeks earlier. His bedroom was quite large, and the machine was permanently positioned and ready to use in one corner.

Jen was also feeling the effects of insufficient exercise and was as committed as Alex to keeping fit. As part of their morning routine, both spent at least twenty minutes each on the machine, by which time the sweat was pouring off them, despite running in lightweight shorts and T-shirts—a source of fascination as each watched the other work out. Jen could have watched for hours the ripple of strong muscles beneath Alex's gleaming skim, while Alex admired Jen's superb physique, her long legs topped by firm butt cheeks that swayed from side to side as she kept up a fast pace. The shower that followed was refreshing and stimulating, both succumbing to intense sexual activity within the confines of the shower cubicle.

Jen felt very comfortable living with Alex and was always singing. Her current favourite was Kelly Clarkson's 'Stronger', which she sang at every opportunity but particularly when preparing food in the kitchen. Alex always enjoyed listening to her yet did not join in, as he admitted that his voice did not lend itself to singing.

By late morning, Alex was wondering about the two Romanian girls and phoned Adrian for a progress report. Both had been in contact with their parents, who had given up all hope of ever seeing their daughters alive again after such a long time without hearing any word from them. Naturally, they were delighted to hear from the girls and were looking forward to having them home again. This would not happen until they had rested properly, eaten well and given statements about their time in captivity, but they would, hopefully, be home in time for Christmas.

"As for Barry Jones and Phil Turner," Adrian continued, "the IDs they were carrying proved to be fakes, and they're saying nothing." This did not surprise Alex. "One called his solicitor, who told them to say nothing. Since we're pretty certain they're Italian, we've sent their photos and fingerprints to the authorities in Rome. I'm sure they'll have no trouble identifying them and links to the other members of their families. By the way, one of the men was carrying a mobile that was not your average phone."

"Oh? How was it different?" Alex asked.

"It wasn't connected to any of the usual network providers. Our analysts are taking it apart to find out more, but it seems that members of the 'Ndrangheta have their own private network with very deep encryption to avoid detection."

"They do seem very well organised and resourceful," Alex agreed. Soon after, Adrian ended the call, leaving Alex to relay the news to Jen.

She smiled broadly. "I'm very proud of you. If it wasn't for your visions, those poor girls would still be sex slaves. On which note…" She checked her watch: it was nearly two-thirty. "I think it's about time for sleep and another vision."

"Now that you've said it, I probably won't have one today," laughed Alex. Ever hopeful, within twenty minutes, he was fast asleep.

This time, he was lucky, as a new vision started quite quickly. A man whom Alex recognised as one of the two on the canal boat and in the delivery van walked out of a room and into a wide corridor. He was wearing slacks and vest and had a towel around his neck. The corridor was long and had many doors with no clues as to what was behind them. At last, the man arrived at one at the far end and pushed it open. Alex followed as closely as he could and was astonished to see a room about five by eight metres full of running machines, exercise bikes, rowing machines and many weight-training machines. The set-up made his exercise equipment seem quite tame by comparison.

There were two men in the room already, one who looked vaguely familiar on an exercise bike, the other on a rowing machine. Alex recognised the second guy straight away. It was the other one from the canal boat. Both men seemed quite pleased to see the new arrival, who took a second rowing machine. Now that Alex understood Italian, he realised the new guy was challenging the other to a race. The electronic data displays on both machines were initialised, and after a short countdown, both men started rowing vigorously. They were quite fit and of similar strength, and Alex watched with interest to see who would come out on top.

The guy on the exercise bike had stopped pedalling and was also watching this challenge with a slight smile on his lips. Alex was trying to think where he could have seen the man, and then it came to him. That day in Woolpit where they had discovered the cannabis farm: he was sure this was the man he had spotted entering the house. *So the cannabis farm was run by this family of Italian criminals.*

An electronic noise was heard, and the two stopped rowing instantly. The third man dismounted from the bike and inspected the displays. The guy whom Alex had followed had rowed twenty-seven more metres in the set time and was declared the winner. Both men were panting from their exertion, but their competitiveness persisted. Their next challenge was on wall-mounted lateral pull-down machines.

"Sam! Have you a minute?" the man from the exercise bike shouted in perfect English.

From his spot by the door, Alex looked around, wondering where this 'Sam' could be. Suddenly, he was enveloped in a huge, dark mass as though someone had turned off the lights. Startled, it took him a few seconds to realise that Sam had walked straight through him. Alex stared in astonishment at the ebony-skinned man, easily the tallest man he'd ever seen at around seven feet in height, making Alex feel quite small by comparison. The man strode confidently over to the lateral bar machines and began to adjust the tension to calibrate them to provide equal resistance.

"Thanks, Sam."

"No problem, Franco." The voice was as big as the man with a deep, resonant baritone quality.

Adjustments made, the two men pulled on their bars, both managing without too much effort to bring them down to the same level. They released their grip, and Sam once again adjusted the weights. This time, both men strained, grunting and grimacing with the effort to pull the bars down past their faces. Muscles bulged and sweat poured down their backs. All the while, Sam watched closely until, seeing one bar move slightly more than that of his opponent, declared a winner.

"You're still the champion, Franco, but your brother is improving and may soon overtake you." Sam's voice boomed around the room, the hard walls adding to the resonance.

Belatedly, it occurred to Alex that while this friendly competition had been going on, he could have been looking around the place and finding out as much as he could while his vision lasted.

Cursing himself for his stupidity, he moved back into the corridor, chose a door on the opposite wall and walked straight through the wall adjacent to it. He was shocked to find himself sharing a shower cubicle with a young woman. It was strange not feeling the water cascade down over his body, and if he had been solid, their bodies would have been touching. It was an erotic thought that made Alex smile, but he pushed it aside to take in features by which he could later identify her.

She could well have been Italian with her long, black hair and Mediterranean complexion. This was confirmed when she started singing along to the music playing in the cubicle. Alex recognised it as 'Moves Like Jagger' by Maroon Five and Christina Aguilera, and although the woman's words were plainly English, her accent could only have originated from Italy.

He tried to assess her age, and after studying her small, firm breasts, slim waist and nicely rounded buttocks perhaps a little too closely, estimated she was around thirty. Alex, of course, was equally naked but had the advantage that the woman could neither see nor feel his presence, not even his arousal at this stunning vision.

If only he knew her name, it could be another clue to the identity of this large group of Italians, but with nobody else in the room, he was unlikely to find out.

Alex was about to drag himself away from this location in search of other useful information, but to his annoyance, the vision quickly faded. What determined where, when and for how long these visions lasted?

Chapter Thirty-Five

JEN FOUND ALEX'S latest vision intriguing and after hearing that he had shared a shower with a beautiful unknown woman wondered if he was teasing her. Eventually, she believed him, and together they tried to analyse the vision. Alex had not seen any windows in the few areas he had encountered and thought the family might be living underground. But where? It seemed likely it would be in London, but that did not help in any way. In a city of over eight million people, it would be the proverbial needle in a haystack.

Jen agreed. "If it is an underground base, how do they get there? It would need to be somewhere members of the public and security services are not aware of."

"Perhaps Adrian will have some ideas," said Alex. "And at least we know the names of two of them—Franco and that huge guy Sam. I wouldn't fancy my chances against him. Anyway, I'd better update Adrian."

When the intelligence officer heard of the shower incident, he laughed and said, "You lucky devil. I wouldn't mind a vision like that!"

Alex wanted to say, *"Get a life, Adrian! Find yourself a good woman and stop being so frustrated!"* but he thought better of it.

"These Italians obviously like to keep fit, judging by all the equipment in that fitness room. If we're lucky enough to find their location, we'll have to be careful with that huge guy! He's obviously their muscle and there to stop people like us invading their territory."

Adrian agreed. "Keep on having your visions, Alex."

Alex was about to disconnect when he had a thought. "Those two criminals who were found in the Thames—didn't you say they'd been strangled by somebody who had great strength?"

"Yes, I did," Adrian confirmed. "And from what you've said, it certainly sounds like this guy Sam could be our culprit. Well thought, Alex!"

Chapter Thirty-Six

December 2011

"IT MAY BE a good idea for you two to take a break from the drug runs."

Gianni was quite relaxed as he spoke to Franco and Georgio in his comfortable lounge area. His sons, however, were not relaxed. When their father had called them in for 'a little chat', they knew that significant changes were about to be made. Changes that would have a dramatic effect on their immediate future, perhaps even in the long term. Neither of them liked change, preferring to stay with what they knew and had done over the past few years.

Georgio was annoyed. "I suppose that's because we lost forty kilos of high-grade cocaine on that Birmingham run!" He was still smarting from his father's harsh words over the unfortunate incident.

Gianni remained calm and impassive. "It's not just that. Experience in other areas would benefit both of you."

Franco was more restrained than his brother and accepted that they had made a serious mistake in losing so much of their valuable cargo. "What do you have in mind, Papà?"

Gianni smiled. He'd known Franco would be more cooperative and 'flexible' than his volatile, younger brother. "The supply of weapons is proving to be very profitable, and we have recently sourced a new supplier in Russia. They are keen to increase volume, and their prices are unbeatable."

"What about demand? Surely, most gangs have sufficient weapons already."

"You would think that, wouldn't you, Franco? The truth is that right now, the requirement for more weapons is at an all-time high. There have been many recent police raids in London, Birmingham, Manchester and Glasgow where large caches of weapons were seized. The gangs are ready to re-arm, and they'll pay good prices for reliable weapons with no questions asked."

Georgio still looked doubtful, but Franco had no such reservations. "Okay, Papà, we're ready to move on the weapons circuit."

Gianni breathed a sigh of relief. He had anticipated some resistance to his suggestions, particularly from his younger son, but thankfully, Georgio made no further comments. "Good! There's only one thing you must remember. If a customer in London is keen to buy, supply him, but tell me and I will inform our friends."

Georgio was puzzled by this request. "Why?"

Gianni looked directly at his son. "It's quite simple. If someone is after a gun in London, there's a good chance it will be used against us. Many are envious of our wealth and power. By revealing their names to the police, we can let the authorities do our dirty work for us by removing the problem. Think about it. After all, we still make a profit on the arms we supply."

Georgio smiled at his father's plan. It was very useful having friends in high places to take out the competition.

However, Gianni was using this tactic with great caution since he did not wish to be the person responsible for the riots, as had happened in August. He could not have predicted such an unfortunate outcome but would be much more careful in the future.

"I want both of you to talk to and learn from Francesco. He has many years' experience in the supply of weapons, so please be open to taking his advice seriously." It was asking a great deal, as Georgio and Francesco had always been confrontational. Francesco was the older of the two cousins with far greater experience and an unfortunate way of expressing his assumed superiority.

ALEX WAS DISAPPOINTED that the vision only lasted a couple of minutes. He recognised Franco and his brother from the canal drug run and the delivery van in Birmingham as well as in the gymnasium, but this was the first time he had seen their father. How he wished he knew the older man's name, but the only names mentioned were Franco and Francesco.

"Drugs protection, prostitution *and* providing illegal weapons," Jen remarked when Alex told her of his latest vision. "No wonder the 'Ndrangheta is so rich and powerful."

"If they were honest, they would probably do a better job than the present British Government," Alex remarked dryly.

Jen laughed. "I thought you were a fan of David Cameron and the governing Conservative party."

"Oh, don't get me wrong. Of all the political parties, the coalition between the Conservative and Liberal Democrats is probably doing as good a job as possible. I just meant that if the 'Ndrangheta were legal, their experience would be of great benefit to the British economy. Think of all the taxes they would have to pay into the Government coffers!"

"Well, there's not much chance of that happening," Jen said, "but at least your visions are helping to build a better picture of the 'Ndrangheta. I get the sense that it's like an iceberg where most of the bulk is still hidden. If only your visions could locate their headquarters."

"That's exactly what I'm hoping for. Rest assured, when I do, I will be doing everything possible to end their reign of terror."

"I'm certain they'll soon be found, Alex." Jen knew that the discovery of the Romanian girls forced to work as prostitutes had touched a raw nerve and deeply affected him. "It's just a matter of time."

ADRIAN WAS EXCITED when he phoned later that morning. "The Italian Police have provided us with names and mugshots of the members of the 'Ndrangheta who managed to escape arrest. The Capocrimine—their head man—is a guy called Gian Battista Lamancusa, aged seventy-eight. I think we can safely assume that all of his extended family members are holed up here in England."

Alex was thrilled at this news. "Great! Can you send us the full details of this family of criminals?"

"Of course. I'll send it in a few minutes. Just keep on having your visions and we may yet find out just where they are."

Chapter Thirty-Seven

ACCORDING TO THE Italian Authorities, there were thirty-eight members of the Lamancusa family probably living in the United Kingdom. Three generations of this dangerous family had escaped capture when a large contingent of Italian Police swooped down on all Calabria-based known members of the 'Ndrangheta. There was a suggestion that news of the raid had been leaked by an insider but not in time to save almost three hundred members of the organisation.

As Alex scanned through all the information, he recognised eight faces. Gianni was the older man in Alex's visions while the two men on the drug run were Franco, whom he already knew, and Georgio. The two men charged with holding the Romanian girls as sex slaves were Brando and Carlino. There were also photos of Lorenzo and Paolo, the two men who killed the Scottish protection racketeers and took over their territory.

The last one he recognised was Agostino Lamancusa. It had been such a brief glimpse of the man entering the house in Woolpit four months earlier and on the exercise bike in the gym.

Examining the details of this family of criminals, Jen realised that some of them could have been responsible for Jason's brutal murder. Looking at those satisfied smiles, she wished she could line up every one of them against a wall and mow them down with a high-powered automatic rifle.

Alex noticed the grim determination on Jen's face but didn't need to ask to know what was on her mind. In an attempt to distract her from the bitter memories of losing Jason, he gestured to the photos and remarked, "There doesn't seem to be many females in the group." Of the hundreds of photos, only nine were of women.

Jen agreed. "The question is are they active members of the 'Ndrangheta or wives and sisters?"

"It doesn't really make any difference, does it? Even if they did nothing illegal themselves, they knew exactly what all these men were doing."

"Very true. Either way, I would like to see all of them behind prison bars."

At the very least, Alex thought. For now, he'd seen enough of this violent Italian family and was about to close the file on his computer when he realised and pointed to one of the younger women. "That's the one I shared a shower with!"

Jen's eyebrows raised in a quizzical smile. "You do sound as though you enjoyed the experience."

He ignored her taunt. "I'm fairly sure it's her."

"*Fairly* sure? I suppose you weren't really looking at her face, were you?"

Alex cracked, finally, and smiled broadly. "Okay, so I was a bit distracted by her nakedness, but I can tell you this. Her body cannot compare to yours, honey!"

Jen laughed and kissed him, accepting his compliment with grace and only a little envy. She was happy with their relationship and confident that Alex felt the same.

WHEN HIS SISTER Lucy phoned to remind Alex of her wish for him to spend the festive period at home with his family, Alex felt under pressure to say yes, but at the same time, he couldn't relax until their mission to find the 'Ndrangheta was complete.

"Sorry, sis, but I'm in the middle of a project and have to wait a bit longer before I can take a break."

"Really? Is it that important? Sounds like an excuse to me. You just want to spend more time with this mystery woman of yours. I mean, who needs a military advisor at Christmas?"

"You'd be surprised," said Alex, laughing at her naivete but also surprised she'd read him so well. Last Christmas, he'd been on active duty in Afghanistan, and it seemed this one would pass without celebration too, but in truth, he didn't mind as long as he was with Jen. "I'm sorry, sis, I really am. I promise that very soon I'll come see you all and we can enjoy a meal together."

Disappointed, Lucy relayed the message to her sister and parents. His mother worried that he was working too hard and blamed the army. At the same time, she was very proud of her son's contribution to the safety of British army personnel.

Alex together with Jen ordered items to be delivered to their families in time for Christmas, hopeful that this might help to stop both families from worrying too much about them. That done, they ordered plenty of festive food and drink for themselves and prepared a memorable Christmas dinner of turkey with all the traditional trimmings and even Christmas pudding with cream to follow.

Annoyingly, over the days that followed, Alex slept peacefully without a single vision. Frustrated, he and Jen experimented with different sleeping patterns, indulging in heavy sex before sleep and sometimes refraining from sex altogether. It made no difference at all, and he began to worry that he had lost the power.

As an alternative, he and Jen spent hours reading through the mass of information on the 'Ndrangheta during their reign of power in Italy. Ever hopeful of discovering something useful, they read and reread all the text. The drugs, prostitution and protection rackets were similar to what they had discovered in the UK, but there was one area in Italy which, to their knowledge, had not been apparent in England.

"Gambling has been a major earner in Calabria, so why would they not be doing the same here?" Alex asked.

Jen shrugged. "They probably are, but how can you find out?"

Alex in reply carried out an internet search on high-end casinos in London. As expected, it brought up quite a list.

Avoiding the online casinos, he selected each one in turn and eventually narrowed down a list of the most probable venues run by the 'Ndrangheta.

"It's only a guess, but I think there are eight possible locations."

"That's a start. Should we tell Adrian?"

Alex pondered on this point for a moment. "The trouble is that Adrian can only deal in hard facts. If I hadn't been able to identify the location of that brothel, those girls would still be working as sex slaves. No, I think we have to do a little investigation for ourselves."

"How? What can we do?" Jen was worried, and not unreasonably, about the dangers if they were to be discovered by the Italian family.

Alex studied her, gearing up for his suggestion. "They may still be looking for you, Jen. Perhaps I should pay a visit to some of these casinos on my own."

"I'm not sure that's a good idea. You could be putting yourself in extreme danger."

"I don't have much choice. My visions seem to have dried up for some reason. I've got to do something!"

Jen could tell that Alex had made up his mind, but this gave her great concern about the new man in her life. The last thing she wanted was to find Alex's body hacked to pieces by the dreaded Italian mob. "Are you going to tell Adrian what you are planning?" She knew that Adrian would try to talk Alex out of the idea.

Alex again considered Jen's question. "I think not. It's such a long shot, there would be little he could do to assist."

This did not ease Jen's mind. She watched him as he selected the clothes for his evening out in London. He really did look good in the suit he had bought from the Cad and the Dandy; it gave him quite an air of sophistication.

Alex was equally pleased with his tailor-made suit. The material and colour were perfect, and the fit was better than anything he'd worn previously. *The expense had definitely been worth it,* he thought.

Alex had again dyed his hair black, making him look very different from the man Jen had met five months earlier. "Just like James Bond," she said, running her hands down his chest.

Alex arched his eyebrows in true Roger Moor style. "Really? Which one?"

Jen laughed. "You could have passed as Daniel Craig until you had your hair dyed. Now perhaps more Pierce Brosnan or Roger Moore." Her face took on a more serious expression. "It would be more natural if we went together. I could wear my wig, and with one of my better dresses, I'd be completely unrecognisable."

It did make good sense. A man on his own could appear a little strange and out of place. "Okay," Alex agreed, checking his watch. "I guess Elsa will be fine on her own for a few hours. I'd like to get to this place by nine-thirty and be out by midnight."

Happy with his change of mind, Jen prepared for her night out in London.

Elsa seemed to know she was going to be left on her own and watched with sadness in her eyes as the couple prepared to leave.

"Sorry, Elsa, not tonight. Be a good girl."

Obediently, she remained on her bed as the door closed behind her master.

Chapter Thirty-Eight

THE COUPLE WALKED for about ten minutes before hailing a taxi. Within twenty more minutes, they had arrived at the Rendezvous Casino on Old Park Lane, Mayfair.

Alex had chosen this casino as the first to visit, as he felt certain this was not one controlled by the 'Ndrangheta since it had been well-established for many years. His thought by coming here was to establish a standard by which he could compare any other casino.

Dress code was obviously important, confirming Alex's idea of purchasing a suit of high quality. He had to admire Jen, who looked very classy and absolutely stunning in her evening dress and brunette wig. As he glanced around, he noticed that everybody was dressed smartly with not a single pair of jeans in sight.

The place was busy with many people collected around the numerous gaming tables. Alex walked over to the cashier's desk and purchased a couple of hundred pounds' worth of chips. He had decided to watch some of the other players before taking part himself.

Next, he bought drinks for Jen and himself, casually sipping while they watched several players losing their money. These players always seemed to think they would win on the next spin of the wheel and became more and more despondent as their losses mounted.

Jen and Alex were careful not to use their real names in conversation and tried to give the impression that they were trying to decide whether to play blackjack or roulette. There were quieter areas where three-card poker or stud poker were being played, but Alex thought it best to avoid these games partly because he was uncertain of all the rules and didn't want to lose money because of his lack of knowledge.

Eventually, he took a chance on the roulette wheel, placing a few chips on one of the squares on the table. He had no idea why he'd picked red eighteen but was both surprised and delighted when the ball landed in his chosen slot. The croupier slid an increased pile of chips towards him.

Jen smiled at him. "Beginner's luck, darling?"

"I don't know. We'll have to see." He placed some, though not all, of the chips on black eleven and was even more surprised when the ball locked into this very slot on the wheel's next spin.

Jen clapped enthusiastically. "Well done! You could be on to a winning streak!"

Not wanting to draw too much attention to himself, Alex gathered his chips but did not place them on the table, preferring instead to sip his drink while watching the other players.

After a gap of about fifteen minutes, Alex again placed some chips on red fifteen, fully expecting to lose this gamble. He was more surprised than anyone when he yet again had picked the winning number. He now had four times as many chips as when he had started.

Of course, the casino owners wanted players to put all their winnings on one last number, which would almost certainly result in the loss of all their chips. Alex had the good sense to stop while ahead and after watching players on the blackjack tables cashed in his chips. He was thrilled to discover that the two hundred pounds he had initially converted to chips had grown to eight hundred and forty pounds.

"Not a bad return for a few hours," he said with a broad smile. He could understand the almost-hypnotic attraction to gambling by millions of people, but he also had more sense of the risks than the average player.

"Are you hungry?" he asked. He knew from his online search that the casino's restaurant had a good reputation.

Jen checked the time. It was eleven-thirty. "Okay, as long as it's just a light meal at this time of the night."

"A light meal it is."

They did not have to wait long for their meal. It was superb, and both left quite satisfied and ready for home.

The couple collected their coats and walked arm in arm out into the chilly January night, picking up a taxi a short while later.

It was a great feeling as they entered the apartment after their evening out and five hundred pounds in profit even allowing for the meal and drinks. "I didn't expect to come home with more money than I had started with," said Alex.

Jen agreed. "I've never been in a casino in my life, but I quite enjoyed it. How did you manage to keep winning?"

He shrugged. "I've never been lucky enough to win anything in my life before. I wonder if it's related to my improved intuition since my injury. The same as when I sensed that bullet aimed at your head."

Jen shivered, remembering how close to death she had come on that night. "Same as with the bomb in the hotel room."

With those sobering thoughts, the couple went to bed, agreeing that over the next two weeks they would visit a different casino each night in the hope that eventually they could discover which ones were run by the Italians.

What Alex had overlooked was the connection between his eyes and Adrian's monitoring system and thus was surprised when, the following morning, Adrian phoned and barked, "What the fuck do you think you were doing last night?"

Realisation dawned, and Alex cursed himself for not thinking about his 'transparent' eyes. He explained how his visions seemed to have dried up and he and Jen had wanted to find out some information for themselves, finishing with, "We did adopt our different identities."

"I still think it was a fucking stupid idea, disguised or not!"

Alex didn't appreciate Adrian's hostility. "We just can't sit in this apartment forever waiting for all the 'Ndrangheta family members to die. I'm sorry if you don't like it, but we have to do something!"

Adrian had to admit that if it led to the Italian family then it would have proved worthwhile. "Just take care and don't attract too much attention by winning against the odds."

He's envious of my winning streak, thought Alex. "Don't worry, Adrian. We'll take great care."

Jen had heard both sides of the conversation, Adrian's voice being louder than usual. She also noticed how Alex's face had coloured at the criticism aimed at him. *Poor Alex*, she thought. *He does seem quite sensitive to Adrian's harsh comments.*

After this, Alex's good mood plummeted, but with Jen's encouragement, particularly in the bedroom, he soon recovered to his more usual relaxed style.

Chapter Thirty-Nine

B RANDO AND CARLINO Lamancusa were relaxing on their bunk beds in their remand cell when they heard their door being unlocked. Two stony-faced armed officers entered. Both were over six feet in height and quite muscular, but one was about ten years senior and probably in his mid-forties. The older officer, a dark-haired man with a sallow complexion, spoke.

"Right, you two. Time for your courtroom appearance."

Neither man made any attempt to move.

"Stand up! Both of you!" The officer's tone was a little sharper now.

Without any sign of urgency or a word, the Italians got to their feet. The officers attached handcuffs to the two and led them out of the cell and the remand centre. The rear door of a police van was opened and the two bundled roughly inside. Their cuffs were removed from the officers' wrists and fastened to bars within the van. Bench seats ran along both sides, and the officer indicated that the prisoners should sit down and not make any trouble. The two prisoners said nothing and looked impassively at their confined surroundings.

The rear doors slammed shut and were securely locked, after which the officers took their places in the front of the vehicle.

It was eight-thirty on a Wednesday morning as the van pulled out into the slow-moving yet busy London traffic.

The journey from the remand centre to the courts was only about three miles, and considering the location, nothing should have gone wrong with the transfer. With only about half a mile before their destination the van turned into a narrow road, and to the surprise of the two officers, their path was blocked by a council refuse truck. Unable to pass, they had no option but to wait, wondering if it was a genuine traffic problem, a question that was soon answered when the van was rocked by a huge explosion and the rear doors blew off.

Two masked, helmeted figures jumped inside and fired stun darts through the metal grille at the officers in the front, taking them completely by surprise. They were unharmed yet unable to prevent their prisoners escaping as they collapsed unconscious from the effects of the quick-acting drug.

The assailants acted swiftly and without hesitation. Using a bolt cutter, they sliced through both sets of handcuffs, releasing the criminals. It was as though they had been expecting this attack, as both jumped out of the van and followed the men who had released them.

Passers-by gawped at the scene in disbelief but made no move against the escaping criminals. Could this really be happening in the centre of London? By the time anyone could galvanise themselves into action, the four men had escaped on motorbikes, which had been concealed in a nearby side road.

When Adrian heard of the escape, he was understandably furious. An alert had been put out in an attempt to recapture the criminals without delay. He phoned Alex, whose first thoughts were for the girls who had been used and abused by these criminals. With anxiety in his voice, he asked, "Where are Jacqueline and Rosita now?"

"Don't worry. They're already home with their families in Romania. They're quite safe now. They asked me to thank you again for helping them."

"Good! I'm just happy we managed to save them from such a horrible life, but it's a pity those bastards managed to escape. I imagine they will be back in their underground bunker by now."

"Don't be so pessimistic, Alex. They will be caught," Adrian said with conviction in his voice.

Chapter Forty

THE NEXT EVENING, the couple repeated their visit to a casino, but this one was not as quite upmarket as the Rendezvous. Alex had drawn up a list of casinos in Central London from the internet and had chosen one at random.

The place was still busy with punters who, although always hoping to win, were destined to be losers. The only winners, of course, were the owners of the casino. Some did win, but as Alex had already noticed, all their winnings were lost in subsequent games. *Why do they never know when to stop?*

As with the previous night, he played the roulette wheel. Again, his luck was in, but with Adrian's words still ringing in his ears, he stopped before his winning streak was noticed.

Nevertheless, Jen spotted some envious glances from those players who had won and then inevitably lost all their chips.

In the background was the constant noise of slot machines with greedy punters always hoping for that elusive jackpot. Both Alex and Jen glanced unnoticed at the staff, looking for any signs of the faces they had now in their minds while aware that the actual 'Ndrangheta members were not likely to be seen walking around the casino. They would be in other rooms watching closed-circuit cameras trained on the gaming floor in the hope of spotting troublesome punters.

Jen was amazed to find a young woman trying to chat up Alex. This woman had played and lost but had noticed Alex winning several times.

"What's the secret of your success?" she asked admiringly.

Alex looked at the woman. She had long blonde hair framing delicate, possibly Scandinavian features and bright-blue eyes. She was wearing a very close-fitting black evening dress which left little to the imagination. *This gets more like a Bond movie every minute*, thought Alex, smiling. "Luck, I suppose." As an afterthought, he added, "And knowing when to stop."

She gave him a coy, inviting smile. "I could do with a guy with your luck. What's your name?"

Alex was surprised that this woman had not noticed Jen who was not far away. "I'm sorry, miss, but I'm with my partner." He indicated Jen, who lifted her glass in a mock toast.

The woman looked disappointed for a moment but soon regained her composure. "That's a pity. If you ever fancy a bit of fun, you'll find me here on most nights. Just ask for Lindi."

She gave Alex a lingering last look and then disappeared into the crowds.

Jen returned to Alex's side. "Interesting conversation?"

"I can't help it if I find women attracted to me," he said with a mischievous smirk.

Jen laughed. With his height, build, handsome features, calm manner and, this evening, so well-dressed, Jen could appreciate why other women were attracted to the man who had become such an important part of her life. If he'd uttered a few words of Italian, he'd have had Lindi falling at his feet.

After another drink, Alex cashed in his chips, and as he and Jen made their way through the crowds, he caught a glimpse of Lindi. She was watching another punter playing blackjack. She spotted Alex and gave him a wide, inviting smile as if to say, *"Please come again. I so want to see more of you."*

Alex smiled to himself. *She certainly doesn't give up easily*, he thought.

AFTER FIVE NIGHTS at different casinos, Alex and Jen were beginning to realise how difficult their task would be. The late evenings were tiring, and they both slept in the following morning, as it was between one and two a.m. before they managed to get to bed. For all they knew, they had unwittingly already been in one run by the 'Ndrangheta, yet Alex was convinced their search would eventually prove fruitful.

On the sixth day, he looked through his list of casinos and muttered to himself, "Come on, which one should we pick?"

Jen heard his frustration. "Don't blame yourself, Alex. Who knows, maybe we'll get lucky tonight."

"I just wish we had some clue."

Jen was thoughtful. "Okay, how about this? I'll jot down the ones we have been to yet, you close your eyes and point to one. At least then, your choice will be completely random and not influenced by the name."

"We can only try." He handed the printout to Jen and waited for her to write down the names of those they had yet to visit. Then he closed his eyes and brought his finger down on the paper in a somewhat exaggerated, dramatic style. "That's the one!"

Jen laughed. She lifted his hand, and both looked at the name he had selected. The King Louis Casino was not far from the one they had visited two nights earlier, but the decision had now been made.

"The King Louis it is." In truth, Alex had little confidence that anything would come of their visit and could already hear Adrian gloating at their failure.

THE ENTRANCE TO the casino was hardly impressive, which made the interior even more of a surprise. The place was richly decorated in the decadent style of the last ruler of France, and the staff continued this theme with their extravagant costumes and wigs. As usual, Alex exchanged two hundred pounds into chips, then watched others playing roulette before trying his luck. When he thought the time was right, he placed several chips on black five. As with every other casino they had been to, Lady Luck was with him, and he gratefully accepted his winnings when the ball fell into this particular slot.

Resisting the impulse to immediately put more chips down, he waited a while before making his second choice. Again he was correct, but as he took his chips and placed them in his pocket, he was distracted by another punter.

This was a bald, rather rotund man in his late fifties, who'd clearly had too much to drink as confirmed by the redness of his fleshy face. He reminded Alex of the comedian Harry Hill but without the giant collar.

He was loud and did not seem to care who heard him. The man was a little unsteady on his feet, and as he rushed to put down more chips, he caught the hand of a smartly dressed younger man standing to his right. The man's drink spilled and chips were knocked onto the floor.

"Get the fuck out of the way!"

The drunken man's face reddened even more as in a slurred voice, he retorted, "There's no need to talk to me like that! It was an accident!"

This inflamed the younger man even more. "No, *you're* the fucking accident! Get out of my way, you fucking idiot!" He bent to pick up the chips off the floor, and as he descended so did the drunken man. Heads collided, and the scene was reminiscent of a Laurel and Hardy slapstick sketch.

Unfortunately, those involved did not seem to think it humorous at all, and the offended man grabbed the other by the lapels, drew back his fist and was about to hit him in the face when security officers appeared and grabbed him from behind. Reluctantly, he loosened his grip and dropped the older man, who fell heavily to the floor.

"There's no need for that, sir. Please calm down."

"Get your fucking hands off me!" He struggled against the stronger force of two burly security men while a third assisted the drunken man, who by now was lying flat on his back with blood pouring from his nose and moaning loudly.

Suddenly, a space opened around these individuals and a woman took over. "I'm sorry, ladies and gentlemen. The games are suspended on this table for now. Please use other tables to place your bets." She then addressed the offended man with a calm relaxing voice. "I'm sorry, sir. The casino will make sure you are not out of pocket."

This woman was obviously in charge and appeared to resolve the situation quite amicably. The drunken man was helped into a chair where his damaged nose was attended to, and soon gaming resumed as though nothing had ever happened.

Jen excitedly tugged on Alex's sleeve and spoke quietly. "Isn't that the woman you showered with?"

Alex had been enthralled by the sequence of events and nearly choked on hearing Jen's unexpected question. Recovering himself a little, he studied the woman. With her hair styled and her smart suit, she looked completely different with her clothes on, but it appeared Jen was right. To confirm this, a message appeared in the top of his vision.

Name: Francesca Lamancusa
Date of birth: November 21, 1979
Place of birth: Calabria Italy
Member of the outlawed 'Ndrangheta.

The face-recognition software was working well.

"Bingo!" he whispered to Jen.

The couple, though excited by their discovery, did their best to carry on as normal, casually sipping their drinks and watching punters lose their money. Once the two men were seen to be placated by the efforts of the woman, she disappeared into one of the backrooms. Alex assumed that she only came out when situations such as this one demanded her special attention.

WHAT FRANCESCA SAID about those two men once she was in her own space was far less comforting and certainly not ladylike. These incidents were an irritation resulting in punters being temporarily distracted from gambling, which was not the idea of this high-earning establishment.

In normal circumstances, she remained in the background keeping a watchful eye on both staff and punters but had, on this occasion, decided to assist in bringing everything back to a peaceful conclusion. Francesca had grown up in a family of tough individuals in the Italian Calabria gangland and was quite capable of looking after herself, as her employees knew by experience.

The man with the injured nose had sobered up quite quickly after the confrontation, and Francesca ordered her staff to arrange for a taxi to take him either home or to an accident and emergency unit. The other man had similarly calmed down and accepted a voucher for two hundred pounds of chips as compensation. It was not really a hardship, as this could soon be recouped on subsequent visits to the gaming tables.

THE FOLLOWING MORNING, Alex phoned Adrian as soon as he thought his section leader would be in his office. "Adrian! We found a casino run by the 'Ndrangheta last night."

"How do you know? Are you certain?" Adrian was sceptical, but at the same time, he hoped that Alex and Jen's visits to the casinos would turn up something useful for him.

Alex described the altercation between the two men and how Francesca Lamancusa had emerged from the backroom to calm the situation. "Check the video from my eyes for last night. It would have been around eleven-thirty. It was at the King Louis Casino near Leicester Square."

There had been little chance of finding the correct casinos by visiting them at random, but if Alex had really seen one of the 'Ndrangheta, then the young captain's intuition was proving more useful than Adrian had anticipated. "Okay, I'll check the videos as soon as we finish this call. The next step would be to place an observer outside the casino in the hope of spotting her leaving."

Adrian, like Alex, found it amusing to watch the confrontation between the two men in the casino but was intrigued to see the young Italian woman doing her best to resolve the problem. *Pity there's no audio to add to the video recording,* her thought, but that would have been far too intrusive, and Alex would never have agreed to this level of monitoring.

Chapter Forty-One

ADRIAN ARRANGED FOR two of his men to keep a watch on the King Louis Casino and was disappointed when they reported back the following day. They had been issued with pictures of Francesca taken and enlarged from the videos captured through Alex's eyes in addition to the photo released by Italian security forces.

Even though they had watched from six in the evening for a twelve-hour period, the two had no sightings of the woman.

Adrian kept his observers in place for the following nights in the hope that they struck lucky, a task that the two men found extremely boring and tiring and took it in turns to be on the lookout from their car while the other rested.

What none of them realised was that Francesca ran seven casinos and spent one night in each, and if Adrian had not decided to keep his men for a full week, they would have completely missed her.

Michael, one of the two assigned to keep watch, was using night-vision optics and noticed a woman who certainly looked like the Italian leave the club around three-fifteen in the morning. She took a seat in the back of a large black Volvo. Michael shook his sleeping colleague, who was gently snoring. "Wake up, Jim! The target just appeared."

With a sudden rush of adrenalin, his partner jumped out of his slumbers and switched on the engine. It was difficult without being noticed, but they did their best to follow the route taken by the Volvo.

After a tortuous thirty-minute route, they were frustrated to find themselves back at the casino. "Fuck! It must have been a trick!" To add to their frustration, the male driver left the Volvo, locked it and entered the casino on his own, seemingly oblivious that he had been followed.

"The woman's not there!" Michael could not believe their bad luck and knew he was going to be asked some awkward questions. *"Why is it so difficult for two of my officers to follow a lone woman around central London at three in the morning? After all, she can't suddenly disappear."*

Jim scratched his head. "She must have been dropped off somewhere, but why didn't we spot her?"

That was the first question Adrian asked when they reported to him later that morning.

"We couldn't follow too closely or else she would easily have spotted us. The number of turns they took, we were very lucky to keep track of the car at all," Michael explained.

Adrian knew this was true and that what they were trying to achieve was a difficult if not impossible task. Even though these two men were experienced in surveillance techniques, the Volvo driver could have spotted them.

Fortunately, their route had been electronically recorded and Michael replayed the data, all three watching the display on the monitor of a road map of the capital, starting at the casino, with times displayed at each point on the journey, but this still did not yield any helpful clues. "I'll send this data to Alex and see if he can spot anything significant about the route she took."

Alex was equally frustrated and disappointed to discover that Francesca had evaded their surveillance. He studied the map in great detail, but after over an hour, they were no further forward. Since it would do no harm to have another pair of eyes to study the problem, Jen also followed the data outlining the now-so-familiar route around London.

"There just doesn't seem to be any part of the journey where she could have left the car without being noticed," Jen admitted. After a moment's thought, she said, "Why don't we ask Adrian if the surveillance guys could take us around the route during the daytime? We may spot something useful."

Alex thought this was a good idea and phoned Adrian with the request. The older man at first felt it would be a further waste of time and resources but eventually agreed to the suggestion. "On one condition."

"What's that?" Alex braced in preparation for what his boss was going to demand.

"That you wait until tomorrow. Michael and Jim are resting now after their overnight surveillance, and I don't feel like disturbing them out of their slumbers."

"I don't have a problem with that," Alex conceded. This was not an unreasonable demand, and one more day would surely not make any significant difference.

Alex had seen no more visions for a couple of weeks, and as he lay in bed that night, he wondered why they had dried up. Jen was already fast asleep, her gentle, rhythmic breathing sounding somehow reassuring. His thoughts, however, were with another woman, Francesca Lamancusa, whom he reasoned was probably only on the fringes of crime as a result of being born into the Lamancusa family. His thoughts were still with her as he fell into a deep sleep.

THE TWO WOMEN in front of the bank of screens scanned through all the images of punters playing roulette, poker, blackjack and even the slot machines. Sometimes they would adjust controls to zoom in or pan around the punters. There was an air of calmness and strict organisation in this viewing room. To his amusement, it struck Alex that in this instance he was actually snooping on the snoopers.

"Look! The tall guy in the dark pinstripes on camera seven Angela!" Francesca directed the other woman to take a closer look.

"Yes, you're right. It is the same guy. What do you want to do about him, Fran?"

"Let's just watch him again to make absolutely certain."

Alex was puzzled by their interest in this one man. What were they looking for? The tall man in pinstripes looked a bit like Alan Rickman in his younger days with a slim build and neat, black hair. The air of confidence and composure displayed by the man added to that impression.

"See there!" said Francesca excitedly. "He's moving around until he's behind one of the players." Alex could not see closely enough to make out what the man was doing but was intrigued by the interest shown by the two women.

"Show me what he's doing with his left hand!"

Angela followed her boss's directions and zoomed in. "It's in his pocket. Are you certain he's up to something?"

"Well, there's no smile on his face, so I don't think he's playing with himself, but he's definitely using something in his pocket to relay the player's cards to the opponent. I've been in this game long enough to recognise an illegal operation."

Alex had to smile to himself at the double standards of this strong-minded Italian criminal.

"Just keep an eye on the game, and if the guy being assisted wins we'll take care of both of them."

It did not take very long for their suspicions to be justified. The man who presumably was receiving the signals made a substantial win.

"Okay, I've seen enough." Francesca spoke into a microphone connecting her to the earpieces worn by her employees. "Greg and Dan, you know the guys we're interested in. Take them into the interview room, please."

The two women and Alex watched closely as two heavily built men, Greg and Dan, Alex presumed, moved towards the gaming table. One of them put a hand on the shoulder of the tall man while the other moved to the opposite side of the table. It was obvious that the couple was surprised and convincingly acted offended, but they complied, knowing better than to try any violent moves. They were escorted, looking somewhat sheepish and uncomfortable, to a door at the back of the room. As soon as Francesca saw this, she jumped up and made her way across the studio. She pushed a door open and walked confidently into the interview room. The heavies pulled chairs out from a desk and offered them to the two punters, who didn't hide their surprise at finding themselves facing the good-looking young Italian woman.

"Good evening, gentlemen. I take it you had a good night playing in my casino?" Her voice was strong, calm and confident with only a slight trace of her native Italian accent. She took a seat in a large, comfortable-looking leather chair. "I'm sure we can clear this matter up quickly."

It was the Alan Rickman lookalike who spoke, though he was noticeably rattled. "I was just enjoying an evening in your superb casino, so what am I doing in here with this man?" He looked at the other man with obvious disdain, trying to emphasise that they had absolutely nothing in common and did not know each other in any way.

"Ah, well, I'm sure we can soon settle this matter. Please empty your outer jacket pockets, sir."

He began to object, but the big security guy behind him bent over and, ignoring his protestations, reached into the man's left pocket and pulled out a small device about the size of a mobile phone. He handed it over to Francesca, who studied it with interest.

It was thicker than a standard mobile, and instead of the usual display and keypad, it had twelve buttons and a two-line Braille cell matrix on its upper surface. "What is this?" She seemed more curious than angry. That would come later.

The man cleared his throat. "My grandmother's Braille phone. She's both blind and deaf and is lost without her communicator. I've had it repaired and will be taking it to her tomorrow."

"Really?" Francesca nodded very slightly to the heavy behind the other man. On this simplest of commands, he reached into the pocket of the other man who had not yet spoken. He retrieved an identical device and handed this to his employer.

Francesca smiled. "What an amazing coincidence! Do you also have a grandmother who is both blind and deaf?"

The man seemed lost for words. "No, I—"

"Come on, gentlemen. Don't piss me off. We've been watching the pair of you on CCTV, and it's obvious you were communicating with each other using these clever little devices to win unfairly." She looked at the two men, who were no longer hiding their nervousness. Scooping up both devices, she offered them to one of her heavies. "It was an ingenious plan and the first time we have encountered these devices. We'll pull them apart for our own amusement and analysis. Unfortunately, there won't be much left by the time we've finished with them."

One of the men reared in his seat as if about to protest or try to grab back the devices but stopped when he once again felt the heavy hand on his shoulder.

Francesca smiled broadly, her voice strong and menacing as she said, "Let me give you some good advice, gentlemen. I don't want to see either of you in the Prince of Clubs Casino ever again. Nor any other of my casinos. Ignore this advice, and both of you will end up just like these clever little gadgets—broken and incapable of anything! Do I make myself clear?"

Both men nodded meekly.

She really does know how to make them feel small, thought Alex.

"Please escort these gentlemen off the premises. Nice meeting you both." Francesca stood and returned to the observation studio. Alex began to follow, but at this point, the vision faded and he returned to his sleep, once more disappointed that it had not lasted long enough to uncover the location of the family's bunker. Why was it that these visions always stopped before any useful information could be gathered?

Jen was intrigued as Alex described his vision over their breakfast. "Now *that* is a really clever way of cheating at cards. I had no idea that Braille mobiles existed."

"Same here," admitted Alex. "I don't think Francesca had come across them either, judging from what she said.

Chapter Forty-Two

A LEX WAS EAGER to relay the information about Francesca to Adrian, who listened with his usual cool interest. "So she has other clubs as well?"

"Seems like it, but we don't know how many. Are we still okay for the journey around London this afternoon?"

"Yes. Michael and Jim will be at your place around one o'clock." With a firmness in his voice, Adrian added, "Just observe and try to avoid being seen, Alex."

"No problem." Alex knew how important this exercise was but had a feeling they were getting closer to the 'Ndrangheta's hiding place. Was it misplaced confidence? He was certain there would be a breakthrough before very long.

The intelligence service was always very precise, and it was exactly at one when the two men arrived. Alex bent down to talk to Elsa and stroked her head. "Sorry, girl, but you can't come with us. You need to keep a watch on this place while we are out."

Her reaction was much the same as a child's, and the German shepherd's shoulders seemed to drop at the realisation that once again she was being left on her own. The mournful look in her eyes made Alex feel guilty.

"I'm sorry, Elsa. We'll be back soon."

Resigned to her role, the dog lay down and watched as Alex and Jen closed the door behind them.

Michael was driving with Jim in the passenger seat while Alex and Jen sat in the rear of the dark-grey Toyota Prius. Even the government's intelligence service realised the advantages of driving a hybrid car on Mayor Boris Johnson's busy London roads. From Alex's apartment, they drove to Leicester Square where, just over a week earlier, Alex and Jen had spent the evening at the King Louis Casino run by Francesca Lamancusa. From there, they drove west along Panton Street turning left onto Whitcomb Street, following the route Francesca's car had taken.

All four were scanning the roads, looking for anything that could give them a clue. They took a few turns until they drove along the notorious Fleet Street to Ludgate Hill and then left past the Old Bailey.

The traffic was heavier than it had been during early morning, but in less than thirty minutes, they were back at Leicester Square.

"Can we do it one more time, please?" asked Alex, frustrated by their lack of progress.

"No problem," replied Michael. "But any more and somebody might notice us."

"Agreed." Alex concentrated all his efforts on finding the point where Francesca could have left the Volvo, and this was his last chance. The car moved at a leisurely pace and again followed the route precisely. Shortly before Newgate Street, they had to wait for traffic lights to change, and it was this that gave Alex an idea.

"Michael! When you were following the Volvo, did you have to stop at these lights?"

The surveillance man had to think, recollecting the early morning journey. "Yes, I believe we did! I remember cursing that the Volvo had made it through the lights and turned right while we had to wait for them to change."

Jim added, "And when the lights changed and we turned onto Newgate Street, we managed to pick it up again."

This encouraged Alex to study the surroundings as the lights turned to green allowing them to turn. Jen was using her iPhone to make a video recording of the journey and she collected footage of all the buildings as they passed.

Alex felt the pressure on him. His head was spinning as he forced himself to look ever more closely before the traffic took them out of the area. Then, from the corner of his vision, he spotted the railings on the island at the west side of Newgate Street where there was a junction with King Edward Street. "What are those railings for?"

The others turned to look where he was pointing. It was Jim who provided the answer. "It's a ventilation shaft for the Tube."

"Of course!" These ventilation shafts were dotted all around London, providing fresh air to the deep tunnels used by London's Underground. "Any idea which line it's for?"

Jim shook his head. "Sorry, I've no idea. I don't use public transport if I can help it."

Taking his gaze off the surroundings, Alex switched on his iPad and performed a quick query. "That's strange. The nearest station is St. Paul's on the Circle line." After a few more searches, he exclaimed, "That must be it! It says there used to be a station on Newgate Street, but it was closed many years ago with the station moving to what is now St. Paul's." He read on a bit more. "And get this! During the Second World War, the electricity board had a control room for the whole of London and the South East built within the service hall beneath that ventilation and lift shaft!"

All inside the car fell silent as they realised the significance of this discovery. If Alex had found the information so easily, the 'Ndrangheta could equally have found it and seen its potential as a hiding place. However, Jen had spotted a flaw in this supposition.

"How would they get into it? I can't imagine Francesca slinging her leg over the railings to climb down to the service hall."

Alex smiled to himself at the image of the cultured Italian woman doing what Jen had just described. "I accept that," he agreed, "so there must be another way into it. When we get back to the apartment, we'll study the videos, particularly of Newgate Street, and hopefully find our entrance."

Within twenty minutes, they returned to the usual boisterous welcome from Elsa as if they had been away for many weeks. Her tail was wagging vigorously as she greeted her master and mistress.

When she had calmed down, Alex and Jen sat together on the sofa to study the video footage. Jen restarted the recording and then fast-forwarded to the junction before Newgate Street. The buildings were quite tall, fairly anonymous and old-fashioned in appearance. Even after replaying the recording several times, they still had no idea where Francesca had gone.

Feeling a little less confident, Alex decided to phone Adrian to let him know what they had discovered.

Adrian was in good humour. "Leave it with me, Alex. I have access to many historical files about London. What we need to know is where the original station was situated on Newgate Street. And I'll get Michael and Jim to keep a watch for this woman close to where we think she is going. Good work, Alex!"

The praise was gratefully received, but Alex had to wonder if they were getting any closer to the truth.

Chapter Forty-Three

ONCE AGAIN, MICHAEL and Jim were on night duty, parked where they had a good view over a large part of Newgate Street. They had arrived around two-thirty in the morning and, using night-vision equipment, began their vigil.

Francesca arrived shortly after three. As before, she was in the Volvo. Her car stopped briefly and then moved quickly away. The Italian woman walked quite casually towards what looked like an apartment block. She pressed some buttons near the doorway, entered the building and disappeared inside. The place looked old but presumably had been refurbished internally to provide modern apartments. Satisfied that they had the information, Michael pressed the ignition and, using battery power only, the Prius glided away silently.

IT WAS ADRIAN who phoned Alex the following morning. "Good news! We have the address where Francesca entered the building, and thanks to the archived data, we know it's adjacent to the site of the old Underground station."

"Fantastic!" Alex was elated at the news. "I feel that we are really getting somewhere at last.

Adrian agreed. "What we mustn't do is to rush into this. We need to gather as much information as possible before we make any move."

"Of course. It reminds me of Afghanistan in a way. Just because we knew where the Taliban were hiding, we wouldn't rush in with an attack. It still took time to work out the best line of approach."

What Adrian said next took Alex's breath away. "I would prefer it if you could leave this operation to us now, Alex."

"No way! You know fucking well that over the past two months, since they attacked Jen, I've thought of nothing except finding where these bastards are hiding. If you think I am going to hand it over to you on a plate you can go screw yourself!"

Adrian had expected some resistance but was surprised at the strength of Alex's feelings. "I'll need clearance from the brigadier general."

"I don't care if you need the queen to approve it. Just accept that I am going in with you guys." Alex turned to look at Jen, who had been listening to this heated conversation. "Do you want to go in with us?"

"I wouldn't want it any other way. I need to see these killers caught. I owe that much to Jason."

Alex again spoke to Adrian. "Here's the deal. Jen, Elsa and I must be included in the raid or else I will kick up such a stink you'll never forget it. My eyes could be our best asset."

Adrian was tired not only of this battle with one of his operatives but also with internal difficulties within the department. Ever-increasing demands were getting him down. Wearily, he said, "Okay, I'll see what I can do. Just don't do anything until we're absolutely ready. It's going to take a few days to prepare for an assault."

"Understood." After a moment's contemplation and a slight change of heart, Alex said, "Sorry, Adrian."

Adrian sighed. "It's okay. I did have a feeling that you would want to go in with us."

The call ended, and Alex turned to face Jen. "It looks as though we're getting close to the 'Ndrangheta and their underground bunker."

She smiled a smile which Alex always enjoyed seeing on her beautiful face. The trouble was that he was now even more concerned about her safety. After what he had said to Adrian, it would be hypocritical of him to try to prevent Jen from actively joining in with the attack.

ADRIAN NOW HAD plans for the apartments on Newgate Street and was studying them in great detail. After the Underground station was closed the buildings remained derelict for many years. As London was becoming an attractive place to live and work, it became ever more viable to develop new offices and apartments. Newgate Street with its proximity to important areas in East Central London was no exception, and even though many buildings were of listed status, developers spent millions on providing comfortable accommodation and office space behind the preserved facades.

What puzzled Adrian was how the 'Ndrangheta had managed to acquire an apartment block, which would house many innocent people to suit their own ends. Then he spotted it. Looking through all the ownership records, it was obvious that after development, the apartments had been owned by several different property companies, sometimes through financial difficulties and others by pure speculation. The present owner was a private venture-capital company based in Calabria, Italy. What better way to launder the millions gained from their illegal rackets in what appeared to be a perfectly legitimate investment? What did surprise him was that the purchase of this particular block of apartments was made in 2007, long before the swoop and arrest of most of the 'Ndrangheta in 2010. Was this an insurance policy that had been planned well in advance, or was it just a lucky coincidence?

Armed with this new information, Adrian called Alex and explained his findings.

The excitement could be heard in the young soldier's voice. "Any chance you could email the building plans to me? Preferably both before and after the property was changed into apartments?"

"No problem, but I don't want you going to look at this place for yourself, Alex. Any tip-off at this stage could compromise the whole operation."

Alex laughed. "Adrian! Would I do such a thing?"

"I've been in this business long enough to know that it only takes one mistake by one person."

"Don't worry. I'd just like to see the plans. I promise not to do anything stupid."

WHEN ALEX RECEIVED the email with the plans for the apartments on Newgate Street, he forwarded a copy to Jen's notebook so they could both study them.

Alex found the original Underground station drawings fascinating, the style contrasting sharply with the modern plans for apartments. By the end of that day, both Alex and Jen had heavy eyes after hours of staring at what were relatively small screens. Within minutes of putting their heads on the pillows, both were sound asleep.

Alex felt very confused when he found himself standing, stark naked, on the pavement. Francesca had just stepped out of the Volvo and was thanking the driver. As the car drove away, she walked over to the entrance door to the apartment block. She pressed a few keys; the door opened automatically, and she stepped inside. Alex rushed to follow her, although there was no need for haste. He could probably have moved straight through the solid door or even through the wall. Still, he took the conventional route and then followed her along a corridor, almost slipping through her body when she stopped abruptly at a doorway. Francesca removed a key from her handbag and inserted it into the lock. To his surprise, there was already a light in the room, although it seemed more like emergency lighting since it was of low illumination.

Locking the door behind her, she began moving around the room. To Alex, it looked like an ordinary storage room with items stacked all over the tiled floor. Then he saw it. In the far corner, there was a low concrete wall, which separated the room from a staircase leading downwards.

Francesca wasted no time and began to descend the steps. Again, Alex followed, but moving about in his visions had never been easy. It was a bit like swimming in air and meant that his progress was hampered, as there was nothing to provide much purchase to aid his progress. *Oh, come on, you idiot! Don't lose her when you're so close.*

Francesca was not rushing but seemed to move with great purpose and confidence. *If she only knew that I can see everything she does, she wouldn't appear so bloody confident.*

After four flights of stairs, the Italian and her unseen stalker entered a wide, tiled corridor. Occasionally, there would be an arch, which originally would have taken the passengers towards the Underground platform but was filled in now, providing no option but to continue along this obviously still-maintained hallway. After a few minutes, the end of the dimly lit corridor lay directly ahead.

Where to now?

All Alex could see was an old-fashioned gate to a lift, but to his surprise, Francesca opened the gate, walked in and pulled it shut behind her. Quickly, Alex followed and very nearly walked straight through the back of the lift cage. Francesca pushed a button, and the lift began to descend. There was nothing derelict about the lift. The movement was smooth, indicating that someone was maintaining the electrics and hydraulics.

The lift halted, and Francesca opened the doors to let herself out. Alex was praying that this vision would not end until he had more useful information for Adrian. The area in front of the lift was not large and had just one door in the opposite wall. Again, she retrieved a key from her bag and inserted it into the lock. Opening it, she walked through and locked the door again behind her. They were in yet another corridor, and this one looked vaguely familiar. Alex thought of the vision where he had passed from the exercise room into a corridor and then into Francesca's shower. This was that same, hotel-like corridor. There were many doors on both sides, but she walked another twenty metres or so and pushed the door open. It led into a small hallway with five doors leading off it.

Francesca opened one of these as though she was trying not to disturb the occupants. Alex was more curious than ever to discover the secrets of this huge underground labyrinth.

"Mama?" The head of a small child lifted off the pillow and looked towards Francesca, now framed in the doorway.

"Gemma! Why are you still awake?"

"I couldn't sleep, Mama. I keep having bad dreams. A really big monster keeps following me everywhere."

From what Alex could see of the girl, he guessed she was about five years old. To his surprise, another voice could then be heard.

"Gemma's a real nuisance, Mama. She keeps waking me up." The girl who had spoken was around eight or nine years old.

"Well, I'm back now, and I want both of you to settle down." She walked over to the younger girl and gave her a hug of reassurance. "Come on now, Gemma. There's nothing to be afraid of. They're just silly dreams. Okay?"

"Okay, Mama." There was a slightly happier tone in the young girl's voice now that her mother had returned.

"And please try not to disturb Serena. She needs her sleep as much as you."

The girl yawned and relaxed back on her pillow. "I'm okay now, Mama."

"Good! Just remember I'm only in the next room." Francesca kissed both her daughters and quietly closed the door. She pushed another door open, switched on the light and walked into what looked like her own bedroom.

No husband? thought Alex. There was something about the room that made him think it was a single woman's room rather than that of a married couple. He moved around, looking for any helpful clues. On a bedside table, there was a photograph of a young, handsome man who was probably in his late twenties. Another photo showed the same man holding a beaming Francesca close in a warm embrace. Alex recognised the older girl in the photograph, who looked a little bored, but she would only have been around four years old. A baby sat sitting in front of Francesca trying to attract her attention. That must have been Gemma.

Alex had guessed correctly. Francesca and her husband Grecco had been blissfully happy together with their two young daughters until 2008 when Grecco was killed in a gun battle with Italian police forces. An informer had revealed the mobster's location, but thanks to the loyalty between 'Ndrangheta family members, the informer did not live long enough to enjoy the substantial reward offered by the authorities.

As he turned around to study the rest of the room, Alex realised that Francesca had taken off her clothes. Standing quite naked, she was hanging her dress in a wardrobe. What was it that made this woman want to remove her clothes whenever Alex was around? *Ah, well, mustn't complain. These fringe benefits are all part of the job!*

She walked into a bathroom where she used the toilet and then brushed her teeth. Alex had gallantly stayed in the bedroom, not wishing to see every intimate detail of this attractive Italian's private life.

Francesca returned to the bedroom and took something from a drawer, placing it on the bedside cabinet. Suddenly, Alex realised what it was. A vibrator! That did suggest the man in the photo was not around anymore. Francesca slipped into her bed and pulled up the covers, taking hold of the vibrator.

Alex was thinking of what he could do for this lonely woman when the vision suddenly faded and he was back in his own bed.

Chapter Forty-Four

WHEN ALEX TOLD Jen of his latest vision over breakfast, she said with a resigned sigh, "Why is it that when your body is in bed with me, your spirit is somewhere else with another woman?"

Alex smiled at her comment. "Sorry, sweetheart. You know it's beyond my control."

"I bet you would've liked to replace her vibrator with something of your own?"

"The thought never crossed my mind!" He crossed his fingers as though it would make any difference.

"Liar!" Jen laughed. She always enjoyed teasing him. "Only a gay guy could resist such a temptation." Neither was dressed yet, Alex in his boxers and T-shirt while Jen was wearing a somewhat brief nightdress and knickers. She jumped up and ran around the table and pulled at Alex's boxers, exposing his manhood. "See! You've got a hard-on just telling me about your vision."

"I can't help that. What do you want me to do?" All thoughts of breakfast had disappeared, and he was laughing as she ran her fingers along his erect member.

"I want you inside me, not in that Italian woman!" She was giggling as she pulled him towards her. Placing a towel on the cold granite worktop, she slipped off her underwear and sat on the edge, facing Alex. "Come on now, Romeo! Do what you can just for me and nobody else!"

Elsa watched with curiosity at the humans doing strange things in the kitchen of all places. Both Jen and Alex were laughing, but Elsa could not understand why.

Alex was elated by Jen's crazy, energetic antics. She was completely sexually driven, unlike the more reserved Helen, though Alex appreciated it was unfair to compare the two very different women. Helen had many good qualities and would probably have made a very good mother for their children. On the other hand, Alex had difficulty imagining Jen changing a baby's nappy, taking children to school and all the other things that went with parenthood. *Don't think too far ahead*, Alex told himself and focused on the here and now.

After their vigorous activity, both were extremely sweaty and needed to shower, which they did together before Alex phoned Adrian to relay his latest vision, the only omission being information about Francesca's vibrator. Of one thing Alex was certain: his knowledge of the underground bunker and its access made his role in the assault even more essential.

"There's just one thing that bothers me," Alex finished. "Francesca's daughters. If we go in with all guns blazing, we could have the deaths of two innocent girls on our conscience." As an afterthought, he added, "There may be other children in other rooms."

Adrian agreed. "It does complicate the assault, but we'll do everything to avoid any collateral damage."

Alex had always loathed that term. Calling the deaths of innocent children 'collateral damage' was the military way of avoiding a difficult issue. He'd seen it in Afghanistan when the Taliban used innocent people to shield them from assault like the cowards they were.

"The other difficulty is that lift," Adrian said, bringing Alex's mind back to the present. "It's going to be pretty difficult getting to the target without alerting them. For all we know, they have cameras close to the lift. Leave it with me to work out a plan of action and I'll call you when we're ready."

IT WAS TWO days later when Adrian phoned back. "I'd like you all to come here for a briefing ready for the assault. I'll send a car for you this afternoon."

As before, it was Terry who arrived at their apartment. Alex had thought it might be him and had warned Jen about this strange uncommunicative man. Still, he was always efficient, and very soon Alex, Jen and Elsa were at MI6, where Adrian was waiting for them. He took them to a briefing room that already seemed to be full of young though experienced intelligence officers.

Many pin boards adorned the walls. On some of these, the photographs of all the 'Ndrangheta family who had so far evaded capture were pinned, along with pictures and maps of Newgate Street and in particular the address where Francesca had been seen entering the building.

Adrian addressed all within the room. "This exercise, ladies and gentlemen, is aimed at capturing, preferably alive, all the remaining members of the 'Ndrangheta currently living underground in the Newgate area of London. You've seen the records of all these individuals, and believe me, they are extremely professional dangerous and very well organised.

"We will start our operation at 0215 tomorrow morning. We'll wait for Francesca and, with her unwitting help, enter the complex. Two officers will remain in the apartment block just in case anybody else turns up." Adrian looked at the attentive faces of his audience. "We know that there are at least two small children, maybe even more. For this reason, extreme care must be exercised to avoid injuring any children."

"Don't forget about Sam!" interrupted Alex.

"Of course. From Officer McCloud's observations, Sam is the 'Ndrangheta's muscle. He's a man of African origin, estimated height and weight, two point one metres and about one hundred and twenty kilos."

The thought of taking on such a formidable individual showed on the officers' faces, yet each person would have liked to be the one to 'bring him down to size'.

"The biggest problem we have is the lift access. My thoughts on this are that myself, Officers McCloud and Sherlock, Elsa the dog and two other officers use the lift first to reach the lower level and the others follow by flexible ladder through the lift's emergency access. In this way, we're not wasting time waiting for an ancient lift to go up and down several times."

Alex felt both excitement and fear as the plan of action was outlined. It reminded him of the times in Afghanistan when attacks on the Taliban had been planned and discussed. There was always an unknown factor. A *what-if* factor. What if there are booby traps? What would they do if Francesca refused to cooperate? What if the lift would not move? So much to think about.

Adrian continued, his tone sounding more like that of a maths lecturer to a class of young students. "The priority once we have reached the level where the targets are living is to terminate the power source. We all have night vision, and with that advantage, we should be able to complete the operation without too many casualties." He paused for effect. "Any questions?"

One of the officers asked, "Why are we going in at two-fifteen?"

"This is a short while before Francesca normally arrives back. We want to surprise her as she enters the apartment block. Hopefully, she will cooperate with us. Even if she doesn't, if anyone hears the lift, they'll just assume it's her returning. That's why the timing is critical. I suggest that you all get some rest now and be ready to leave here at one-thirty precisely."

Chapter Forty-Five

ALEX FOUND IT difficult to sleep, but at least he was rested when all officers were called to prepare for the assault. Jen was not the only female officer. She and three others were issued with the same dark tunics as the men. Black and light in weight, the suits were reinforced with Kevlar. This super-strong material was also used in the headgear ensuring maximum protection for the wearer.

Even Elsa wore a Kevlar-reinforced suit and headgear, giving her an unusual, almost supernatural appearance, but her tail was still wagging, which was always a good sign.

Once everybody was ready, they filed into the underground car park of the MI6 building. Three black minibuses were waiting for them, Adrian again organising who went into which vehicle. The engines were already started, and as soon as everybody had taken their places, the vehicles moved out into the darkened London streets. They moved at quite a leisurely pace. Alex was sitting next to Jen, and Elsa relaxed on the floor between them. Alex looked sideways at Jen and smiled to himself on seeing her camouflaged face. She looked different and had the confidence of a very determined individual. Jen sensed Alex was looking at her and smiled back. They arrived near Newgate Street exactly on time, and all the officers, swiftly and silently, left their vehicles. Aware that the underground criminals may have cameras close to the apartment block, the team split into small groups in an attempt to blend in with the surroundings.

They did not have long to wait. Within minutes, the black Volvo turned into Newgate Street. Francesca exited the vehicle, glancing around as it drove away, and headed towards the apartment entrance. As soon as she opened the main door, Alex and Adrian who had been hiding nearby, ran up behind her. Alex put his hand over her mouth to silence her and quickly dragged her inside.

"Don't scream if you want to see Serena and Gemma again!"

The mention of her daughters' names did the trick. Francesca's tense body relaxed into submission.

"What do you want?"

Alex could see the fear in her eyes and knew that he had guessed correctly in using the names of this woman's two young children. He knew that exploiting weaknesses was the best way to survive. As he restrained her, he could feel her heart pounding. "You will help us to reach the underground base where your family members are hiding."

"I…I don't know what you mean," she stammered.

"Yes, you do! I know that you go down the stairs in this building into the old underground station and then into a lift to reach your base."

Francesca stared at him. "*How* do you know?"

"Never mind that. Just cooperate with us and you and your children will be safe. Okay?"

She nodded submissively, her eyes darting from Alex to the many others dressed like him entering the building, along with Elsa. Thankfully, she didn't seem to recognise him from the time he and Jen had visited her casino, probably because of their military-style camouflage.

Alex held out his hand. "Give me your keys."

She opened her Louis Vuitton bag and took out a ring holding several keys, dropping it reluctantly into Alex's outstretched palm.

"Which key opens the door in this area?"

"That one." She pointed to one. Alex used it in the lock of the door from his vision. Francesca gasped in surprise.

The room was just as he had seen, containing many large boxes and crates. He wondered what was inside them but would leave that until later.

Still holding on to Francesca, he walked across the untidy room and found the staircase leading downwards. "Are there any cameras between here and your rooms?"

Francesca shook her head. "What's going to happen to my family?"

It was Adrian who answered. "The 'Ndrangheta members will be arrested and eventually deported back to Italy, assuming they put up no resistance. But if you help us to capture them without any problems, we'll keep you out of prison to let you and your children stay together. That's a promise."

Alex wondered how far this woman would go against her extended family to save the lives of her children and herself. From what he had read about the 'Ndrangheta, there were severe punishments for any traitor within the family, but the fact that she was giving the information under duress may help to keep her and the girls safe.

He led the group slowly down the stairs, aware that it would be foolish to assume she would not lead them into a trap. As they reached the underground platform, there was a low level of illumination from occasional wall lights, which presumably were left on permanently. Floors and walls were tiled; considering how old the station was, they were in remarkably good condition.

Approaching the gate at the end of the corridor, Alex could imagine crowds of commuters filling this space with noisy excited chatter as people made their way to their places of work. Now there was just the muted sound of the officers' footsteps as they followed the Italian woman.

As they reached the gate, Francesca hesitated. Impatient to move on, Alex pulled it open and strode into the lift, dragging the woman along. Adrian, Jen and Elsa followed. When they realised how large the lift was, four other officers joined them. Pulling the gate back into position, Alex motioned to the Italian to press the button but then had second thoughts. If one of those buttons were to alert the 'Ndrangheta members, their task would be that much more difficult. Remembering which one Francesca had pressed in his vision, he dealt with it himself, and the lift began to descend to the lower level. For a brief moment, his eyes met Francesca's, and he saw the fear and confusion in them. Did it mean that she was not as criminally minded as the others?

The lift stopped, and Adrian opened the gate, allowing all but two of the officers to leave. The remaining men removed the access panel from the roof of the lift cage. A lightweight coiled ladder dropped through the opening; within seconds, the remainder of the officers began to climb down to the lower level.

After only a couple of minutes of activity, all the officers were assembled within this now somewhat cramped anteroom.

Alex held out the small group of keys in front of his captive. "Which key now?" The Italian woman again hesitated a little. "Remember, Francesca, we are very close to your children, and I know exactly which room they are in."

She stared at him, understandably incredulous that he could know such detail. "This is the one," she replied nervously.

Starkly aware of how close they were to a highly organised and dangerous group of criminals, Alex turned the key in the lock.

Chapter Forty-Six

Aᴛ fᴛᴇʀ Aʟᴇx ʜᴀᴅ gingerly unlocked the door, it was Adrian who led the way. The officers spread out along the dimly lit corridor with at least two outside each door. Alex indicated the room in which the young children would be sleeping. There was no need for their room to be invaded.

At a signal from Adrian, each door was kicked in and flares together with smoke bombs detonated. The officers rushed into the rooms, shouting and trying to intimidate the occupants into rapid submission. Not surprisingly, it was not going to be that simple.

Several of the men had weapons at their bedsides and fired at the intruders, probably as an instinctive reaction.

Jen escorted Francesca into her room to look after her two girls, who huddled, tearful and terrified by all the shouting and confusion. Their mother beckoned them to her, and the three sat on the bed, holding each other.

"Are there any other children down here?" Jen asked.

Francesca shook her head. "No other young children like my two," she said with a strong sense of fear in her voice. "Will you really keep us safe?"

"We will," Jen promised, hoping she wasn't overstepping.

"It will be a relief to end this…underground existence."

"Have you lived here a long time?"

"Since my husband passed. At least I get some reprieve working in the evenings. My girls…they don't have the same luxury." She kissed their heads and held them closer still.

"What about their education?" Jen asked.

"I teach them here. When I'm at work, my mother cares for them." She became quiet and thoughtful for a moment. "I will need to find other work now. A small price to pay if we are safe."

PURELY BY CHANCE, it was Alex and Elsa who entered Gianni's room, where he and his wife Carina were in bed and awoke, startled, though it was Carina who seemed to resent this intrusion the most. With typical fiery Italian temperament, she threw anything she could lay her hands on at Alex, all the while cursing him in Italian.

"Attack!" he shouted as he was bombarded by books, a bedside lamp and even part of a trouser press.

Seeing Carina as the greater threat, Elsa sank her teeth into the woman's arm, effectively disabling her. Carina screamed. That was when Alex noticed Gianni had a gun, and it was aimed directly at Elsa's head. Even with her Kevlar protection, that would kill her. With only a fraction of a second to spare, he shot at the Italian's gun hand. Gianni's weapon fired, missing Elsa by inches, and then fell harmlessly to the floor. Alex fired another shot, hitting Gianni in the leg, effectively disabling him. *Must keep the bastard alive.*

The noise was sheer hell as gunfire, screams and shouts reverberated throughout the warren of rooms.

"Where is Gian Battista? Where is the Capocrimine?" Alex demanded.

Gianni had collapsed to the floor where his wife was trying to support him.

"You seem to know so much, you find him—if you're not too late."

"Too late for what?"

Gianni smiled through his pain. "That would be telling."

At that instant, all the lights went out, plunging the maze of rooms into complete darkness. Presumably, one of the officers had found and disabled the power source as instructed. For Alex, this made no difference at all. His implanted eyes afforded him perfect night vision. Similarly, the other officers would have switched to night-vision goggles so should be able to cope equally well.

Alex wasted no time. Grabbing Gianni's weapon from the floor, he tucked it into his waistband and ran back into the corridor followed by Elsa.

Adrian had burst into the room where the two brothers Lorenzo and Paolo were sleeping. "Out of bed, you two!"

They did as instructed, both standing in their boxer shorts for a second before Paulo made a dive towards the bed and smoothly threw a knife that had been concealed under his pillow. It had been directed towards Adrian's face with remarkable accuracy, but Adrian instinctively dropped down, and the blade skimmed over his head, missing him by a few millimetres before embedding itself in the doorframe. Adrian had intended only to disable these two and took a shot at Paolo's arm, but with the Italian's movement, the bullet entered his chest. Blood spurted everywhere as he sank to his knees.

"Paolo!" Lorenzo dropped to his knees and held his dying brother, staring at Adrian with horror and absolute hatred in his eyes.

Adrian had no need to apologise yet managed to say, "I'm sorry, but if he had not thrown that knife at me, he would still be uninjured. There may still be a chance to save him—we have medical support coming soon." Adrian called for another officer to keep watch and make sure Lorenzo didn't try anything. By the time medical support arrived, Paolo would be dead. The loss of blood was too great to allow any chance of survival.

During all the noise and confusion, a large figure slipped silently along towards the end of the corridor assisted by the darkness. The man quietly opened the door and entered one of the rooms. With cat-like precision, he made his way towards another door.

In this bedroom, Gian Battista had been enjoying a rare, alcohol-assisted deep sleep when he awoke to find Sam shaking him. "Wake up. We are under attack."

"What? Are you certain?" As Gian listened, he could hear the shouts of the officers in the corridor and was in no doubt about the truth of Sam's warning.

For his age, he was quite quick in pulling on a pair of trousers, shirt and jacket, a task made more difficult by the absence of lighting.

Sam had locked the door to delay any assailants and quickly helped Gian into his shoes. "You'll need a weapon, sir." He handed a gun to the elderly man, who tucked it into his belt. Last of all, Gian Battista grabbed an envelope containing a large amount of cash out of a bedside drawer. Hastily, he stuffed it into his jacket pocket, ready to make his escape.

While he was doing this, Sam had already opened a hidden door in one of the walls. He ushered the old man through the opening, saying, "I will do my best to delay them to give you time to escape."

"My stick! I need my stick!"

Sam quickly found it and placed it into the old man's grasping hands.

"Thank you, Sam. You have been a great help."

Knowing from this that his comfortable way of life had come to an end, Sam closed the secret door and effortlessly moved a large chest of drawers in front to conceal the opening. It was only a matter of time now, but at least he had done his best to save the Capocrimine.

SOME OF THE officers were dragging the Italians out into the corridor, and as Alex turned to look the other way, he spotted the huge bulk of Sam purposely striding towards him, a look of grim determination on his face. The man seemed even bigger than when Alex had seen him in his vision. He must have weighed well over a hundred and twenty kilos, but it was all well-toned muscle and the man's fitness could not be doubted.

Elsa did not need to be given the instruction to attack, as the threat to her master was obvious and imminent. She ran swiftly towards the fast-approaching giant, who barely flinched as the dog sank its teeth into his calf. If this had been any other man, he would have collapsed where he stood, but not Sam. He simply swatted the dog away as if it were merely a troublesome fly. Elsa crashed into the wall with a howl of pain.

That was when Alex made a potentially fatal mistake. He aimed his weapon at Sam's leg, in an attempt to cripple rather than kill, and pulled the trigger. To his amazement, Sam hardly flinched as the bullet sank into the firm flesh, allowing blood to trickle down his leg as he broke into a somewhat clumsy but nevertheless swift run. Ripping the gun out of Alex's hand, he tossed the weapon to one side, and before Alex could reach to get the other gun out of his waistband, Sam had his hands around Alex's neck.

Alex felt the strength draining out of his body as the grip of this huge man became ever tighter. He cursed to himself:. All the Kevlar protection on his body and head was useless. Lights were flashing through his brain, the knowledge that he was close to death pervading his mind and blocking out all his other senses.

Thus, he was only vaguely aware of the huge explosion that ripped through the air until the pressure on his neck mercifully diminished, and he fell to the floor, his oxygen-deprived muscles aching and feeble.

"Alex!"

He heard Jen's voice, though she sounded somehow very distant, and for a second he wondered if he was in fact dead.

"Alex! Come back! Please!"

Hands gripped his shoulders and shook him so hard his head bounced against the floor. It was enough of a jolt to get him to his feet—with Jen's assistance.

"What happened to Sam?" Alex asked, still fuzzy. "I thought he was breaking my neck." Before Jen could speak, the answer came in the form of Sam's huge body, which seemed to fill the entire width of the corridor. As Alex's senses returned, he noticed first the expensive carpet incongruous with an old train station and now covered in blood and brain matter, and then that the back of Sam's head had been blown away. Alex's knees buckled in relief that the big man would never get those deadly hands on anyone else.

"Who shot him?" he asked, although he had a very strong idea who it had been.

Jen smiled. "Just returning the favour from when you saved my life. I managed to get several rounds into his big head while he was concentrating on strangling you."

"Thanks, Jen. I owe my life to you."

"No, you don't. We're quits, okay?"

He gave her a huge kiss of gratitude. "Okay!" As he gathered his thoughts, he remembered seeing his dog flung aside by Sam. "Elsa! Is she all right?"

"I guess so. See for yourself."

A warm nose nuzzled Alex's hand. "Elsa!" He stroked the dog's head and felt a wet patch where a small trickle of blood was already congealing. There would be a scar, but she seemed to be in no immediate danger. "You were terrific!" he praised her, but then it dawned on him what Sam had been up to. "The Capocrimine! I think Sam was meant to delay me to give him time to escape!"

"We've checked all the rooms."

Alex looked at the end of the corridor from where Sam had appeared. "There! Sam came through that door. There must be another way out!"

Forgetting how close he had come to death, Alex charged ahead, followed by Elsa, and pushed open the last door, which was set back slightly from the main wall surface. It opened into a large luxuriously furnished but otherwise empty room. Another door led to a bedroom, which, disappointingly, was also empty. Calling Elsa to him, he ran back out into the corridor where Jen was waiting and started tapping along the wall. "There has to be a hidden exit somewhere."

"What makes you think that?"

"At this stage, it's part guesswork and part intuition, but if you think like these people, wouldn't you have an emergency exit?"

"I suppose so," admitted Jen.

Alex looked back down the long corridor and spotted Adrian. "Adrian! Can you come here a minute?"

The older man jogged towards them, his way clear now some of his men had moved Sam's body to one side. "What is it?"

"I think this may be an emergency way out for the Capocrimine. Can you use some explosive charge to blow a hole in it?"

Adrian smiled, seeming delighted by the idea. "No problem. Pete!" he called to one of his men, who brought a small container of plastic explosive. Adrian explained what they needed, and stepped aside while Pete spread a thick, waxy substance between floor and wall. That done, he pushed a small detonator into the substance. "Stand well back. We don't know what the explosion will bring down." Once everybody was at a safe distance, Pete activated the detonator. The noise in the confined space was deafening and sent a vast cloud of dust along the corridor.

As the dust settled, Alex's intuition was proved to be correct. There had been no solid concrete or brick wall behind the plasterboard. Instead, another corridor opened up in front of them with a smaller one that led off to the concealed door in the bedroom. Knocking away some loose, hanging debris, Alex with Elsa stepped through, followed by Adrian and Jen, both holding flashlights.

The corridor was about two and a half metres high by two wide, quite rough and basic in comparison to the luxurious living quarters. There was a cement finish to the floor, walls and ceiling, but no attempt had been made to give it a smooth finish. It was what it was—an emergency exit—but to where did it lead?

Alex quickened his pace, not running but walking at a speed that allowed him to scan around for hidden dangers. There was still no sight of the old man, but Alex was convinced he had come this way from the little disturbances in the dust on the concrete floor.

Alex had not bargained for what happened next. The corridor split off into two different directions. *Fuck!* "Now why would they do that?"

"A delaying tactic," answered Adrian.

Alex looked closely at the floor, scanning the surface in minute detail. "Well, it didn't work." He pointed the direction they should take while explaining, "The Capocrimine is nearly eighty and I'm almost certain he's using a walking stick."

Adrian and Jen both looked at the floor, but their eyes were unable to discern the regular disturbance in the floor dust where the old man's stick had supported his weight. Once again, Alex silently thanked Professor Goldman for making his artificial eyes powerful enough to spot these telltale signs.

The three continued along the corridor and, after about another hundred metres, came to a door. To their annoyance, it had been locked from the other side.

"No problem," said Adrian. "Just stand back a minute." They did as instructed, allowing Adrian to shoot the lock mechanism. There was an ear-splitting bang as it shattered and the door swung open. They stepped through the opening and to their surprise found themselves on a London Underground platform. The three turned around in amazement to see that they were at St. Paul's station on the Central line.

At three-fifteen in the morning, the platform was deserted, but in comparison to the dark corridors they had come through, the lighting was good, and it was Jen who spotted a figure slowly climbing some stairs. "There he is!"

All three humans and one dog ran towards the staircase, their footsteps echoing around the empty area. The elderly man, not fast enough to escape, turned to face his pursuers. That was when they noticed the gun in his hand.

Jen quickly dodged behind a ticket machine, although it offered very little cover. Alex and Adrian pressed themselves against the wall, but none of them was ever in any real danger. Gian Battista Lamancusa, realising that he could not evade his pursuers any longer, leaned heavily on his walking stick and put the gun against his own head, pulling the trigger. Again, the noise of the gun firing seemed even louder, the sound reverberating around the hard surfaces of the subway. The weapon, walking stick and then the old man himself tumbled down the nine or ten steps back onto the platform. The King of the 'Ndrangheta had finally fallen from his throne. This was the end of his sixty-year reign since being baptised into the 'Honoured Society' at the age of eighteen.

Chapter Forty-Seven

A DRIAN USED HIS radio to call for medical assistance, but it was obvious from the pool of blood spreading across the platform that the old man was well and truly dead. Nevertheless, the senior intelligence officer needed to stay at the scene until somebody could take charge of the body.

"You might as well return to the underground rooms to see if they need any further assistance," he advised Alex and Jen.

Nodding, Alex took one last look at the upturned face of the old man. For a second, he wondered if Gian was, somehow, still alive because despite having bled out on the platform, there was still colour to his face. Then as Alex watched, the dark hue shifted like a dark cloud extending slightly beyond the head, diminishing in intensity as the last dregs of life left the physical body.

Astonished, Alex turned to Jen. "Did you see something around his head?"

"Blood?"

"No. More like… an aura."

She looked closer, clearly puzzled. "An aura?"

"That's the only way I can describe it, but it's just about gone now. It faded as he died."

Jen looked again at the old man and shook her head. "No, nothing, but your sight is far beyond mind. Supernatural, kind of. And a little scary."

Alex wasn't sure he liked that description, but there was no further conversation as he, Jen and Elsa retraced their steps through the narrow corridor back to the junction in the passage.

"I think we should see where this leads," Alex said, gesturing the other path to the one they'd taken.

"I think we should check if everything is all right first," Jen said. "I'm curious too, but we can always check it out later."

"Okay," Alex conceded, and they continued on their way, back to the carpeted corridor where the criminals were lined up against the wall, handcuffed and defeated.

Alex recognised a few of these men. Agostino—the first of the Italian family seen by him at Woolpit—was, like everybody else shocked by this intrusion into their 'home'. Beside him stood Brando and Carlino, whose escape from the prison van had only given them a few short weeks of freedom. After what they had put Jacqueline and Rosita through, that was more than they deserved.

As Alex studied their faces, he again saw that dark-brownish aura he'd seen around the Capocrimine's face.

"Everything okay, Alex?" Adrian's second-in-command, Mike Edwards, drew up alongside him.

"Fine," Alex said. "Did you get them all?"

"We did. Thirty-nine of them including Francesca and her daughters." Mike moved off, gesturing Alex and Jen to walk with him, which they did, Elsa plodding obediently at Alex's side.

"I promised Francesca she'd escape punishment if she assisted us with information," Alex said once they were out of earshot of the other men. "Take good care of her, won't you?"

"Don't worry. She'll probably get a suspended sentence to allow her to stay with her children. Anyway, I need to show you what we found."

The three followed Mike into a large, well-stocked room. The remains of the heavily reinforced door stood against the wall.

"What the…?" Alex was stopped in his tracks by a veritable treasure trove, an Aladdin's cave stacked with gold bars, packages of many different currencies of banknotes, bags full of drugs and, within large wooden crates, many different types of guns and rifles together with a great deal of ammunition.

Jen drew in a sharp breath. "There must be millions of pounds in here. What a fantastic catch!"

Mike smiled. "It's been a very good day so far. Quite a haul!"

"We have one other passage to check on, Mike. Can we borrow your man with the plastic explosives just in case there's another barrier?"

"Of course." Mike called for Pete and instructed him to go with Alex and Jen, who led the way along the by now well-trodden rough-hewn passage to the fork, where they took the other route, no idea what they would find next. It was a very long and meandering journey, the passage sloping down to a deeper level with the ceiling becoming low enough in places that it was necessary for these tall individuals to bend forward.

Alex estimated they had walked at least a mile before the passage opened out into what seemed to be a huge cavern.

It was in darkness, yet with his ultra-sensitive eyes, Alex instantly recognised the view in front of them. They were in an underground cave with water lapping gently against a low harbour wall. A submarine was securely fastened to low bollards on the quayside. The craft had a sleek, low profile with a strange, black plastic-like finish, presumably to make detection by underwater sonar equipment very difficult.

"This is what I saw in my first vision when they were transferring the bags of cocaine from the sub to the narrowboat."

Pete and Jen did not have Alex's super vision and had to use their powerful torches to make out any detail. As they raised them to the roof, Alex pointed. "That's the hoist they used on their drug run."

Spotting a row of switches on the rear wall, Alex went over and flipped them one at a time, and soon, the underground cavern flooded with light. The three gazed around the huge area.

"It must have cost a fortune to set up all of this," Jen said in wonderment.

Pete was more interested in the stealth submarine and had walked down the short gangway onto the deck. "This is quite impressive." A cable ran across the ground and into a hatch on the top of the submarine. "Looks as though the batteries are being charged ready for a journey."

Although he had no sense of imminent danger, Alex called out, "Careful, Pete! It may be a booby trap!"

Pete looked cautiously through the part-open hatch. He shone his torch around the interior of the submarine and decided there were no signs of possible traps. "I think it's okay. You two stay there while I check." The explosives expert opened the hatch fully and climbed down into the interior of the craft.

Meanwhile, Jen, Alex and Elsa explored the jetty area, curious to discover more about this underground marina. At one end of the quay, the water lapped lazily against a vertical wall.

"No obvious way of escape here," said Jen.

"Unless it's under the surface. I remember from my vision the submarine moving carefully through a tunnel and then surfacing over there." He pointed towards where the craft was now moored. "Let's check the other end."

The trio walked about a hundred and fifty metres to the far end of the quayside. In some places, the quay was about ten metres in depth, but at this end, it was less than two metres wide. Alex was surprised to feel cool, fresh air on his face and shone his torch around the wall closest to them, searching for an opening. "There!"

"What is it?" Jen could see nothing of particular interest.

"I think this is where the canal boat enters and leaves. There's a tunnel in that wall surface—it must lead to the canal system. I can feel fresh air coming through."

"How on earth did they manage to create all this without being detected?"

"I don't think they did," Alex mused. "My feeling is that it was constructed during the Second World War to provide safety and shelter during air raids."

Jen was surprised by this possibility. "Really?"

"Many subway stations were used as emergency evacuation areas, and that tunnel leads directly to St. Paul's station. This might even have been an emergency exit for senior government officials or the royal family."

They were discussing this as they walked back towards the gently floating craft. Pete emerged from the submarine with a wide grin on his face. "What a fantastic toy! Come and have a look."

Jen, Alex and Elsa walked along the gangway and followed Pete into the craft. It brought back memories of Alex's first vision, and now there were no bags of cocaine, it seemed less cramped than he remembered.

Pete showed them the controls in front of the helmsman's comfortable seat. "This craft must have cost an absolute fortune! It's very sophisticated and crammed with state-of-the-art navigation and stealth technology."

For the next few minutes, the three of them looked closely at every area within the craft. It even had a compact yet well-designed toilet and washroom, which would have been vital for longer journeys. Eventually, they left the submarine and set off on the long walk back to the underground 'Ndrangheta rooms, where the lighting had been restored, now that the criminal gang were safely under their control, and some of the prisoners were still waiting but most had already been taken away.

Alex spotted Mike and quickly told him of their discovery.

"This is quite a catch in many different ways. Come and see what else I have found."

They followed him into what would have been the lounge area for the Capocrimine. It was luxurious in every detail from comfortable seating and expensive ornaments to richly decorated walls and concealed high-tech LED lighting. "Do you recognise anything?" asked Mike.

The others looked around the room, wondering what they were supposed to see. Then all of a sudden Alex spotted them. "Those paintings! They look vaguely familiar."

"Well spotted, Alex. Over the years, many famous art masterpieces have been stolen, and we're looking at two of them here." Mike Edwards had several interests to occupy him when off duty, and as a lover of fine art, he had quickly recognised the treasures hidden away in this underground habitat.

Alex looked at the first of the two paintings. There were three musicians, a young woman playing a harpsichord, a man playing a lute and another woman singing.

"This one on the left is *The Concert* by Johannes Vermeer and is reckoned to be worth over one hundred and thirty million pounds. It was stolen from the Isabella Stewart Gardner Museum in 1990."

Alex looked again at this painting. True, it was impressive, but who would pay a hundred and thirty million for just one painting? He'd never understood how paintings commanded such high prices, but as long as there were billionaires with money to spend, the prices would continue to be over-inflated.

Mike continued as though he was the guide at a national art gallery. "*Poppy Flowers* was painted by Vincent Van Gogh in the late 1800s. It was stolen from Cairo's Mohammed Mahmoud Khalil Museum in 2010 and is worth about thirty-five million pounds. The reward alone for these two paintings would be several hundred thousand pounds! How about that? The 'Ndrangheta and a veritable treasure trove all in one day!"

At this point, Adrian came into the room and did a double-take at the valuable hoard, but Alex remained unimpressed, more concerned about keeping his promise to Francesca.

"Adrian, have you made arrangements for Francesca and her daughters yet? Those girls are innocent parties in all this. I'd hate to think of them suffering because of their family ties."

Adrian looked thoughtful. "If Francesca comes good on her side of the deal, I see no reason why we can't sort out new identities for the three of them and let them get on with their lives in peace."

Chapter Forty-Eight

ALL THE NEWS channels were covering this huge story, but Alex preferred to watch Fiona Bruce on the BBC. Maybe it was the seductive twinkle in her eyes or the slightly teasing tone in her voice; whatever it was, she fascinated him even though she was probably double his age.

"The Intelligence Service yesterday apprehended over thirty members of an Italian family. Similar to the Mafia in ideals, they are called the 'Ndrangheta, originally based in Calabria, Southern Italy. The family was ruled by Gian Battista Lamancusa, a seventy-eight-year-old ruthless gangster who committed suicide when he realised that capture was inevitable. Several other members of the family have suffered gunshot wounds and are being closely guarded in hospital.

"The large family evaded arrest over two years ago when Italian police forces managed to capture and arrest nearly three hundred members of the same syndicate. At this stage, little is being disclosed by the security service, but it appears that this large number of criminals together with family members including two small children had entered the UK illegally and have been living underground in a luxurious dwelling beneath the Old Bailey."

At this point, the image changed from Fiona to that of the superbly comfortable living room where Gian Battista had spent most of his time.

"The organisation made use of secret passages underneath the famous legal courts that were used in the nineteenth century to move prisoners towards Newgate Prison for public executions but had been abandoned for more than a hundred years."

The picture switched from the newsreader to images of the world-famous law courts, and Alex wondered if the members of the 'Ndrangheta would face trial in the very same building under which they had been hiding and living. *That would be true justice for the Mafia members*, he thought.

"Adrian was not surprised by this disclosure," Jen commented. "He said the Ministry of Defence has a building over Brompton Road Underground station in West London. The station is also owned by the Ministry of Defence and hasn't been used for over eighty years. Perhaps there's also an illegal operation running there right under the noses of the MOD."

Alex agreed. "I now believe that anything is possible, so who knows?"

Fiona continued with her report.

"How these Italians managed to discover this place, carry out all the structural work and actually take up residence is still a mystery to the authorities. From this secret location, the family has been running a multi-billion-pound empire based on illegal immigration, prostitution, protection rackets, providing weapons and importing drugs for distribution throughout the United Kingdom. Security forces also found a room containing gold bars, large quantities of banknotes, drugs and weapons presumably collected by the 'Ndrangheta members over a period of many years.

"Two valuable paintings, which had been stolen several years ago, were also recovered. The final discovery was a five-million-pound mini-submarine, which had been used to smuggle both the family and drugs into the United Kingdom. The submarine was found in an underground cave with a connecting channel to the open sea and access to the British canal system. It was packed with stealth electronics to avoid detection by the authorities."

An image of the submarine appeared, and Alex switched the television off.

"You had enough of Fiona now, huh?" Jen teased.

"Never!" Alex laughed. He had seen the report several times already and settled back on the sofa with Jen while Elsa lay at their feet. "What a bloody cheek! Actually living underneath the Old Bailey. That took real balls!"

Jen smiled. It was a cheeky smile specially for the man she had lived with for the past three months. "You mean that yours are *not* real? Perhaps I should investigate and get down to the truth." With those words, she jumped up and chased him into the bedroom.

Elsa remained where she was, relaxing in the living room. While she would never understand the crazy behaviour of these humans, she was, by now, quite accustomed to her master's strange antics with this woman and closed her eyes, knowing she would be undisturbed for quite a while.

Epilogue

IT WAS THE first time Alex's family had visited him at his apartment in London, and all were impressed after looking around the tidy rooms. Alex hoped he had not left any of Jen's personal items lying around for them to spot or else he would always be teased and reminded of this by his ultra-observant sisters.

Lucy was sitting on one side of him on the sofa with Amelia on the other and his parents relaxing in the armchairs. All four had taken a liking to Elsa and made a great fuss of her. Of course, Elsa enjoyed *all* the attention but for some reason favoured Amelia and lay on the floor near the young girl's feet, which pleased his Amelia no end. There was an uncomfortable moment when she noticed the scar from Elsa's recent battle with Sam, but she seemed to accept Alex's story that a Rottweiler had attacked her while out walking. Attacks by other dogs on guide dogs were not unheard of.

They had all commented on how well Alex was looking. *It's a good job that the marks on my neck from Sam's attempt to strangle me have faded*, he thought. Still, to be certain, he had worn a smart black polo-neck sweater.

The occasion was Amelia's fourteenth birthday: when she had been asked what she would like as a gift, all she wanted was to visit her big brother and see the sights of London. Her parents and Lucy also thought it was a great idea and had arranged with Alex to visit him on the following Saturday.

In preparation, he'd had to revert to his original brown hair and blue eyes to avoid awkward questions but it had been easy enough with Jen's help. He'd need to check with her how to change his eye colour by himself, for the immediate future at least.

When he'd told her of the arrangement, she'd said it would be better if she was not there at the same time as his family. "They would jump to the wrong conclusion."

"Is that conclusion so wrong?" Alex had asked somewhat naively. "Do you not want to stay with me?"

She'd looked at him and with a great deal of sadness in her voice said, "You know it's not that simple. Kristin has been keeping the States up to date, but I'm already well over my allotted stay here in the UK. My job is based in the US and my family lives there. It's best I go back sooner rather than later."

It still hurt to think about it, yet when he'd asked her if he'd ever see her again, her answer was matter-of-fact, as if the question was not even necessary.

"Of course you will! I'm not that far away, and I'll visit whenever it's possible." It was definitely not an afterthought when she added coyly, "And you could always come stay with me for a vacation— whenever you wish."

Jen had really caught him by surprise. He wanted to be a major part of her life, but despite her assurance, he doubted they would ever meet again. He had no idea why this feeling should have been so strong, yet he was certain it was the truth.

Alex thought of Jack Reacher in Lee Child's novels. In each adventure, he would find a beautiful woman to bed, but by the end of the story, he would be moving on, leaving the woman behind.

It's not quite the same situation, but the effect is the same. A fantastic, short-lived relationship and now I must move on to a new chapter in my life!

About the Author

John Stephen Raynor was born in 1944 in Oldham, Lancashire. At the age of two, he was diagnosed with a serious progressive eye condition retinitis pigmentosa.

At fifteen, he began working in architecture, eventually becoming a self-employed software developer and marrying his first wife in 1967. Sadly, the long hours building up his business took their toll, and the couple separated in 1989.

It was in the Philippines he found his soul mate, whom he married in 1993. Her experiences are the inspiration for much of John's fictional work including his novel *Cotabato Girl*.

After twenty years of keeping diaries, John drew on these to publish *Necklaces & Knickers* – one of two autobiographical works describing this most traumatic period.

Registered blind since the age of thirty-five, John relies on his computer with speech synthesis for software development and creative writing.

Also by J. S. Raynor

Cotabato Girl

In the land of Ferdinand Marcos, you quickly learn to be tough. Born the eighth and youngest child of a family on the Philippine breadline Lisa Tiguelo knows she must take revenge for the past. But the price will be higher than anyone can imagine.

Cocktales & Nibbles

Cocktales & Nibbles is a collection of twelve stories ranging from the shortest such as 'Lite in the Sky' which was my first story written in 1973 to the lengthy 'A Universal Threat' written in 2017. The title of this book is meant to signify the short stories as 'Nibbles' while the longer stories are representative of the 'Cocktales'. Please forgive my change to the spelling of 'Cocktails' – this is how my mind works! These stories were written over a period of forty-four years.

Necklaces & Knickers

It was 1991 and John Raynor's life was in a bit of a mess. At forty-six, two years after his divorce, he was living on his own and the future seemed bleak. And then there was Carole, a divorcee two years younger than him, and suddenly everything changed. Their bond was immediate and intense. This is the true account of a sixteen-month relationship that changed John's life dramatically.

Find out more about John's previous and upcoming works on his website: www.jsraynor.co.uk

Beaten Track Publishing

For more titles from Beaten Track Publishing
please visit our website:

https://www.beatentrackpublishing.com

Thanks for reading!